savage VOW

USA Today Bestselling Authors

J.L. BECK & S. RENA

Copyright © 2022 by Bleeding Heart Press

Cover Design: C. Hallman

Editing: Kelly Allenby

Proofread: Editing for Indies

All rights reserved.

No part of this book may be reproduced in any form or by any electronic or mechanical means, including information storage and retrieval systems, without written permission from the author, except for the use of brief quotations in a book review.

VOW

1

ALICIA

What am I supposed to do? Where do I go from here? Probably no more than an hour ago, I was about to kiss my husband for the first time. I was dazed and shaken, but I made it through the ceremony—what little ceremony there was. I knew what I had to do to make it out of this alive, even if I was sure the entire time that my supposed father was going to spill the beans and ruin everything.

He did, too. Just not in the way I imagined.

Now, here I am. Locked up again in the same room as when I first got here. The difference is I'm wearing a bloodstained wedding dress. And a band around my ring finger, a symbol of the mockery of a union I'm now a part of.

I'm waiting for my husband to decide what he's going to do with me.

A heartbroken sob tears itself from my chest before I can fight it back. I don't understand what happened. Like things weren't bad enough as they were. Forced into the wedding, having to pretend those people were my parents. I've told so many lies and half-truths that I can't keep track of any of it.

All I know now is that there is no lying my way out of this one. That

Alvarez guy told Enzo I'm not who he thinks I am. He's just as disgusting and cruel as the rest of them.

I thought Enzo was better than that. In fact, deep down, I know he is. I didn't mean to blurt out my feelings for him, but they're real. I love him. I was terrified for those brief moments when I didn't know if he was hit by a bullet. The idea of being without him... Even now, it's not something I want to imagine. Even though he's locked me up again. Even when I know there is a high chance he will kill me.

The click of the lock makes my head snap up. My eyes are on the door. My heart starts to race, and a sickening wave of nausea ripples through me. This is it. I honestly didn't think it would take this long for him to come up here and take his rage out on me. I hold my breath, ready to face my fate, but it isn't Enzo who comes into the room. I blink, confused for a moment, when I realize it's a guard instead.

He glares at me for a split second before leaving a tray of food on the floor. I don't have time to take a breath and ask what's happening before he closes the door again, clicking the lock into place.

"Please, somebody, talk to me!" I rush from the bed and knock on the door when what I want to do is pound my fists, but I know that won't get me anywhere. The best thing I can do right now is play it cool. As cool as a person can play it in a situation like this.

I have to settle for picking up the tray covered in food we were supposed to be enjoying as part of our wedding dinner. Yet another symbol of what this day was supposed to be and what it eventually evolved into. It's kind of cold now, the wine sauce coating the chicken somewhat congealed, but I have no idea the next time someone will think to feed me, so I doubt I should look a gift horse in the mouth. Even though I'm about as far away from hungry as I can remember ever being, I force myself through it, eating potatoes and sauteed vegetables without really tasting much of it.

If it wasn't all so stressful, I might have to laugh. Could this entire situation be any further from what I would have imagined my wedding to be like one day? All my youthful illusions, gone at once. I'm sitting alone in a locked room with only a tiny window through which to see the outside world. My dress—one I didn't get to choose for myself—is covered in blood and grass stains. I'm eating cold food from a tray, forcing myself to swallow every bite even though it tastes like sawdust. Waiting for my husband to barge in here and make good on his promise of killing me.

And all the while, my brain is churning. What am I supposed to do here? What should I say? I doubt he'll believe anything I come up with, but I have to try, don't I? I can't roll over and die without at least trying to save myself.

I hate the sense of returning to where we started, especially when it seemed Enzo was starting to come around. He was actually sweet toward me, tender. I'm not fooling myself by remembering the concern etched all over his face and dripping from his voice when he checked me over to make sure I was okay. He could have protected himself alone but threw himself over me instead. That has to mean something.

Can I make that work in my favor now?

One thing is obvious: Josef Alvarez was lying when he said he wasn't responsible for this shooting. Who else would be?

The more I think about it, the more I wonder if all of this isn't partly my fault. I could have told him the truth from the beginning or at any point during this whole ordeal. Clearly, all Alvarez ever cared about was the drugs. Now I understand a lot of things I didn't before. The shooting at the airplane hangar—obviously, he figured they were bringing the drugs to the meeting and wanted them back, no strings attached. Meaning killing the people who brought them back to him.

Meanwhile, Enzo thought it was me he was looking for. I guess it's easy to look back now and see all the mistakes and all the ways this could have been avoided. At the time, they only thought I was doing my best to survive. I never meant to get anybody killed, not even that wicked old man.

I have no doubt Enzo is going to put that together sooner rather than later. Maybe I can somehow get ahead of him. I'll tell him the full truth, all of it. I might be able to get through to him, especially if I tell him what Alvarez was really looking for all along. If all he wants is the drugs, it's a simple matter of returning them.

Or… if Enzo still has the drugs, which I have no doubt he would, maybe he can use them in some other way. If Alvarez is that desperate to get them back, they must be something special. I don't know anything about that, but I remember Enzo's reaction when he tested them. He tried to hide it, but when I look back, it's clear something about them intrigued him. Maybe he could sell them himself or find out how they were manufactured. He could still come out of this having gained something.

No, that won't bring his grandfather back, but it might put Enzo in a better position to get his revenge. I have no doubt that's what sits at the forefront of his mind since it's what I would want if the only father figure I had was suddenly assassinated in front of me. How he's going to get vengeance for the old man.

Even though he couldn't have been a very nice man, and he certainly made me feel like a cheap piece of trash. I'll never forget how pitifully Enzo reacted when he knew there was nothing to be done. That the man who had raised him was gone. Just remembering it now stirs pain in my chest. It's dangerous to think of him as a lost little boy, but I can't help it. That's exactly who he was at that moment.

One thing I know for sure. There's no way he's going to be thinking clearly. I know he'll hate it if I try to talk sense to him, but that's what I have to do. I have to get through to him somehow. I have to make sure he sees the big picture and doesn't get lost in his pain and rage. Not even only for my sake but for his own. He was dangerously close to losing it out there. People don't make smart decisions when they're in that state of mind.

And even though he's got me locked in here, I still care. Probably too much. I don't want to see him hurting any worse than he already is, and I wish there was a way I could take it away. Since I know that's not possible, all I can do is try to keep things from getting any worse.

I have no idea how much time passes. I only know the light outside the little window changes as the sun moves across the sky and the day progresses. There isn't even that much noise coming from the rest of the house, which strikes me as odd. I imagine Enzo throwing things around, screaming, threatening to burn the whole place down unless somebody starts giving him the answers he wants. Somehow, the silence is even more frightening than what I just imagined. Too many ugly possibilities exist in that silence.

The lock clicks. My heart is going to explode. My stomach feels like I'm on my way down the first big hill of a roller coaster.

The door opens, and the sensation only intensifies when Enzo steps through it. He's wild, his eyes blazing, hair mussed like he's been running his hands through it. His normally healthy color has drained away—now he's gray, drawn. But I don't get a sense of illness or weakness from him, far from it. He looks like he's ready to kill.

And he's glaring at me.

I force myself to stand but can't hide the way I'm shaking. It isn't weakness. Anybody in their right mind would shake if a man like him was looking at them the way he's looking at me. Like he wants to slaughter me and watch the blood drip out on the floor.

Is he waiting for me to speak? I lick my lips to moisten them. "Enzo. You might not believe this, but I'm so sorry about your grandfather. If there was anything I could have done, I would have."

That's as much as he lets me get out before crossing the room and grabbing me. A squeak escapes my lips as his fingers dig into my cheeks while he backs me against the wall. I know I shouldn't be surprised, just like I shouldn't let it hurt me. But it does. It hurts my heart. I'm looking into the eyes of a stranger when I was so sure things between us had changed.

"Let me give you a piece of advice." He hardly even sounds like himself, more like a wild animal with its teeth bared, and it's clear from the smell of his breath that he's had at least one drink already. "You are never, ever to speak of my grandfather again. I don't want you to mention him. I don't want your sympathy. All I'll ever get from you is lies and more lies, anyway. So don't waste your breath or my time."

"I wasn't—" I suck in a pained breath when his fingers dig deeper into my flesh. Pain ignites in my cheeks. Much more pressure, and he'll break my cheekbones. I'm sure he'd like that.

"You will only speak when you're answering a direct question. I don't want to hear anything else from you." His voice shakes with barely restrained rage. "Nod if you understand."

My head bobs up and down as much as I can move it.

"Now. Tell me who the hell you are," he snarls. "Before I kill you."

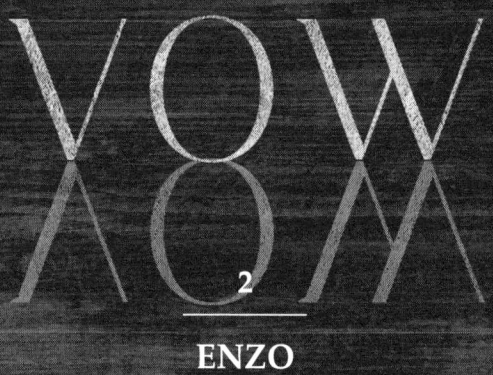

2

ENZO

I probably shouldn't be in this room with her. Not while I feel the way I do. Certainly not while I'm touching her this way when it would be so easy to hurt her. That's all I want to do. *Hurt her.* Make her scream, make her beg, and watch her blood run through my fingers like a river.

Focus, dammit. Why are you letting a woman rule your emotions?

Maybe I am truly going insane. For a moment, I hear Grandfather's voice in my head so sharp and clear, as if he were standing beside me.

But that's impossible. He's dead—his life snuffed out right in front of me, his blood is on my clothes. This suit another symbol of the charade that went on here today. Another symbol of how easily I was led around, as well.

My grip on her tightens, and I feel her delicate facial bones beneath my fingers. I could destroy her beauty in an instant, ruin her, break her.

"By the time I'm finished with you," I whisper, barely hanging on to the last threads of my control, "you won't even recognize yourself. No one will."

She's tough, I'll give her that—or at least she's attempting to be. She doesn't blink. A tremble courses through her body as she sucks in a pained breath as I dig my fingers deeper into her flesh. But she won't blink nor back down.

"Well?" I growl, leaning in close. If she isn't careful, she'll hyperventilate, her rapid breaths short and shallow. "Start talking."

"Can't," she manages to whisper. She looks down at my hand, covering half her face.

That's all that's stopping her? Fair enough. I take hold of her throat instead, pivot, and throw her onto the bed. She lands in an ungraceful heap, but instead of scrambling around, trying to sit upright to have a little dignity, she remains that way, gasping and coughing on her back.

I don't know what part of her I want to injure first. I have too. It's the least she deserves. "It's amazing you're still breathing," I whisper, and even my voice shakes with my barely controlled rage. I'm going to lose it completely, aren't I? I hope I do. I hope I blackout from the rage and wake up covered in her blood.

When I reach out and touch her ankle, it seems to stir her to life again. She attempts to pull herself away, to escape to the other side of the bed, but her legs get lost in the long dress, the heel of her shoe caught in the hem and tearing it. Her wedding dress, now stained and destroyed, is the perfect symbol of what was destroyed today. Thanks to her, all thanks to her. My grandfather's life. Any hope of my family securing their place here.

And somewhere deep in my chest, beyond family loyalty, is me. My wishes, the hopes I didn't dare voice even to myself. And here it is, proof of the wisdom of my reticence. I knew there had to be a reason I couldn't open myself fully to her. Why I couldn't imagine a future for us. There was never going to be one because she was never going to be better than she is, more than she is. A liar, a nothing. No one. And certainly unworthy of the name De Luca.

I reach down and grab her torn hem, laughing as I do, even though nothing about this is funny. "Look at you. The nerve of wearing a white dress. What a charade. What an absolute joke."

I take her by the ankle again and haul her across the bed until she's close enough that I can reach the top of the dress, over her tits. "You don't deserve to wear this." One quick tug and the seams give way, but the sound of her anguished cries as I do touches the place deep inside me that needs to make her pay the most. I haven't begun to take back what's mine.

"Please, please, Enzo..." Her words mean nothing to me. Now I take the dress in both hands and tear it, growling as I do.

"A white dress. Innocence. I'm sure that was the biggest joke of all, wasn't it?" It's shredded now, hanging from her arms as she once again tries to crawl away from me. The ultimate symbol of everything lost today. Hanging in tatters, ruined beyond repair.

It's a game, and I almost enjoy it. Pulling the dress from her, I leave her in nothing but a white thong and bra I suppose were meant to entice me somehow. And dammit, they would, too. If she were anyone else and my grandfather was still breathing, we would be having a much different encounter in this room. Wasn't I only just beginning to entertain the idea before—

No. I can't think about that now. I won't. I won't put myself through it when there's so much more to be done. This lying bitch? She's nothing, a distraction, just as she always has been. The fault lies with me for allowing myself to lose perspective.

I won't make that mistake again.

"Enzo, please, listen to me..." She lifts her head, her makeup smeared and running down her face, hair hanging in tear-dampened tangles on either side. This is how she deserves to look. Ruined. The way she's ruined so much.

"I would have listened to you. You had countless chances to speak up for yourself. To tell the truth. Instead, you chose to lie over and over."

"What choice did I have? You wouldn't have killed me if I had told you the truth before now? Please, we both know that isn't true. I was trying to save my own life!"

"Then you wasted your time because your life isn't worth saving."

"I know you don't mean that!"

I ball up the scraps of fabric in my hands, well aware of the dried blood touching my skin. Grandfather, I let you down. I let everyone down. It's that thought alone that revives me, that gives me strength in the face of her pitiful state. Her anguished cries. "Don't you dare tell me what I do and do not mean," I warn in a growl. "The next time you do will be the last time you breathe, mark my words. You mean nothing to me. I look at you, and I feel nothing inside. Do not fool yourself, whatever your name is."

"Alicia," she whispers, but I hardly hear her over the rush of blood in my ears and the screaming that has not yet let up in my head. It still doesn't feel real. None of it feels real.

"I don't care. You're nothing. You are no one. And as far as I'm concerned, you can rot here." With that, I throw the ruined dress at her, and the sound of her sobs is a twisted symphony as I leave the room and lock the door.

It's easier to breathe when I'm not in front of her, when the temptation to snap her neck or crush her windpipe isn't so strong. I hear her through the door—somehow, knowing she's still weeping, even though I'm not there to watch, pleases me. She isn't putting on a show for my benefit. She's genuinely distraught. Good.

As for her distress, it's nothing compared to mine. As long as I live, I will never get the image out of my mind's eye. The way he laid there, staring up at the sky, seeing nothing when those eyes of his were so shrewd, all-seeing, all-knowing. The man could convey an entire history with the slightest glance and could go on a vicious rant with nothing but a quirked eyebrow. And now, he'll do neither of those things again. He sees nothing. He knows nothing. All that's left is the shell when what I need is the wisdom. The guidance. What's the next step? How do I make these bastards pay for what they've done?

How does my family come out of this stronger than ever because, of course, that is the only acceptable conclusion. We cannot merely survive this. We must come out on top, better and stronger.

And if that involves hanging the head of one Josef Alvarez in my study, so be it. I'm going to take great pleasure in paying him back for every bit of what he's done.

One step at a time. That's a piece of advice I know my grandfather would hand down were he here. I can't look too far ahead, for the big picture would overwhelm me. The best I can do now is keep it in mind while taking the first of many steps. The rest will fall into place as time passes.

And what is the first step? That, no one needs to tell me.

I walk down the stairs and through the kitchen. The house is quiet except for the tumult taking place in the guest bedroom. I wonder how long she'll cry for. I wonder if anyone will hear her. In the kitchen, looking at what would have been our wedding feast—now in foil containers keeping warm on the stove and in the oven, it strikes me as a terrible, twisted joke. Look at us, making all these plans, and for what? None of it was ever real. Not even my bride's name.

I turn away from it, more important things on my mind. Such as where the hell everyone went.

Because I have questions for them.

They aren't in the yard, where what's left of our ceremony lies on the ground. The flower-covered arch is now in ruins, petals strewn across the grass. A patch of blood on the ground is all that remains of my grandfather, whose body the men carried away. He's somewhere in the house now, I imagine. My head spins at the idea, and I tighten my fists, willing myself to hold it together. This isn't the time to lose myself in emotion. One day, I will mourn the man who raised me, who gave me a second chance at life—if not my first chance since I doubt my bastard of a father would have given me much of one even if he hadn't tried to kill me.

Now, however, there are much more important things to be done. I continue searching, finally arriving at the garage. The door is ajar, and the smell of cigarette smoke carries my way on the breeze. I don't hear anything—no speaking, no accusations. But they're chain-smoking; that much is for sure. All of them nervous, and rightly so.

I swing the door open, and they all jump as one, all of them. Big, hulking, brutal men, seemingly terrified by the sound of squeaking hinges.

I say nothing at first, stepping into the garage and closing the door behind me. My gaze lands on each of them in turn and lingers while I slowly remove my jacket, hanging it over a folding chair which one of them jumped up from upon my entrance.

I unbutton the collar of my shirt before removing my cuff links slowly and deliberately. Occasionally, I glance around, gauging their reactions. Every passing moment ratchets the tension a bit further, which is precisely the idea. Eventually, one of them will crack under the pressure. Whichever one of them is responsible for the assassination that took place today.

Once my sleeves are rolled up to the elbow, cuff links safe in the jacket pocket, I turn to all of them. "So" I murmur, my gaze sweeping the group. "Which one of you would like to explain how my grandfather was killed on your watch?"

3

ALICIA

Once again, my life has become nothing but a series of brief moments where things get a little better before getting bad all over again. I'm only allowed out of the room for a few minutes at a time to use the bathroom. Then I'm locked back up. Nobody talks to me. Hardly anybody even looks at me. All they do is unlock the door, drag me to the bathroom, and wait outside, then drag me back to the room and lock the door. In all, not a difficult job.

I must be cracking up. How much more of this can a person take before they completely lose their mind?

It's been days since the wedding—at least three if I'm reading the light outside the window correctly. There's nothing for me to do but hang around and try to sleep as much as I can. That's my only way of escaping—when I'm asleep. Not that my dreams are exactly wonderful since they're generally filled with screaming and blood. Sometimes my blood, sometimes Enzo's, mostly his grandfather's. The horror of that day is still so vivid, like sometimes when I close my eyes, I feel like I'm right back there. Realizing in horror that the man was dead, no matter how much Enzo wanted me to save him. Knowing I would have to break his heart. Knowing if the shot had gone even slightly wild, Enzo would have been hit.

I go through every possible variation of the event in my sleep. It's morbid, but there's not much I can do about my subconscious. I guess it's a way of working things out, making them make sense. There's no making sense of any of this. No matter how I look at it, it's completely hopeless.

Only once has Enzo visited me after the wedding night. It almost makes me laugh thinking of it that way. Our wedding night. Not exactly how I imagined it—I'm sure he feels the same. I doubt he imagined mourning his grandfather and learning everything that was supposed to be cemented between the two families was based on lies and more lies.

And what did he do during that visit? He threw clothes on the bed, then left and locked the door behind him without uttering a word.

And now here I am. Just as clueless as I've been all along. With no control over anything—my life, what happens next. I don't know what he's planning. Any minute, he could storm in here and shoot me in the head. I have no way of telling if and when that's ever going to happen. This is no way to live, yet I know I don't want to die, either. I don't know what I want anymore.

When I start hearing more movement downstairs, though, I can't help but be afraid. Something's happening.. Wondering what it could be is enough to drive me out of my skull, but I can't stop. I listen at the door, pressing my ear to the wood, but the best I can make out is muffled conversations. I can't make out a single word.

Enough is enough. I can only stand so much of this helpless feeling. I knock on the door, praying I'm not shooting myself in the foot by doing it. "Hello? Somebody? Anybody?" I hold my breath, listening hard, and at first, I hear nothing. Ten seconds pass. Twenty. Finally, after half a minute, somebody unlocks the door, and I scramble back to make room for them.

It's one of the guards, and to say he looks put out by me would be an understatement. "Just wait a minute." Then he closes the door and locks it without giving me an explanation, or any idea of what's happening. I don't know whether to be afraid or what. I don't know anything.

More time passes, time spent pacing and wringing my hands, chewing my lip, and chewing my nails. I'm falling to pieces in this stupid little room, practically wearing grooves in the floor from all my walking back and forth. I have to do something. I can't lie in bed and fester.

I'm close to the door when it swings open to reveal Enzo. He looks better than I've seen him since the wedding, fully dressed and well-groomed. When he dropped off those clothes yesterday—or was it the day before?—he was unshaven, his eyes bloodshot. Now he at least looks like he's showered today and bothered to take care of the basics. That has to be a good sign.

What is not a good sign is the way he grabs me by the arm and, without a single word, drags me out of the room. Instead of dragging me to the bathroom the way he normally goes, he pulls me down the stairs and straight out the front door. The car is waiting, the passenger side door open. He practically throws me inside before slamming the door, then marches around to the driver's side and drops behind the wheel.

I'm afraid to breathe too loudly. I'm afraid to do much of anything. But I can't sit here and not say a word when it's obvious this is my last car ride ever. "Where are you taking me? Where is it going to happen?"

It isn't until we're out of the driveway and leaving the development where the townhouse sits that he bothers to acknowledge me. "What? What are you talking about?"

"Where are you taking me? You're taking me someplace to kill me now, right? I can see why you wouldn't want to do it back there. Too much cleanup. What, are you putting me in a hole someplace? I only want to know. I want to be able to prepare myself."

He taps on the wheel with his fingers, the muscles in his jaw ticking. I wish I could see inside that head of his. The slightest clue, the slightest hint of what he's thinking. I would take anything right now over this unnerving silence.

"You've watched a lot of movies, haven't you?" he finally asks in a flat voice.

"What does that have to do with anything?"

"Here you are, assuming I'm going to put you in a hole. Who said anything about putting you in a hole?"

"Okay, then in the swamp. There have to be swamps around here someplace, right?"

"That would be easier and more efficient," he mutters. "Let the animals do the work for us. But no, we won't be doing that, either."

Something inside me snaps. "For God's sake, what are we doing? Can you at least tell me that? Or do I have to be in the dark until the very end?"

"A few days spent on your own clearly did nothing to quiet you down."

"A few days spent on my own worried sick and wondering if I was living my last day. Sorry if I'm a little bit unnerved."

"You can stop being so unnerved. I'm taking you home."

I can't stifle the little gasp his announcement stirs up. Home. I'm going home! Of all the crazy scenarios that have run through my head, that was the single one I didn't dare imagine because it seemed impossible. Why break my own heart by imagining the impossible?

As if reading my mind, he continues, "My home. We're going back to Italy, where we belong now."

"Why? I don't understand."

"That's where I'm from. It's where I belong. And since you are my bride, you belong with me, so you're coming along. We'll be safer there."

He hesitates, then adds, "Besides, I can't bury my grandfather here. He belongs back home with the family. See that car behind us?"

I check out the side mirror, and my eyes widen at the sight of a hearse behind us. I don't think I can be blamed for not picking up little details like that when I was so sure I was being driven to my murder.

"So we're going right now? As in, today?"

"As in, as soon as we make it to the airport and the jet takes off. Yes. That's what I mean."

Italy. I'm going to Italy. "I don't have my passport."

He laughs for the first time in days, and it's not exactly a warm or friendly sound. "You have a lot to learn, *Alicia*." He says it like it's a curse, a condemnation, instead of my actual name. He might as well call me bitch instead. It would have the same effect.

Italy. So this is it. Even the slightest semblance of my old life is gone, forgotten. Nobody asked me. Never once was my opinion sought out. I just have to go along with it. He's taking me across an ocean to another continent, and still calling me his bride. I mean, I am, but hearing him say it is so strange.

This airport is a lot different than the one we visited during that disastrous meeting. For starters, it's still in use and well-maintained. There's a plane sitting there, and I guess it's ours. Or rather, his. It's amazing to think his family has that kind of wealth. Who needs to buy plane tickets when you have your own plane?

We're close to the plane when I notice another car already waiting, and the most startling thing happens before we come to a stop. A man who looks exactly like Enzo steps out, followed by a pretty girl who takes his hand and holds it while they wait for us to reach them.

"My brother, Christian. His wife, Siân," Enzo explains before putting the car in park and killing the engine. I search my memory but can't recall this person. He's got a twin brother? There are two of them in the world? Now I have to wonder what this guy's story is and why Enzo never brought him up. The way he made it sound, it was only him and his grandfather. What's the story there? I know better than to think I'll ever get it, or at least that I'll get it anytime soon. Eventually, he might warm up to me again, but that's going to take a while.

Enzo opens my door, and I step out, wrapping my arms around myself and following him to where he shakes hands with his brother. "Christian," Enzo murmurs.

Christian nods. "I wanted to pay my respects before you leave."

"That's good of you. I know he would appreciate it." Enzo then nods in acknowledgment of Siân, and she offers a faint smile that I guess is supposed to be friendly or encouraging or maybe offered in sympathy. What's her deal, I wonder. Wouldn't it be funny if she came into Christian's life in the same messed up way I entered Enzo's? But no, I'm sure the odds of that verge on the impossible.

I certainly can't ask for clarification. That much is clear. All I can do is watch as the casket is unloaded from the hearse. It's very nice, as far as caskets go, snowy white. It gleams like a pearl as the men load it onto a wheeled cart which they then roll over to the plane. I sneak a quick look at Enzo from the corner of my eye and see he's struggling, his jaw is tight, and his throat is working like he's trying to swallow back emotion.

Even now, when he's treated me so brutally, I want to reach out and comfort him. At least Christian has Siân's hand to hold, but Enzo might as well be alone. He would probably slap my hand away if I tried to touch him right now. It hurts to think of him suffering through this alone, silently. I wish there was something I could do.

"Thank you for coming," he murmurs to Christian, then nods to Siân. "And be sure to take care of yourself. You're carrying my niece or nephew. Precious cargo and all that." The three of them share a soft laugh while I merely wait, silent and trembling, to be told what to do next.

As it turns out, Enzo tells me nothing, only climbing steps up into the cabin without bothering to check whether I'm following him. Christian and Siân head back to their car—hardly acknowledging me.

I guess this is it. I'm about to step into my new life in a country I've never visited, in a world, I know very little about.

I touch my foot to the first step, take a deep breath, and continue to climb.

ENZO

I suppose this house is mine now, and the land upon which it sits. I suppose all of this is mine. I should feel something, anything, but I don't. The best I can do now is drag myself through the halls upon returning from the funeral. Eventually, I might be able to process the implications of all of this. The fact that I'm now head of the family and it all falls upon my shoulders.

Instead of coming to terms with my new reality, too much of my bandwidth is caught up in hating myself. I'm unable to process what I just went through today, watching Grandfather's coffin being lowered into the ground, and so I must turn to what's been at the forefront of my consciousness all this time.

How I'm the one who did this. How all of this started because of one stupid, reckless decision on my part. I could hardly bring myself to greet the many mourners who shook my hand today, all of whom pledged loyalty to the family and expressed their deepest sympathy for the loss of a great man. All the while, through all of their weak attempts at bringing comfort, all I could do was blame myself. I came close to telling them more than once that it was me, that I was the reason the man is now in the ground, that all of this is the result of a rash decision.

No, that would be childish, not to mention foolish. Nobody needs to know. I'm sure they all have their theories on what might have happened, though I've been tight-lipped on the subject. Suffice it to say, one of our enemies got to him, and they're going to pay. In our world, discretion is key. They respect that, I'm glad to say.

My footfalls echo in the large, otherwise silent house. I'm drawn to the first stash of alcohol my gaze lands upon like a moth to a flame. The first gulp of whiskey burns its way through my chest, and I savor the sensation, relish it. It does nothing to lessen the much more potent fire blazing away there, but then I doubt the entire bottle would have such an effect.

If only, if only. The words run through my head as I go to the window, gazing out upon the gardens Grandfather so enjoyed strolling through during his rare moments of peace. He always said he did his best thinking out there, but he could not have named a single one of the flowers now in bloom. He appreciated beauty, even if he could not understand it.

If only I hadn't fucked up and taken her. If only I had questioned the logic of the situation. Why would Alvarez have his own daughter waiting at the warehouse? Surely, he would not have sent her as a liaison; there was no reason for a member of his own family to have his prized product hidden in her bag when it was so clear she was on her way out. She'd been trying to get away when Prince and I caught her. She wasn't leaving the drugs for someone; she was sneaking off with them. Now, why would a member of that family do such a thing?

My hand tightens around the glass until I'm afraid I might shatter it, but then I would deserve the injury. I deserve much worse than that. So fucking stupid. And I'm supposed to lead this family now? When I so blindly, so carelessly, led us to this point?

If only I hadn't taken her. Brought her home. Kept her locked away. What did I think I was doing? Scoring points for us? How pathetic.

And she's here, locked in this house, in a room far grander than the one she was given back in Miami. She's scarcely left it since we arrived, and I've only set eyes upon her when necessary. This morning, for instance, when I entered the room just long enough to inform her, I'd be leaving for the funeral. She was smart enough not to say a word. A part of me expected her to offer condolences, which might have finally been what broke my resolve and pushed me to break her.

I pour another drink after draining the glass, wandering out of the parlor and up the stairs. There's no question where I'm heading. She's the only thing on my brain, the image of her face permanently etched at the forefront of my mind's eye. No amount of drinking could erase her, no more than it could erase the bitter, burning sense of betrayal. The rage.

I unlock the door and swing it open slowly, not saying a word, wondering what I'll catch her doing. There's nothing in here she can use against me—I've already searched thoroughly—but she's a clever one. Cunning. How else could she have pulled the proverbial wool over my eyes all this time?

She isn't creating a rope out of bed sheets or fashioning a weapon. She's only sleeping, lying on her back with one arm folded over her abdomen while the other is bent, her hand resting on the pillow, close to her face. She's peaceful, without so much as a care lining her smooth brow. Her breathing is soft and even.

Something moves in me, shifts. I swallow hard against whatever is trying to work its way out of my chest—whatever it is, it isn't rage. I'm far too familiar with that emotion to mistake it. This isn't the rush of heat brought about by mindless rage.

It's warmth. Something close to tenderness, perhaps.

She is the last person in the world who deserves it. I stand a bit straighter and lift my chin in defiance. Of what? My own weakness, I suppose. The very thing that brought me here. The very thing that killed my grandfather, no matter who pulled the trigger. It was I who put him in that position. I might as well have placed the gun in the murderer's hand.

She doesn't stir when I enter the room, though the carpet beneath my feet muffles my steps. I place my glass on the nightstand before sitting on the edge of the bed, perching carefully, knowing anything more would wake her immediately. I don't know why, but I want to have this moment with her. A moment of peace. A moment in which she has no idea of the danger she's in while she sleeps peacefully. The wolf sitting beside her.

It would take no effort at all. A hand over her face to stop her breathing. Not a pillow; I would want to watch her panic, not simply imagine it from the other side of the pillow. I could crush her throat. Snap her neck. Or I could do it the old-fashioned way and simply put a bullet in her head.

I'm considering this when suddenly, she stirs. Does she sense me? Probably not, because her absolute shock is not the sort of thing that could be feigned. Immediately, she begins scrambling away, tears springing to her eyes as she attempts to leap across the bed away from me.

I'm too fast, and I reach out wrapping an arm around her waist, while using my other hand to cover her mouth. "Stop crying," I growl, holding her tight. "I'm sick to death of hearing you cry. Was it your grandfather who was murdered in front of you? What the fuck reason do you have to cry?" Eventually, she calms herself, her mouth still covered. But there are no more tears, and her breathing has calmed to something more normal, less hitching and gasping.

I lower my hand, then take hold of the glass I set down. "It's over," I inform her as if she couldn't put that together on her own. "He's in the ground. Congratulations. We did it. We got him killed."

"I know it doesn't mean anything, but—"

"Don't waste your breath," I mutter, staring down into the glass. I should have brought the entire bottle. This won't be nearly enough. The warmth of her body calls to me. I merely glance at her, watching her out of the corner of my eye. Dammit, there's still something about her body. She has a way of making me react, though it's the last thing I want to do. I can't afford to be weak, not again, and certainly not because of her. But the memory of her lusciousness, her sweetness, it's all still so fresh. And she is right here, lying only inches from where I sit.

I shouldn't, but there's no helping it. My fingers fairly twitch with desire, especially now that the nightgown she's wearing has worked its way up her thighs, thanks to her attempts to escape me.

I shouldn't, but I have to. Her creamy skin demands to be touched. I run the backs of my fingers over her thigh, just above her knee, and her breath catches. "Now," I murmur, staring down at her skin because I can't bring myself to look her in the eye, "you are going to tell me everything I want to know. Do you understand?"

"Yes," she whispers.

"Good. I don't think I need to tell you what will happen if you lie, and from now on, I will take nothing you say at face value. I will do my research. I will know if you are lying to me. Understood?"

I glance away from her thigh in time to see her nod, her gaze steady. "Yes."

"Very well. You can't say you weren't warned." I throw back the rest of the whiskey before speaking again. "Now. Tell me, exactly who are you, and how you ended up at that warehouse?" Meanwhile, my hand inches up her thigh, a silent warning. I'm giving her a chance to speak her peace, and the moment she displeases me, it's over.

I will hurt her. I know exactly how to do it, and she knows I do.

"My name is Alicia, which I told you before. I'm just a normal person. Before I met you, I was an average college student, nothing special. Only I didn't have enough money to stay enrolled. I would have had to wait another year to take the classes I needed, and I didn't want to wait another year to finish my credits and graduate. The whole thing was hopeless. And a friend of mine…"

"Go on."

"My friend told me about a way to make a lot of money in one night. She's the one who sent me to the warehouse to pick up that package. I was supposed to deliver it to another location. And that was it. That was all I was supposed to do. I didn't know anything about what I was picking up; she didn't tell me a thing, I swear. I mean, I sort of figured it out, but I was desperate. And she promised all I had to do was pick it up and then drop it off. That's it."

A likely story. "Who is this friend of yours?"

Her cheeks darken, and for the first time, she averts her gaze. "Her name is Elena. I only know her through school. But she made it sound like this was a job she was doing for her family, and she had done it before lots of times. It's how she makes her money."

"So you knew you were doing something that could have been very dangerous, but you did it anyway."

"I just told you. I had no money. And it's not just tuition," she continues when I scoff and click my tongue. "I'm not saying I was living on the streets, but I came close once or twice. This place?" She waves a hand, indicating the luxury in which she was peacefully sleeping only minutes ago. "I guess this is where you live when you're not in a townhouse like the one back in Miami. My entire apartment could fit in this single room. I never had any extra money. I couldn't afford to go out with friends. My clothes have to be literally falling to pieces before I replace them. So yes, I was willing to trade all of that for a little bit of comfort, even if it meant doing something that might have been dangerous. But Elena insisted it wasn't, that she does it all the time and nobody ever has a problem with it, so I was desperate and stupid enough to go along with it."

I hear her. I do.

But a great deal of my concentration is also focused on the feel of her. She is the ultimate escape, the ultimate release. That's what I need most right now. Not explanations, not reflection, not even planning out what comes next. I need to forget. There's not enough liquor in this entire house to make that happen, but it could happen so easily with her. Alicia. Aly. Whatever she calls herself.

Her breath hitches when I slide my hand over the silky fabric that looks as though it was poured over her curves. My fingertips skim her chest and the curve of her tit. "And it never once occurred to you to tell me the truth? That you only went there to make a little money because a friend told you about it?"

"Would you have believed me?"

"It doesn't matter, does it? Because you weren't willing to take the chance."

"You were practically choking me to death. Even when I told you I had no idea what was in that package, you wouldn't believe me. You were determined to think what you wanted to think. Now, tell me. Do I have any reason to believe you would suddenly be reasonable?"

"Did I ask for your reprimands?" When my hand closes over her tit and squeezes, she grits her teeth together. "I think you're forgetting your situation here, but I would be more than willing to remind you."

"I'm not forgetting anything," she grits out, trembling, her body frozen stiff.

It's a heady feeling, knowing I completely control her life. There she was, worried she would never earn the credits she needed to graduate. I wonder if she's even given thought to her schooling since I captured her. Isn't it strange how our priorities shift at the drop of a hat? The way mine did the day of my wedding.

I should not want this woman. I shouldn't give her the opportunity to explain herself. She doesn't deserve it, doesn't deserve to live.

Why can't I stop craving her? She is a weakness I cannot afford. I stand suddenly, fighting for control that seems to slip away no matter how tightly I try to grip it.

"Where are you going?" she blurts out. I lift an eyebrow in surprise, though she looks as surprised as I am at her sudden question. Like it came out without her intending it.

"Since when is that any of your business?"

Her cheeks go pink, and she averts her gaze, looking out the window before lowering her gaze to the heavy silk blanket covering the bed. "I was only wondering. I've... barely seen you since we got here."

She flinches at my disbelieving snort. "Is my faithful wife missing me?" I venture, watching her reaction. Where is this coming from?

"Forget it." Her arms fold, covering her chest.

"Is there something you wanted to discuss?" I'm willing to entertain this. Perhaps too willing. Perhaps looking for an excuse to linger a little longer, inhale her scent, and watch as light streaming through the big windows caresses the curves of her face, her body. Lucky light. My hands ache to do the same.

"Not really. I mean... I just figured..." She lifts a shoulder. "I thought maybe you'd want to have somebody around after..."

She can't be sincere. There's no way she wants to spend time with me after how I've treated her. This is another way of twisting me up, as she did before. Tricking me into caring. Pushing me to forget why she's here. What she's done. "After the funeral? After burying my grandfather?"

"Yes." Her features pinch together in a pained expression that quickly fades. "You don't have to be alone, is all. I'm here. I'm not going anywhere."

"You're right. You're not going anywhere."

"You don't have to be alone," she whispers. She still won't look at me. I can't read her. Could I ever? "That's all I'm trying to say."

"Who said I'm going to be alone? You're the one who doesn't deserve company." She flinches, and that's a good thing. Better for her to remember her place.

If anything, I'm glad she reminded me of my priorities before I did something idiotic like sit down with her—or worse, like pulling back that blanket and crawling into bed to do anything but sleep.

Every moment I spend with her is another moment I'm risking my resolve breaking entirely. That's why I leave her without another word, closing and locking the door, putting at least that between us so the temptation isn't quite as strong.

I have no idea what to do with her, especially since the memory of how good it feels inside her refuses to let me go.

5

ALICIA

It's the strangest feeling, the sense of being a princess locked in a tower. Like my life has suddenly become a fairy tale, the sort of thing I used to read and watch movies about when I was a kid. The poor, plucky princess who, through no fault of her own, has to suffer indignities and pain, wishing with all her might for someone to rescue her.

Right about now would be a nice time for my fairy godmother to show up. Maybe she could get me out of this because I certainly can't do it on my own.

In the absence of such a presence, there's nothing for me to do but look out the windows, pace my bedroom, and take long soaks in the deep bathtub. I can't pretend that isn't nice—the thing is practically the size of a small swimming pool. Sometimes I soak well past the point where my skin prunes, just for something to do with my time.

There are books up here, but they seem more decorative than anything else, dusty old hardback copies of obscure works. I'm desperate enough for some way to pass the time that I've read a few of them, only to find myself with no memory of exactly what I read by the time I finished. It's like I read the words, and I process them, but nothing sticks.

How am I supposed to get out of this? That question is always on my mind and the reason I can't focus on anything. There's always the fear lingering in the back of my consciousness that Enzo will come charging in at any moment, threatening me, touching me, making me feel small, helpless, and totally under his thumb. It's like living in limbo, never able to settle down or relax. I sleep so lightly now that the slightest noise wakes me. And in a house this big and this old, a lot of creaking is going on. Rattling pipes and windows that shake a little in a stiff breeze. Sometimes I sit up in the darkness, staring at the windows until I can start to make things out, thanks to the early morning light.

If this goes on much longer, I'm going to go insane. If Enzo thought he had a problem on his hands before, he's in for a big, unhappy surprise when I go off the deep end.

Two days after the funeral, there is a knock on the bedroom door. The fact that anyone is knocking surprises me enough on its own. "Yes?" I call out. The door swings open wide, and Enzo appears before me, sliding his hands into the pockets of his slacks. I wish he didn't look so good. I wish my lonely heart didn't immediately want to reach for him and beg for his forgiveness. It felt like we were so close to something real. I couldn't have imagined that. No matter how he's acting now. I can't shake the feeling that I met the real Enzo at some point back in Miami, the one underneath the mask he wears now.

A mask I'm sure his grandfather fixed in place a long time ago.

"Are you hungry?" he asks. "I thought it would be nice for us to have breakfast together out on the terrace. It's a beautiful morning. And I would like it if you joined me."

I wonder how much it took for him to get all of that out. It's like every word was torture.

Is this a good sign? I wish I knew. I wish I didn't always have to wonder what's behind every comment, every simple invitation. "Sure, it would be nice to eat somewhere other than this room."

"I thought it might." He looks me up and down, and for a moment, I find myself hoping it means he's taking an interest in me again. My heart sinks when all he says is, "I'm glad I bought you all those things back in Miami. At least you have something to wear."

"Thank you for having everything sent over for me." After all, we sort of left in a hurry, and I wasn't exactly allowed to pack. But my clothes and other items arrived the day of the funeral, after Enzo left me, once I finally told him everything. For all I know, he was holding it back, waiting for me to fess up before giving me the dignity of wearing actual clothes. I'm not sure I even want to know where he dug up the nightgown I was wearing at first.

I have to follow him from the bedroom since this house is an impenetrable maze to me. I haven't exactly had the opportunity to take a tour and learn the layout—and once I get an idea of the true size of the place, I have to wonder how long it would take me to figure it all out. It's so huge, sprawling, and nobody has to tell me where the money came from to build this kind of palace. I think back to the drugs I had in my bag and wonder how much the De Luca family is responsible for spreading all over the country and maybe even further than that.

Downstairs, past the bright, sunny kitchen, are a set of doors that lead out onto the terrace he spoke of. And while I'm trying my best to be dignified and quiet, always keeping my eyes and ears open, I can't help but gasp like the out-of-touch, unsophisticated rube I am when we step outside.

It's one thing to survey the grounds from upstairs, but it's another thing to be out here. The heady aroma of so many luscious flowers makes my head spin. A pergola spans the terrace from end to end, and around the wood slats above me wind flowering vines. Bees buzz here and there, almost lazy as they go from blossom to blossom.

And in front of me is a garden that brings to mind the word paradise. Fruit trees, enormous roses, all other kinds of flowers I can't identify but would love to. I wonder if there's a book around here somewhere that could help me name them all. There are paths cut out and neatly kept, without so much as a weed marring their beauty, winding almost aimlessly through acres of meticulously manicured land.

Beyond this sits rolling hills, and in the distance, a lake shimmers in the morning sun. Like diamonds, sparkling, making me wish I was in one of the handful of boats already out there. I don't think I've ever longed quite so hard in all my life.

"This is stunning," I breathe, stepping up to the railing separating the stone terrace from what lies before it.

I turn to Enzo, startled into smiling, and his lips twitch. "Would you believe it if I told you this was my grandfather's pride and joy?"

"I'm not so sure. It doesn't seem like..." I really should stop while I'm ahead, shouldn't I? He doesn't need to know what I really think about that old man. Sure, he meant a lot to Enzo, but he was kind of a pig, too.

He knows what I was thinking and now flashes a brief but genuine grin. "You'd be surprised how many hours he spent out here, thinking and planning. He always said he thought better when he was out from behind his desk. Please, have a seat."

He even pulls out a chair for me, then takes a seat opposite mine. Between us is an array of different foods: cheeses, fruit, bread, little jars of jam and butter. "Coffee?" he asks, and I nod eagerly. The aroma is even stronger than that of the flowers, and the taste is rich, better than any coffee I've ever tasted at home. It shouldn't come as a surprise, I guess.

"I normally take a light breakfast. I don't know why, but my appetite changes when I'm out here." He helps himself to various items and fills his plate, then I do the same. "The baker is second to none. I'm almost anxious for you to taste his desserts." He sounds friendly, almost. Like he hasn't been keeping me prisoner all this time. I almost ask him what he's trying to get at? His moods are giving me whiplash.

"So there's a lot of staff on the grounds?"

"A handful." I guess he's not in the mood to answer questions. All I want is to get a feel of what I'm up against here. I've been secluded all these days and nights, with nothing to do but think and wonder and worry. It's a good thing I've never had a problem with my own company. I know some people might go out of their mind, if forced to be alone for very long.

He's already pouring himself another cup of coffee by the time he starts to talk about what he really invited me out here for. ""Now that I've had a few days to think, I believe the two of us ought to get a few things straightened out. I'm sure you have many questions you would appreciate having answers to, as well."

"Yes, now that—"

"I will answer them in my own time, if at all." Just like that, the very thin veneer of politeness dissolves, leaving me with the man who has countless times threatened to kill me.

He settles back in his chair, slicing up an apple in his hand. Obviously, he knows the effect it has, that knife, even if it is small. It takes conscious effort, but I force myself to look into his eyes rather than follow the knife's progress. He flips a slice into his mouth, crunching loudly. "We have a problem."

Just one?

"We are officially married. You are a De Luca now, for better or for worse. There's no going back. Putting it mildly, I know this isn't what either of us signed up for." There's a bitter edge to his voice that I guess doesn't come as a surprise.

Married. Now I understand that I hoped we could declare the whole thing null and void and get it over with. I could bring up the fact that we haven't consummated the marriage yet and could have it annulled, but something tells me all I'd get in return would be a quick, hard fuck on top of this table. Anything to remind me I have no say in this.

He gazes out over the gardens, looking almost wistful for a heartbeat. "In the end, Grandfather had only one wish for me. It was one of the last things he said to me just before the ceremony. That I need to carry on the De Luca name. Through all of this, that has been his only goal. I can't tell you how many times he tried to set me up with random women he thought would be a good wife, a good mother. Somebody to provide me with plenty of heirs to carry on the family name." He glances my way, his mouth drawn into a thin line. "He thought you fit the bill."

I hope he doesn't expect me to be flattered by that. The man looked at me and treated me like some broodmare, like only what I have between my legs gives me any value. I suppose that was the case to him.

"With that in mind, I want to make a deal with you." He tosses the core onto his empty plate but keeps his grip on the little knife. I already know how fond he is of knives, so this doesn't exactly thrill me much.

"What kind of deal?" Is my voice shaking? My voice is definitely shaking. I get the feeling he enjoys that, anyway.

"I will allow you to go back to your life, no strings attached."

I wait, holding my breath. Finally, it's too much. "If?" I prompt since obviously there's something else coming.

"If you give me a son."

A handful of words, but they hit me like a cannonball. I can hardly believe what I'm hearing. "A son?"

"Yes. A baby. That's what I want."

"But not just a baby. A son." Even saying it out loud doesn't make it any easier to understand.

His brows draw together. "Yes. What part of this is so difficult for you to comprehend? I thought you at least had a little sense."

I do my best not to snarl. "You're aware there is always a fifty percent chance that it could be a girl, and then I am stuck back at square one."

"Then we continue trying till we have a boy."

He's lost his mind. There's no freaking way to guarantee I'll get pregnant, and if I do and the pregnancy is healthy and whatnot, there is still a fifty percent chance the baby will be a girl instead of a boy. I could end up stuck in this damn marriage with ten daughters. And I highly doubt he'd stop there, even if my body was falling apart.

"Well?" He says it like a man who knows he's got me cornered. He has no reason to doubt I'll go ahead with this because he doesn't see me as having any other choice.

"Well... Is there another option?"

He blinks rapidly. "Excuse me?"

"I'm saying, is that my only option? Is there another condition I could choose instead?"

"Certainly." The man moves fast. In a flash, he withdraws a gun from his waistband and points it at me, aiming between my eyes. I stiffen, staring at him, holding my breath. This is it. He's finally going to do it. I'm going to die.

"Option number two: I become a widower much sooner than expected."

If he was going to do it, he'd do it. I don't know where that thought comes from, but it rings out loud and clear in my head. He doesn't want to kill me—not yet, at least. Not when he has a wife to give him what he thinks he needs more than anything. Like he's a king, and the succession is in jeopardy.

That doesn't mean I can push too hard. I don't want him losing it and firing anyway to spite me. I'm thousands of miles from home. It would be so easy for me to simply disappear without a trace. Nobody would even care.

So I keep my voice low, my gaze fixed on the gun. Asking him to lower it will only make things worse. I'll go in the opposite direction. "Then do it."

The gun jumps a little before steadying. "Don't bluff with me."

"Who says I am?"

"You're not going to like how it turns out."

"If the only other option is becoming a real-life Rapunzel, living locked up until you decide you've made good use of my uterus, who's to say?" I glance away from the gun long enough to meet his gaze.

His eyes narrow. I don't want to die, but I'm not going to whimper and beg the way he so obviously wishes I would. The best thing is I know it's driving him crazy—I'm surprised there isn't steam coming from his ears. Not that I can afford to get cocky. He could still snap.

"Why don't we talk about this like two rational people?" My mind is racing almost as fast as my heart, but I think I'm getting through to him. Maybe. "Without the gun? I can't think well with a gun in my face."

"Nobody asked you to think," he grits out.

"No," I admit. "But I think there might be a way we can both get what we want out of this—"

"Beyond me being allowed to live," I add before he can throw that in my face.

If he wants his heir, he's going to have to play ball. I doubt he wants to go through the hassle of divorce and finding another woman willing to have his child. For once, I have the upper hand or at least a fighting chance.

He knows it, too. And he hates it. "Fine." He lowers the gun, allowing me to breathe easier. "Let's go inside. This had better be good."

I hope it is, too. Now all I have to do is come up with a way to convince him to return to Miami, where I'll have a better chance of getting my life back. I think there might be a way to make this all work.

VOW

6

ENZO

What is she thinking? What's this all about? I'm willing to give her enough rope to hang herself with by letting her dream up a way for this to benefit both of us, but I only have so much patience. There will be hell to pay if this is nothing but a stall tactic.

She's pensive, brows drawn together, lips pursed while examining the shelves lining three walls of the study. Along with countless books, there are framed photos taken decades ago, along with assorted treasures from the many cities Grandfather visited on cartel business. Not that he was a sentimental man. I always imagined he enjoyed looking at certain pieces and remembering the deals he put in place on those particular trips.

I would tell her about it, but I don't want to interrupt her reflecting upon my offer, which was truly not an offer at all. She has no choice.

So why didn't she jump to accept it? There he goes again, my grandfather, still speaking in my head while buried beneath six feet of earth. Taunting me, challenging me. Forcing me to look at the problem from all angles, dissect it, and dig into it until I reach the heart of the matter.

And what is at the heart of the matter? The fact that no matter what I do to her, it gets me no closer to justice. And that is what I need—sitting here, where my grandfather should be seated, drives the point home.

Yes, I want a child, an heir, but I want my heir born into a world with as few bloodthirsty enemies as possible. I want them safe.

That means I'm going to bring down the Alvarez cartel if it's the last thing I ever do, though I have no intention of it being that. I'm going to win. Even if I'm not certain at this very moment of just how I'll go about it.

And I'm not going to get any closer to that understanding if I spend all my time sitting here at what was only recently my grandfather's desk, gazing upon my wife as she putters around and quite possibly stalls for time.

Wife. The word still boggles my mind. I have difficulty wrapping my head around it, no matter how I present the matter to her. For better or worse and all that. She is my wife. And I will see to it that I get what I deserve out of this arrangement.

Even if she has to think about it. Her reaction boggles me, too. She is in no position to think things over, or weigh her options, especially because she has no options. It's either this or she dies. What, does she intend on challenging me, pushing me, seeing if I mean it? And what happens when she finds out I do, that I mean it very much? She won't be alive to reflect on her foolishness.

I have to turn my attention away from her or else risk exploding. On the desk is the file Grandfather presented me with before sending me to Miami. All of the information we have about Alvarez and the cartel. At the moment, it does me no good. I need to find a way to get closer, deeper inside. It might be easier now, ironically, since I have no doubt Alvarez is crowing and celebrating up a storm, thinking he got one over on us. The limited time I've spent with the man has told me at least one thing: he's extremely full of himself, deeply certain of his cleverness. I might be able to use that to my advantage. I only have to figure out how.

"This is a beautiful room." She slides the book she was examining back into its slot, then runs her fingers over the spines along the rest of the row. "Really gorgeous. Your grandfather put all of this together? Or did your grandmother do it?"

"I never knew her, but this was the way he liked things. His special room. I doubt he would've allowed her to decorate it for him."

Her lips twitch. "That sounds right. No offense, but this is the second time today I find myself surprised by him."

"We De Luca men are complex creatures. It isn't all violence and greed."

"Obviously." She crosses the room slowly, her hands folded in front of her. Even at this moment, when I'm so fucking frustrated I can barely breathe, I can't help but admire the dignity with which she carries herself. That's one thing I've always appreciated about her from the beginning. She might cry and beg, but she doesn't break easily. There I was, attributing that strength to her upbringing in the middle of a cartel, but now I know it's simply who she is. And I'm sure the hardships she's endured have only toughened her further.

She looks down at the file, spread open on the desk. I watch as her eyes light up. "I know a way to make this work for both of us," she murmurs. Do I hear sly excitement in her voice?

She is amusing, if nothing else. "Where did you get the idea that this was open for discussion or negotiation? Or that I want this to work out for anyone but myself? Did I not make myself clear enough? Because I would be more than happy—"

She holds up a hand, shaking her head. "You made yourself perfectly clear, thank you."

"You're welcome," I retort. "So? What's the point of this?"

"I hear your offer… and would like to make you a counteroffer." Only the slight twitching of her jaw gives away her nerves. Otherwise, listening to her, I would think she was made of ice. Cold, perfectly composed. Damned if it isn't a turn-on, too. It's as if everything about this woman was created to tempt me, tantalize me, even when I know that's the last thing I need right now.

I lean back in the chair, tenting my fingers beneath my chin. This might turn out to be interesting, come to think of it. "Very well. And just what would that counteroffer consist of?"

She arches an eyebrow. "You're willing to hear me out?"

"I'll listen," I grunt, nodding slowly. "But understand me. If I don't like what I hear, I'm going to take what I want anyway. Nothing you say right now is going to change that. But please, do go on. I'm curious."

Her jaw twitches again, and I know, I just know she's fighting to maintain herself. What she wants is to smart off, to tell me to go fuck myself or something similar. She's too smart for that.

She gestures to one of the chairs facing the desk, and I nod, watching as she takes a seat. She sits perfectly upright, at attention. "I've been thinking a lot about how I ended up here. Like I told you, a friend of mine gave me the information about the warehouse, the package, and all of that. It's her fault I got into this in the first place. Whether she did it on purpose or not, she set me up for this. And I think it's wrong for her to get off scot-free."

I barely suppress an amused snort. "By all means. Go right ahead. I would never refuse the impulse for vengeance, but I'm still not sure what this has to do with me. Or our arrangement."

She ignores my response altogether and continues, "I only know her through school, really. That's how we met. We've never socialized outside of school because, as I told you, I never had any money for that kind of thing. No time, either." Her gaze fixes over my shoulder as she stares out the window for a moment, almost like she's reflecting on her life.

Her old life, now.

"And?" I prompt.

She shakes herself out of it, her gaze colliding with mine. "And that means I need to go back to school if I'm going to get to her. I need to pretend everything is going okay."

"You want me to allow you to return to school so you can get back at the girl who sent you to the warehouse?"

"Yes. That's exactly what I want."

"Why would I do that? What do I get out of it? I need you with me, remember? If I'm going to breed you, I need to be with you."

She leans in slightly, lowering her brow, fixing me with a cold stare. "I don't know for sure if she is Josef Alvarez's niece, but she did mention her uncle more than once, even if she didn't drop his name. And remember, who did you assume I was when I told you my name was Elena?"

I look at the file and remember finding the information inside. "His daughter."

"Exactly. My so-called friend was named after Josef Alvarez's dead daughter. Obviously, the family connection is strong. You want to find a way to get to him? Then let's get to her. We'll both benefit from this. You know we will." The need for revenge seeps into her words. I never took her for the type that would want vengeance, but I'm sure she's never been in a situation like this. We never know how far we'll go until we're pushed.

"Don't tell me what I know," I warn.

"Think about it," she urges. "We'll both get what we want. I'll go along with your... offer... without complaining, without any trouble at all. But I want this. And I know you want him."

She settles back in the chair with a soft grunt. "Hell. I do, too." I like this side of her. She's showing me glimpses of the sort of woman who'd make an excellent wife for a man in my position. Strategic, levelheaded. Calm despite a gun aimed between her eyes.

While I see the truth in everything she said, part of me feels I should stay here and settle family business, making sure I present an image of strength in the face of tragedy.

At the same time, I can do that from Miami just as well. It isn't as if my grandfather sat and festered in this chair. It isn't as if we'll be there forever, either.

And this might be just what I need to rid myself of Alvarez once and for all. I might not have succeeded by kidnapping his supposed daughter, but the niece named after his dead child? That could get me a lot further.

Naturally, I cannot reveal my true feelings about the idea to Alicia, not yet. I can't come off as too eager, too willing to take her lead. "It isn't a bad idea," I murmur. "I'm willing to consider it. But..."

Her eyes narrow while her mouth pulls downward at the corners. "But?"

"I'm afraid you're going to have to convince me of your dedication."

For the first time since she faced me down outside, her expression slips to reveal some of her anxiety. "What does that mean?" she asks, her nostrils flaring as she fights to control her breathing. Surely, adrenaline is pumping through her veins, now tainted with cold fear. It's delicious.

"I'll need collateral. Proof of commitment to your plan. Otherwise, how do I know you won't run off on me the moment you're on campus? You do realize I'll be taking quite a risk. I need to know I have security."

"Exactly how do you plan on having me prove that?"

"I thought you'd never ask." I push back from the desk but remain in the chair. "For starters, you can prove your submissiveness. I need to be sure you know how to follow orders when they're given."

"And how do you want me to prove that?" She's not fooling me. There's a note of flat, cold understanding in her voice.

"I want you to crawl to me on all fours and show me just how eager you are to be of service. You're going to help right the wrongs to which you've contributed. And you're going to get your vengeance, which you so richly deserve. So now, show me. Show me how much you want it."

I do my best to hold back the grin threatening to appear on my lips. If she clenches her teeth any harder, they'll crack. I can't pretend I'm not enjoying the sight of her processing this, fighting with herself, knowing she doesn't have any option but to submit, yet fighting against that knowledge just the same. She's stubborn, prideful, and I can't pretend not to admire that at least a little.

When she all but slithers out of the chair, sinking to her knees, I can't help but twitch behind my zipper. She's mine, mine to do with as I wish. And she knows it. It's a heady feeling, rich with possibility. What couldn't I make this woman do if I had a mind to?

For now, it's enough to watch her slowly, grudgingly crawl on hands and knees to where I'm seated. I swivel the chair and face the side of the desk where she'll arrive. She takes her time about it but eventually makes it to me, every movement deliberate until she finally comes to a stop between my feet.

"Good girl," I whisper. My chest is so tight it isn't easy not to reveal my excitement.

"What do you want me to do?" she asks, lifting her gaze. When her eyes meet mine, I'd swear a bolt of sheer electricity leaps from her to me.

"Come here," She moves maybe an inch forward. "Closer," I grunt. "Show me how much you miss my cock. It's been a while, hasn't it? Is your pussy lonely? Or maybe your mouth is. Show me how much you miss me."

She hesitates for the briefest moment before coming closer, raising herself up on her knees alone, sliding her hands up my legs from ankle to knee. Fuck, I didn't expect to react so strongly, my cock stirring to life in an instant. Heavy desire pulses through my veins. I need to be careful, or I'll forget the point of this exercise in favor of sheer indulgence.

She begins the slow, excruciating climb from knee to thigh, inching her way up. "How would you like me to show you?" she whispers. Is she fucking with me, or is there a throb of desire in her voice? I wish I knew. I wish I knew if this was all an act.

No, that isn't what matters. Dammit, I need to keep my thoughts in check. "I want you to place your lips over it. Don't unzip but kiss the bulge you've stirred to life here. Worship it. Worship me, and, baby, you better make it believable," I add, reaching for her and threading my fingers through her thick, soft hair.

Rather than break eye contact, she remains fixed on me as she lowers her head. I can't look away, either, staring into those green orbs. She's a siren, calling me into dark waters, and I'll be damned if I don't go. She presses her plump lips against my crotch, and I jump and throb. Fuck me, how I long to take her over this desk, in this chair, against the wall. Anywhere and everywhere. I want to fill her with my seed over and over until it's dripping out of her and onto the floor. But now isn't the time for such an indulgence.

"You can do better than that," I snip, "Come on. Show me. Prove to me how much you want this."

She brushes her lips over me, turning her head back and forth, sighing softly as she does. And that sigh goes straight through me like yet another bolt of electricity. Now I can't help myself, and I let my fingers tighten in her hair while I push her head down, thrusting my hips upward at the same time. Burying her face against me until I know she can't breathe. She digs her fingers into my thighs, grunting, but I hold her in place just the same.

"You will do what I say when I say," I grunt, humping her face, relishing in her increased desperation. "You will be where I want you to be when I want you to be there, and you will ask no questions. I will control every aspect of this situation. You will do nothing without my say-so. And if I find you've done even one thing to go against me in any way whatsoever, it's over. I'll find some other bitch to fucking breed. Yours isn't the only pussy in Miami, Alicia. Do you understand?"

Her high-pitched, strangled groans are enough for me, and I release her, allowing her to fall back. She lands in a heap, gasping for air and all I can do is stare down at her. She's a beautiful, dangerous mess that I've tangled myself in. Still on her knees, and fighting to regain composure, I watch as she swipes at her eyes, where tears are starting to form. I feel like an asshole, but I can't allow my feelings for her to control me. I gave in once before, and look where it got me. I am many things, but I will not be made a mockery by my people, nor will I allow her to think she can bend me and use me. This is for the better—for both of us. I stand and straighten my pants and jacket. It's the last thing I want to do, leave without sinking my cock deep inside her, but it's the smart thing.

"I have a few things to arrange before we go. We leave tomorrow night. Be prepared." She gets on her feet without another look at me and hurries from the room.

Leaving me with a painful erection and the certainty that, sooner or later, toying with her won't be enough. I'm going to need her again, and not because I want an heir.

VOW

7
ALICIA

Shit. Here I am again.

I didn't think I'd ever see this place after I was so roughly pulled from it. Will there ever come a time when my life isn't like a giant roller coaster ride? The sense of never knowing what's happening next isn't exciting. It's unnerving. I'm never sure of myself. I don't even know if I should bother unpacking since something could come up, and I might end up having to pack again tomorrow. Or, more likely, things will change so quickly that I won't be able to pack at all, and I won't have time to bring my bags with me anyway. Because I have no say in anything. I'm pulled here and there, thrown into a car, or strong-armed into boarding a jet. I'm a doll, pretty to look at, but my emotions and needs mean nothing to anyone.

And to think, those beautiful gardens are going unadmired right now. That enormous house has nobody living in it but the men who guard it—even then, I don't think they actually stay inside, but rather in separate buildings on the estate. What a waste.

The sooner I get things settled with Elena, the sooner we'll go back. Not that I'm in any hurry to leave the country again, not with my husband. I'm still not used to the idea of that word, especially when it's used in relation to Enzo. He's on the phone now, pacing around the house. Setting things up for himself. Not that he would bother cluing me in, but then again, I'm not sure I want to know what's going on in his head. What he's planning. At least, not when the plans have to do with something other than me. I would love nothing more than to watch Josef Alvarez suffer, but I don't need to know the finer details. I just have to do my job.

And then, I guess we'll go back to Italy, so I can have Enzo's baby. No, not just his baby. His son because that's all that matters. Whether or not my child has a penis between his legs is what counts. I'm sick of this whole fucked-up, misogynistic world of his. Plus, how can he expect me to have a child and simply walk away like nothing ever happened? The idea of leaving any child, let alone our own, with him is unsettling.

I didn't think to ask what happens after I'm finished being bred. He said I could go back to my life—does that mean I'll return to Miami? Do I get money to set myself up? I was too busy proving myself, following his instructions, that I didn't think to ask for specifics. I need to do that. I need to get details. Would he laugh me out of the room if I asked to get it in writing? I should probably do that, too, or at least try. I don't think it's too much to ask.

For now, it makes sense to get unpacked in what has become my bedroom. I would like the much larger room Enzo lives out of, but I'm not trying to share space with him, either. I'll make do with a smaller closet and a smaller dresser. It isn't like I have all that much, anyway. Only what he's bought for me.

I have nothing of my own. Even my son, should he be born, wouldn't be mine. He'd be Enzo's to mold and shape.

This is not the time for tears of frustration and sadness to well up in my eyes, but the timing has been off throughout this entire nightmare. I shove the suitcase aside and sit on the bed, staring at the floor. It blurs thanks to my tears, but I blink them back just in case he walks in and finds me crying. For some reason, putting up a front matters. I don't need him knowing how vulnerable I feel right now, even if I'm sure he could guess. He might be a real bastard when he puts his mind to it, but he does possess a level of emotional intelligence he couldn't possibly have inherited from his grandfather. Like one small part of him wasn't destroyed by that man.

I'm just tired, is all. At least here, in Miami, I might not feel quite so lost at sea. If I'm going back to school, that means having a little bit of myself back. I need that. I need to feel like me, not like some captured, tormented prisoner. I might be able to sleep better at night—falling asleep over my books sounds a lot better than crying myself to sleep.

I didn't bother closing the door all the way, and I barely have a warning signal of Enzo's footfalls before it creaks open. "Bored with unpacking?" he asks, sizing up the situation in a single glance.

"I'm tired. My body can't keep up with the time change, swinging back and forth like I've been doing." Maybe he'll believe that. Right now, I don't care whether or not he does, so long as he leaves me alone.

"You'd better adjust because this isn't a vacation. You have work to do here. I hope you haven't forgotten."

I shouldn't let him get to me like this, but if I don't vent at least a little bit of the bitterness eating me up inside, I'll either explode or crumble into dust. "Thanks for reminding me. It's barely been a day and a half since we made our arrangement, but it's nice of you to remind me, anyway."

"I'll chalk that up to fatigue after all this travel."

I don't really care either way, but I hold my tongue rather than lash out at him. He'll only find a way to make me regret it later, so it isn't worth the effort.

When he doesn't leave, I look his way. He's leaning against the doorframe, hands in his pockets, and I wish he didn't look so good. The man already has me at a disadvantage. I don't need to lust after him. "Is there anything else you want to talk about? Because I could really use some rest."

He doesn't answer right away, choosing instead to stare at me some more. I can't get a read on him—his expression is impossible to understand. Finally, I can't take the suspense anymore. "What is it? What do you want?"

His mouth tugs upward at the corner. "I was just thinking to myself. There you were, practically strutting into my study less than forty-eight hours ago, all commanding and full of confidence. I knew at the time it was an act, but to see the proof in front of me is something else. Look at you. Dejected, realizing you're right back where you started."

"That isn't exactly why I was sitting here this way." Though it was pretty damn close.

"I know it can't be because you're in love with me. That was just another one of your games, a way of using me. Isn't that right?"

I'm not going to do this. I'm not going to let him twist me up. I'm practically biting my tongue against the litany of terrible, filthy things he needs to hear about himself, about his entire fucked-up family. He wants to hurt me. He wants me to break down. I will not give him that satisfaction.

And he knows it, and it's driving him crazy. I can feel it, his frustration, practically reaching across the room to wrap itself around my throat the way he's so often done with his hand.

Suddenly, he changes the subject. "I have something for you. A wedding gift."

Immediately, instinct warns me against reacting. I'm not going to give him what he wants, dammit. He might have me trapped here, but I won't play along. "I never imagined you would get me anything. I don't have anything for you."

"Remember, we're going to take care of that in time." Right, because all that matters is giving him a baby. "Besides, this is not a gift from me. It's from my grandfather."

As if I wasn't already apprehensive. He crosses the room, and I hold my breath, bracing myself for what's coming. He slides a hand inside his jacket, and a sickening chill settles over me.

Until he withdraws his hand and with it a slim, long, velvet box. He opens it and holds it out for me to examine a pair of bracelets. Diamond bracelets, and not just a single row of jewels, either. Both feature four rows of stones. I don't need to ask if they're real, and I wouldn't insult him, anyway. I've already seen the house the old man lived in. I have no doubt he could afford this.

They're overwhelming. Too fine to touch. They sparkle like they're on fire, catching the light and throwing it back in a million little prisms. "I..."

"He wanted you to have them."

"Sure, and that's very sweet, but it doesn't feel right. I don't know if I can accept them."

"Too fucking bad," he snaps. "The man wanted you to have them. They're a gift to my wife. Believe me, I would send them back otherwise, but it's not my place to do that."

He pulls the bracelets from the box, then tosses the box aside in favor of grabbing one of my wrists. As usual, I have no choice in this. I'm going to wear them whether I want to or not.

I look from my wrist up at him, and he happens to glance over and meet my gaze at that exact second. Something passes between us—I can read it on his face, the way his expression softens. For a moment, I have hope. There he is, the Enzo I thought I knew before. The one who said he loved me. The one who almost tenderly recited the marriage vows.

It must be an illusion, his softening because all I have to do is blink, and it's gone. His eyes narrow, and at the last second, he turns the bracelet over so the diamonds are pressed against my skin rather than facing out. "What are you doing?" I ask, but my question is ignored. He's too busy doing the same with my other wrist, and once he's finished clasping the bracelet, he wraps his hands around them both and squeezes hard.

I can't help it. I gasp, then grit my teeth against the pain. "You're the reason he's gone," he mutters. "Yet here you are, wearing the jewels he bought for you. How does that make you feel? Are you proud of yourself?"

"You've made your point," I whisper, shaking from the pain as the stones dig into my skin.

"No. I don't think I have." He holds both wrists in one hand and loosens his tie with the other, then lifts it over his head. I hardly have time to figure out what he's doing before he drapes the loop around my wrists and cinches the tie tight.

"You don't have to do this. Haven't we gotten past this point by now?" My pleas fall on deaf ears. He's too busy tying the other end of the striped silk to the headboard, leaving me sitting up partway with most of my body draped over the bed.

"You're going to have to prove how committed you are to this plan." He looms over me, holding my wrists even though the tie is already so tight. The tie isn't enough to make the diamonds dig into my flesh, and that's what he wants. To make sure I'm hurting as much as possible. He squeezes tighter, and now I can't blink back the tears that spring to my eyes. "I am!" I gasp.

"That's not enough. Your words aren't enough. You've already told so many lies." He mutters to himself in Italian while lowering his zipper. "You're going to have to show it through actions. What's that saying? Actions speak louder than words?"

He's already getting hard by the time he pulls himself free and traces my lips with the head of his cock. Of course, he'd get off on my pain. He's a psychopath. "You're going to suck me so good there won't be any question of your commitment. Do you understand me?"

The very idea makes my blood curdle. Not sucking him off but doing what he wants. Giving in this easily. "Yes!" I gasp out when the stinging pain in my wrists becomes too much.

"I thought so." He's stiff by the time he surges forward, rolling his hips and entering my mouth. All I have to do is hold on until he's finished, then he'll leave me alone. It's the only thought keeping me from gagging when he hits the back of my throat and groans like he's satisfied.

"My wife. Always so eager to please me." He lets out a bitter laugh before driving himself forward again, and again, holding the back of my head in one hand and my crossed wrists with the other. Using me, controlling me like he has from the beginning. "Use your tongue. Show me how much you crave my cum."

Tears roll down my cheeks as pain and humiliation swirl together. I close my eyes, but he squeezes my wrists harder. "No. Look up at me. I want you to watch me while I fill your pretty mouth with my cum." He wears a twisted sort of smile when I force my gaze upward to meet his.

I wish I could tell him it doesn't need to be this way. That we could've had something real, that we were both in a shitty situation but could've made the best of it if it wasn't for the anger he can't control. He doesn't have to force me. He doesn't have to humiliate me this way.

It only occurs to me while he's fucking my face that he doesn't care.

He wants to hurt me. He won't be satisfied until I'm bleeding and begging him to stop. A strangled cry tears itself out of me at the thought, one that's muffled thanks to the dick working its way in and out of my mouth. The sound makes him groan and causes him to twist my hair around his fist and tug so I whimper again.

"Mm, that's right. You know just what I like." He sighs when I do. "So happy to please your husband. So committed to my happiness and satisfaction. Maybe you deserve to wear these bracelets, after all. Maybe I ought to give you a pearl necklace to go with them."

His stare is hard, cold, and I find myself craving the warmth I saw in them before everything fell into a million pieces. "Wouldn't you like that? A pearl necklace? My cum running down your chest like the slut you are?" He thrusts harder, so hard his balls slap against my chin, and my nose aches from banging against his base. His breathing quickens, his pace growing more frantic.

That's not even the worst part, not even close. I'm wet and getting wetter with every slap of his balls. With every filthy word, every snarl, every grunt. He's treating me like trash, and all it's doing is hardening my nipples and making me crave him more. It shouldn't, but it does, and I have no idea how to feel about it.

I want him—need him—to touch me, to make the ache go away. Because I'm aching inside. Aching between my legs, where my clit throbs. It's almost painful—and rubbing my thighs together doesn't do anything but turn my helpless gagging into frustrated groaning because that isn't enough. Only his touch will do, and wanting his touch right now while he's using me, is sick and twisted.

A tear rolls down my cheek, and for the first time it's like he's seeing it. He chuckles darkly. "Poor little wife," he growls with a vicious pull of my hair that sends a delicious tingle through my scalp and down my spine. He has no idea what this is doing to me.

He calls me a slut, and maybe I am because I can't pretend I wouldn't come if he so much as flicked a finger over my swollen bundle of nerves. I don't understand the desire, but the degradation turns me on, even though I know it shouldn't, even though I know he doesn't truly care about me.

How could I be turned on by a man who only wants to use me? *It wasn't always like this.*

"You ready for my cum?" he asks in a tight whisper interrupting my thoughts. I'm almost elated but also dissatisfied for it to end so soon. All I can do is look up at him through my teary eyes. His gaze darkens, and his hold on my hair becomes painful; my scalp burns where he holds me, and a growl escapes his lips. "Don't you dare waste a drop, you lying slut," he warns.

"Fucking Christ. Here... it... is..." It's not another second before the taste of him floods my tongue and coats the inside of my mouth. There's so much I'm forced to swallow or choke.

It's the relief of him letting go of my wrists that really matters. As soon as he does, I feel as though I could weep with gratitude, but I won't. Instead, I swallow what's in my mouth once he's withdrawn, not saying a word even when he unties me and removes the bracelets. I guess I don't get to keep them after all. Not that it matters right now when I have red welts to remind me of them.

"You did good. Now clean yourself up," he orders, disdain dripping from his voice. I look up at him and almost shrink back when he raises his hand. I'm afraid of him for more than one reason, but I've never worried he would hit me, so why do I now?

Something close to anger flickers in his eyes for one moment, but before I can fully register it, it's gone.

"Don't shrink away from me. I've never hit you, and I won't. I might be a monster, but I don't get off on abusing women."

"What do you call what you just did?" I snap, the words escaping before I can stop them.

A wide grin falls onto his lips. "Proof. You could've stopped me. You could've told me no, but you didn't. You didn't want to. Deep down, we both know you wanted my cock in your mouth. The only shame is that it wasn't in your pussy. Cum is such a waste if it's not being used to offer me an heir." His thumb comes out of nowhere and caresses my bottom lip. "You missed some." It's the first time since before the wedding that he's touched me in a gentle manner. It infuriates me how he can go from burning hot with anger to calm and collected the next instant.

I can't believe the words that leave my mouth next. "I hate you!"

"Good, it'll be better if we keep things that way. Wouldn't want the truth to come out now, would we?" My hand balls up into a fist, but I hold myself back. As bad as I want to lash out, I don't really want to hurt him.

At least he leaves the room quickly after that so I can go to the bathroom and run cold water over my wrists, weeping silently while I do.

I had a feeling I was making a deal with the devil back in Italy, but now I know for sure.

VOW

8

ENZO

"If you don't stop jiggling your leg around, no one will ever believe you aren't nervous." I place a hand on Alicia's knee. "Please. Stop. It's driving me insane."

"I'm insane for thinking I'll be able to get away with this."

"Would you relax already?" Nerves are one thing, but this reaction is bordering on morbid. "You're acting like we're talking our way out of a murder rap, for fuck's sake. We're trying to keep you in school. Not exactly death penalty-level business."

She rolls her eyes but stops with the leg, so I'll take it as a victory. "What are you going to say?"

"Don't worry about it. I told you I have this under control." I slide her a look that makes her recoil slightly. "And as you know, I don't appreciate being questioned. So sit back and let me take care of things."

I add a smile and continue when she doesn't respond. "After all, I'm your husband. It's my job to take care of things." Someone should tell her she has a terrible poker face. I can practically see every thought going through her head, none of which are particularly complimentary toward me. Still, she bites back whatever sarcastic comment she would love nothing more than to let fly. The girl knows better than to test me, even in public.

"I just hope they don't put up too much of a fight. We're already not meeting with my usual advisor. At least he and I have an established relationship. I've never worked with this other person before." She cranes her neck to look through the open door into the bustling main office. But then she catches a glimpse of the grimace on my face at the mention of her having a relationship with another man. Her spine stiffens, and she lets out a shaky breath. "Not like that, Enzo. I just mean he's been the person to manage my accounts, provide guidance, that sort of thing."

She's nervous; I can see it written all over her posture. I have half a mind to forbid her from ever meeting with him again. I'm the only man she'll ever need for guidance. But I don't. This is all a ruse to get to her friend, Elena. Once that mission is fulfilled, school will be no more. She won't need it while bringing my son into this world. So instead, I brush a piece of lint from my pants and patiently wait for this new advisor she speaks of.

We are sitting in what is essentially a cubby, waiting for someone to come in and decide whether she deserves to remain enrolled for the rest of the semester after having missed so much time. How was I supposed to know her college education would end up being important?

"Sorry to keep you waiting." The woman who walks in is not exactly young, but she isn't old, either. She could never be described as hot, though I suppose in the right clothes and with the right grooming, she could be attractive.

One thing is for certain: when she sets her eyes on me, something about her changes. Whether she's aware of it or not, she responds to me, standing up a bit straighter and thrusting out a pair of tits that are almost admirable.

"I never mind waiting for a pretty woman," I assure her with an easy smile. "I'm sure you're very busy here. It seems that way, at least."

"You have no idea. I'm sure you're probably wondering why you're meeting with me and not your assigned advisor. Due to the nature of your case, your file has been escalated to me as the Senior Advisor for the university." She extends a hand across her desk. "I'm Catherine."

"Enzo De Luca. It's a pleasure. I promise we won't take up too much of your time." When I take her hand, I make a point of holding on a beat longer than necessary.

"I'm afraid I wouldn't have much to spare, anyway, Mr. De Luca." She offers a breathless little laugh as she takes a seat.

"Then I'm even more grateful you've taken the time to sit down with us. We both are." I turn to Alicia, grinning, and she forces a tight smile in response. She's hating this, which naturally means I love it. This in no way evens the score—she's never going to be able to make up for what she did to me, my family—but it goes at least part way toward it.

Catherine clears her throat before typing something into her laptop. "I understand you've missed quite a bit of coursework this semester, Miss—"

"Actually," I correct with another smile, "it's Mrs. De Luca now. And that's why I've come in to see you, to apologize in person for having swept this incredibly lovely creature off her feet. I know I should have taken her schoolwork into consideration, but I couldn't wait until the end of the semester to make her mine, officially. It was all sort of a whirlwind."

I close a hand over Alicia's, threading my fingers between hers. "And once I set my sights on what I want, you can't convince me otherwise. I can't tell you how many times I've gotten in trouble for my impulsiveness. But I think this time around, I'll only end up being grateful for it."

I smile at my wife, leaning in a bit as if feeling affectionate. "At least, I hope so."

"So that's it? You two got married?" She looks at Alicia, raising her brows. "Without giving a word to your professors? Or even bothering to reach out? Not that I'm not pleased for you. Congratulations," she adds as an afterthought.

I squeeze Alicia's hand, signaling for her to fall in line. "Thank you," she murmurs with a little shrug. "And I know I should have made arrangements. But like he said—"

"I wasn't about to be refused. I mean, the whole thing was like a fairy tale. I couldn't help but be swept up in the moment." I shrug, chuckling. "Call me impulsive, but if there's one thing we Italians know about besides pasta, it's romance."

"That's lovely, and like I said, I'm glad for you. But we do have policies for a reason. If everyone left town to get married at the drop of a hat, how would anyone earn enough credits to graduate? And if we look the other way, we'd have to look the other way for everyone. It just isn't fair." At least she manages to sound sympathetic, even if she isn't telling me what I want to hear.

"And I am sorry about that, really, I am." All right, so there's no point in trying to appeal to her romantic side. It seems she doesn't have much of one—I notice the absence of family pictures on her desk, not to mention her bare ring finger.

I lean forward a little, looking only at her. She's the only person in the world right now. "There must be something we can arrange. What if I promise to make sure Mrs. De Luca makes up the work? I'll chain her to her desk if need be. I'll withhold meals if that's what it takes."

A giggle bubbles up and out of her before she can stop it. "All right, that won't be necessary."

"Whatever you say. I just want to make sure you know how serious I am about this. We wouldn't be having this problem if it wasn't for me. So I am willing to do whatever it takes to make things right." I lower my brow, grinning. "Whatever it takes, Catherine."

That did it. Her cheeks flush, and she averts her gaze, but not soon enough. She's interested. I have her on the hook.

The key here is not to lose sight of the big picture and try to reel her in too quickly. This takes control, discipline. "So what can I do? Could this perhaps be settled via a donation to the school? I'm not sure if you're aware of this, but my family is quite prosperous. Back in Italy, we're well-known and respected. With that comes money—or is it the other way around? Does the respect come because of the money?" I screw up my face like I'm thinking, and she giggles again.

She manages to suppress it quickly, coughing to cover up the rest. "You know, in certain circles, that could be considered a bribe."

"And how many buildings up at Harvard just happened to be named after third and fourth-generation students currently enrolled? It happens all the time. This might not be Harvard, but don't you deserve some nice, new facilities?" I glance around, lifting an eyebrow. "Or perhaps a new administration building. With bigger offices."

She purses her lips. "All right, I get your point. And maybe we can work something out, but that's not up to me to decide."

"But surely, you can make a note somewhere that my wife pledges to make up all of the coursework she missed. Even if she has to work through the winter break. Would that be possible?"

"Well..."

"Aw, come on, Catherine. Between you and me, we both know strings can be pulled. We both understand how these things really work. There are always two sets of standards, two sets of rules." I offer a sly smirk. "And there are ways around all of them. If you know what I mean. I think you do."

She blushes again. "I guess if she promised to have all of the work made-up before the start of the next semester, and if she attends all of her classes going forward, I don't see any reason an exception can't be made."

"See? I knew when I looked at you that I was looking at a sensible person with no interest in penalizing Alicia for a whirlwind romance." I sit back, beaming at my bride, who looks like she sat on a thumbtack and is trying to cover.

"Very well. You've convinced me, Mr. De Luca." She looks to Alicia, grinning conspiratorially. "And now I understand how he convinced you to run off and marry him at the drop of a hat. A very smooth talker."

"One of my many qualities. But I doubt you want to go into the private details of my life." She chuckles when I wink, so I plunge ahead. "Oh, now that I'm thinking about it, I'll need you to add me as the primary contact on Alicia's file."

"What?" Alicia whispers. "I don't think they do that... babe."

Catherine's warm, open attitude turns frigid. "Exactly why would you want me to do that?"

"So I can be sure she's staying on the straight and narrow, of course. I want to make sure we're all working together, and she's living up to her end of the bargain we're making today." I take Alicia's chin in my hand, pretending to be playful for the sake of our audience. "Besides, if there are any financial issues or any problems, I want to be sure I'm made aware of it immediately. I know if you look at the file, you'll see she's been through some hardship before. That part of her life is over, but I'm sure you can understand how reticent she is over the idea of ever visiting the financial aid offices again. I would much rather take that off her hands."

I glance at the advisor, who's frowning. "And between the two of us, she has a tendency to take too many things on her shoulders. She's accustomed to handling everything on her own, having been alone for so long. It's admirable, but I hate thinking of her struggling in silence when I could so easily help."

"That's very sweet of you." She's warming up again, that chilliness thawing.

"What do you say? Could you be a good girl and do it for me?"

Her cheeks flush, and she bites her lip. "I mean..."

"Come on, now. It's simple. I know you can make it work. Especially if it means sitting in an actual office one day," I add, and I'm barely able to bite back a satisfied smile at the open interest that flashes across her face. "I could make that happen, Catherine—if you're a good girl and make this happen."

She looks to Alicia, who's fallen silent and still. "Is this what you want?"

If she knows what's good for her, it is. "It would be nice not having to worry about things anymore. Like my husband said, I've been on my own for a long time. It's a relief knowing he wants to help me take care of things. I can focus on my coursework now."

"See? Really, in the end, this is in everyone's best interest." I turn the full charm on the woman in front of me, who is practically putty in my hands now. If it wouldn't go directly against the loving picture I've tried to concoct, I'd offer to take her to dinner to sweeten the deal. I'm sure it's been a while since she's had a date with anyone but her cats.

"All right," she finally relents. "I'll put you down as the contact person where your wife is concerned."

"Thank you so much. You've taken a stressful situation and turned it into a lovely meeting." I stand and offer my hand to shake. "It's been a real pleasure meeting with you. And I would love to meet again sometime to discuss the other arrangements we hinted at."

"I would be happy to speak with you at a time you find convenient, Mr. De Luca."

Alicia winds her arm through mine. "Now, babe, you said it yourself earlier. She's a busy woman."

"I'm not too busy for that," she assures us.

"I didn't think you would be." I leave her with a wink before escorting my wife from the office. We aren't out in the hall yet before I can't help laughing softly.

If I didn't know better, I'd think my loving wife is jealous.

VOW

9

ALICIA

I have so many reasons to hate Enzo, but right now? The fact that I'm swamped with work is the primary reason. Why did he have to make such a big deal of me making up all the work? Couldn't he have sweet-talked that cat lady at the administration office into letting me slide a little? The way she was looking at him, I have no doubt she would've gone for it. The woman's tongue was practically lolling out of her mouth, for God's sake. It was pathetic.

But no, he couldn't be bothered. He probably gets off on knowing I'll have all this work to make up.

My head is still spinning hours later, stretched out on my bed, for lack of a desk, textbooks and syllabi spread out in front of me. I might as well get used to not sleeping since that's the only way I'll be able to catch up. All thanks to him, of course. Nobody asked him to kidnap me and hold me hostage like he did. This is all his fault. He should be the one doing the homework, not me.

Ugh. Yes, I'm being a baby. All things considered, I doubt anybody could blame me.

"How's my little student doing in here?" The man is loving this, poking his head into the room and grinning when he sees the mess around me. "I know I shouldn't interrupt when you're so busy, but I couldn't help it."

"I'm glad you're enjoying yourself," I mutter, my teeth clenched. "The more you interrupt me, the longer I'll spend digging my way out of the hole you put me in."

He lowers his brow, and I know that was a mistake. Not that I needed to have it pointed out to me. Smarting off like that is a calculated risk. Right now, I'm willing to take it. He needs to hear what an asshole he is.

Rather than back out into the hallway like any sane person would do, he steps fully into the room. "In case you aren't aware. You're treading on thin ice. I'm already displeased with the way you conducted yourself back at the school."

"What are you talking about?" I ask, guarded and searching my memory.

"Don't play dumb with me. You were against me being placed in your file as a contact person. You made the mistake of voicing that disapproval in front of the woman who was helpful enough to pull strings for me." He folds his arms, and I can't help noticing how it makes his sleeves bulge. This is a strong man, a powerful man. He's proven it to me countless times already, hasn't he?

"You took me by surprise," I point out. My voice is shaking. Dammit, I don't want him to hear how he's affecting me.

"You're going to need to learn to hide your true feelings if you'll have any hope of surviving our marriage." There's not so much as a twitch of his lips to tell me he's joking. The man is dead-ass serious. A chill runs down my spine at the implications.

"I won't talk back anymore," I vow. "Really. If I have any questions, I'll wait until we're alone to ask you about them. I won't say anything in front of people."

"I'm afraid I can't believe you, though I appreciate your assurance." He shakes his head slowly. It's the flatness in his voice that makes my blood run cold. "You aren't abiding by our agreement."

"How so? I was confused and concerned that Catherine lady was going to see through your request. It sounded sort of abusive, honestly. Don't you see that? Red flags all over the place."

He raises an eyebrow—something tells me I'm not getting through to him. "I had it under control. The woman was in the palm of my hand." I look down at my books, but not in time to hide the eye roll I can't hold back. "What? You don't like the idea of me finding it so easy to make her do what I wanted?"

"No. It was kind of pitiful, if anything. The way she caved." The way he took advantage of it. I can't say that out loud. I might as well ask him to hurt me.

"Pitiful? Or useful?" He's enjoying this way too much, but that's no surprise. He gets off on this kind of thing. Toying with me. "Because from where I'm standing, we couldn't have gotten luckier. Imagine if a man had walked into the office."

Then maybe I would've been the one who had to turn on the charm. When Enzo's brows draw together in an angry slash over his narrowed eyes, I have to wonder whether he's thinking the same thing. If he is, he doesn't like the idea much.

"Don't waste time pretending." He's grinning again. "You didn't like hearing me talk to her that way, did you? I was almost touched by your jealousy."

That gets my attention. "I wasn't jealous."

"Bullshit. I know a jealous woman when I see one."

"If you say so." I wish he wasn't so good at seeing through me. I wish I was better at hiding what I felt in the office earlier. Not jealousy—I'd never be jealous of the way he speaks to another woman, not after how he's treated me—but disgust. Discomfort. Anger at how easy it is for him to turn on the charm whenever there's something he wants. Meanwhile, it was all I could do to keep from blurting out the truth of who he really is. Wouldn't Catherine have been surprised if she knew the real man she was basically flirting with?

Okay. Maybe I was a little jealous. But I'd sooner bite off my tongue than admit it.

"I do say so." His voice is hard again, the grin having dissolved into something closer to a scowl. "I think you would rather be my good girl. Is that it? Would you rather be the one I call a good girl?" He pushes away from the wall, and now I'm really getting nervous. This is more than teasing, even more than reprimanding me for talking out of turn earlier. That look in his eye. I know that look.

It's enough to make me get up on my knees, torn between wanting to stand my ground and wanting to run away. Far away. "I really do have a lot of work to catch up on," I remind him, but my voice is weak. Shaky. He's going to see right through it.

And he does. "You have plenty of time to catch up on it. Up until the start of the next semester, if I do recall."

"Sure, but I have to sit through lectures and have no idea what the hell is going on, too. I'd rather try to at least catch up with the coursework, if not the assignments."

He reaches the foot of the bed and looks over the work I've spread out before sweeping an arm over it, knocking it all to the floor. "Keep your eyes on what's really important. I could not give less of a fuck whether or not you pass your courses. And I sure as hell don't care if you ever catch up. The idea was to keep you in school until you manage to reconnect with Elena. That's all. I can't believe you took any of the other shit seriously." My heart falls into the pit of my stomach.

"I still want to finish school. I'm not going to give up on it."

"What the fuck do you care?" he asks with a disbelieving laugh. "You don't need it. You'll be taken care of once you fulfill your end of our bargain."

"That doesn't mean I have to give up on my dreams."

"Dreams?" he parrots with a snicker. "Aren't you studying to be a nurse or something?"

I can't help myself. "You weren't scoffing when I was saving Prince's life, were you? It was pretty important then, wasn't it?"

That did it. That was when I stepped over the line.

"Off the bed. Now." When I don't move quickly enough, he takes me by the arm and pulls me the rest of the way, making me stumble and almost hit the floor. "This is what I get for going out of my way for you. Having to sweet-talk that bitch at the school, all so you can get an attitude problem. Maybe that was a mistake. Maybe you'll have to find another way to connect with Elena and settle the score."

He looks down at the floor and lifts his lip in distaste. "Pick all this shit up. Hurry." I'm too confused by his sudden shift in tone to hesitate, following orders quickly, my hands trembling but not so hard they slow me down. I stack the books and papers and place them on the nightstand, keeping my back to him after I've finished.

"Now, I want you over the bed. Like the naughty girl you are."

"Enzo, do we really—" He doesn't give me time to finish my thought before shoving me face-first, bending me over the edge. I don't have time to adjust to this before the sharp crack of his hand against my ass makes me yelp.

"This is the only way to deal with you. The only way to make you listen. You have to be reminded who's in charge." Again, he makes contact, then again. Against the thin material of my leggings and the almost nonexistent thong underneath, his hand might as well be a whip. Every strike leaves me howling into the mattress, the blankets clutched in my fists.

"Don't like that so much, do you?" *Smack!* "You'll think of this the next time you want to smart off to me, won't you?" *Smack!*

It's excruciating, the pain. The humiliation.

And oh, God, it's making me wet. By the time he lands the sixth or seventh below, the crotch of my panties is stuck to my pussy. I'm so ashamed. I shouldn't like this. But then, I shouldn't have liked a lot of what he's done to me, should I? I don't know what makes me hate him more: the things he does or the things he shows me about myself, things I didn't know before I met him.

"You do not talk back to me." He hits me again, and the force of it makes me scream. I'm somewhere beyond pain now and beyond pleasure, too. It's a sensation, pure and simple, and I'm going to shatter from the force of it.

"Don't like that so much, do you? Maybe you should have thought of that before you defied me." He yanks down my leggings, the thong with it. I squeeze my eyes shut at the sound of his knowing laughter. "I knew it. You never let me down when it comes to this." He runs his palm over my tender ass, and I whimper from pain and pleasure. My body acting on its own as I roll my hips and drive my pussy against the edge of the mattress.

"Dripping wet," he whispers. "If I didn't know better, I would think you bring this on to have an excuse for me to punish you. Is that what it is?"

I thought it was a rhetorical question, but I guess I was wrong because he takes me by the hair and pulls my head back, his mouth close to my ear. "I asked you a question. Is that what it is? Do you get off on your punishment?" All I can do is groan in discomfort and dismay. He laughs nastily, pressing my face back down against the mattress and grabbing my pussy with the other hand. "All this time, this is what you're craving. Hoping you can get me angry enough that I'll do things to you." He shoves his fingers inside me, and I cry out my pain and my shame, and yes, pleasure, too. I want this. I need this.

"Fine," he grunts, fucking me hard and fast with his fingers. Stretching me, making me writhe beneath him. He lets go of my head in favor of undoing his belt and unzipping his pants. "You can't say I don't give you what you want."

And then he's filling me, slamming himself against me, deep inside me. There's no pretending we're in this together. He's taking me, using me, holding me by the back of the neck, and pinning me down while he pounds into me like I'm nothing. Like I'm no one, just a hole to fuck and fill. My cries go unheard—either that, or he likes them and responds by fucking me harder, relentlessly, while all I can do is hold on until it's over. There's something unhinged about him, something wild and vicious. I just need it to be over.

"Oh, yeah... fuck, I'm gonna come... you're gonna make me come..." I close my eyes and brace myself an instant before he slams into me one last time, going stiff and then finally still. I feel it, his cum. It floods my insides with a rush of warmth. I let out the breath I was holding, weak with relief now that he's finished.

He hates me. He must truly hate me. How else could he do that to me? And now I'm not crying from the physical pain. There's a much deeper pain in my heart. We could've had so much if only things had been different. If only.

I press my palms to the mattress, ready to get up, but his hand on my neck keeps me pinned in place. "Where do you think you're going?" he pants, still locked with me, his lower half flush with mine.

"I was getting up," I whisper, trembling. What is this? Another game?

"No, you aren't. Not yet." He leans down, his breath hot in my ear. "Remember, we need to get you pregnant. Stay right there, just like that." And he stays, too, long after he should.

All I can do is weep quietly, torn between wanting this to work so it can be over as quickly as possible and hoping it never does because I'm not sure I want to bring this man's child into the world. Not when he shows me the almost endless depths of darkness and depravity he's capable of.

Before long, his breathing slows down. So do my tears. Why bother crying? I've known who he is from the beginning. And I still want him. How pathetic is that? If he had taken it a little easier on me and been less brutal, I might even have come.

But I understand a fundamental truth now: degradation turns me on, but brutal hatred isn't such a thrill. We'll never get back what we had before. What we almost had, what we came so close to sharing.

He sighs and pushes himself up on his palms. "Stay that way. Keep your legs closed tight." He finally separates his body from mine, and now I can breathe easier. From the corner of my eye, I watch him leave the room. How long is he going to leave me this way? Is it a test? I'm not about to find out the hard way, which I would if I defied him.

I'm exhausted, body and soul. Hurting in a way more profound than anything physical. I can't understand why I'd want somebody like him, capable of hurting me in so many different ways. Why do I want him to care for me again? I never saw myself as a broken person, but I must be. Broken beyond repair.

My heart skips a beat when his footsteps ring out in the hallway. He appears a moment later, looking like the past fifteen minutes never happened. Like he didn't leave me with my ass throbbing, and his cum trickling out of me.

He's holding something I realize is a washcloth, crossing the room without saying a word. A sudden shock startles me once he touches the cloth to my ass cheek. "Relax," he murmurs, running the cloth over my tingling flesh. "I thought this might help."

Now I want to cry all over again. Not because he's hurting me, but because I know he has kindness in him. I've seen it before, and here it is again. It might hurt less, come to think of it, if I didn't know about this other side. If he was a flat-out monster without a soul or a conscience, I could write him off. Sort of like the way I wrote off his grandfather after that first conversation.

Enzo isn't like him. No matter how he tries to be.

"For what it's worth," I venture as he tries to undo what he's done, "I think there are other positions that help. When you're trying to conceive, I mean."

"Really?"

"Yeah. Like if I'm on my back with my knees drawn up. I think I'm supposed to stay that way for a while afterward."

"Hmm." He's so gentle it's like he's another person now, going back and forth with the cloth, stroking and soothing. Why can't he be like this always? "We'll have to try that next time. For now, relax. Let's hope nature takes its course."

All I can do is close my eyes and wonder whether or not that will be a good thing. Whether our child will see this side of him or the side forged by the world, he grew up in.

10

ENZO

As far as I can tell, things with Alicia are going according to plan. She's waiting for the perfect opportunity to reconnect with Elena. According to Paolo, her new shadow, there hasn't been much progress in that today. Well, Rome wasn't built in a single day, either. I can bide my time, so long as I don't have to bide it forever.

I'm sure she hates being escorted around school by Paolo, but that's not my problem. There's no way I would get a single thing done in the course of a day if all I did was wonder if I could trust her and if she was more intent on slipping a message to a professor asking for help than she was on finding Elena and putting the plan in motion. She even had the nerve to act surprised when Paolo was waiting for her in the car this morning, and her surprise made me laugh. It's as if she forgets who she's dealing with.

No matter. I have other affairs to put in order this afternoon. The house is full of tight, tense energy, my men—those I still trust—patrolling the grounds while I wait for my two o'clock appointment to arrive.

Out of all the operations I contacted, the Martinez family was the only one to request a face-to-face meeting. While I don't much love the notion of inviting the head of a rival cartel to my home, concessions must be made at times like this. I can't afford to stand on ceremony, not with so much hanging in the balance. I'm sure my wife would roll her eyes and think me a sexist prick—which I might very well be—but the fact that the Martinez family is headed by a woman leaves me better inclined to open the door and invite her in. I have no doubt she'll be guarded, as will I, but I'm not as worried about her coming in with guns blazing.

Still, she's a woman in a man's world, and I have no illusions of her being a pushover. When her father died, the family was left in shambles as his brothers and close associates knifed each other in the back, both metaphorically and literally, in hopes of taking over. The only one left standing, Rosa Martinez not only pulled the pieces together but more than doubled their revenue in two years. She's a savvy, powerful woman and a dangerous enemy. I'd much rather she be an ally in this fight.

She arrives five minutes early, and I wait in my office while my men frisk her men and all the other bits of business that need to be taken care of before she's escorted to where I sit behind my desk. I stand upon the opening of the door, buttoning my jacket—and the sight of the creature who strides into the room threatens to take my breath away. I've seen pictures of Rosa Martinez, but none of them did her justice. Without so much as a glance, she orders the pair of guards she brought with her to wait against the door while she continues into the study.

"Mr. De Luca. Thank you for taking the time to meet with me today." She stops in front of the desk and extends a hand before shaking with a firm grip. "We're both busy people, so let's not waste time. No, I would not like a drink," she adds before I have the opportunity to offer.

Interesting. "Please, have a seat. I must admit, I was somewhat taken aback when you insisted upon meeting in person."

She folds her trim body, lowering herself into a leather club chair before crossing her slim legs. "I'm busy, but I do like to know who is asking for my involvement in what could potentially turn into a war. Until now, it would be your grandfather I was meeting with." Her brows knit together for a moment. "My condolences, by the way."

"Thank you. What would you like to know about me? What could make you more comfortable and more likely to come to an agreement?"

"How much money do you have?" The corners of her mouth twitch in the first sign of humor she's revealed since her arrival.

"I'm offering something much better and longer lasting than a dollar amount, Ms. Martinez. I'm offering the opportunity to rid ourselves once and for all of the entire Alvarez operation. That is the end goal, to take them down. Then once the job is done, we can discuss financial gains. This is the goose that laid the golden egg. You don't want to kill it now to take whatever little you can get when there's the opportunity to make money well into the future."

"And you honestly believe you have a plan in place that could do the trick?"

"Leave that to me. What I need to know is, are you interested? Would you align with me if it meant wiping them off the map?"

She narrows her shrewd, dark eyes. "Speaking frankly?"

"I would prefer we did."

"Very well. I hate those bastards and want nothing more than to see them taken down. As painfully as possible." Her bland expression doesn't shift an inch as she says this. She might as well be describing today's weather report.

"I appreciate your candor. Now, if you wouldn't mind, how does that benefit me?"

"You tell me, Mr. De Luca. What can I do for you?"

Under different circumstances, this meeting would take a left turn, and we might end up discussing issues that have nothing to do with Josef Alvarez and the cartel. But business is business—and I am, after all, a married man. Somehow, the band on my left hand feels heavier than it should.

I don't know who I'm kidding. The fact is, Rosa could be the most beautiful, sexy, enticing woman in the world, but I would only see Alicia when I looked at her. The way I do now. It doesn't matter how I try to distance myself from the woman I married. No matter how I fight it, she pulls me in like a current controlling me under the surface of what looks like still water.

I want to hate her. I wish it was possible. Hell, I can't even stop thinking about her now, in the middle of a critical meeting.

With that in mind, I lift my chin and square my shoulders. Enough letting my mind wander. "What would benefit me most now is distraction. I want them harried. I want them flustered. I want none of them to know a moment's peace. If they're too busy putting out small fires set by other rivals, they'll be less likely to notice the very large inferno I'm setting."

She nods slowly, those keen, intelligent eyes of hers narrowing. "Wouldn't it be a shame if one of their shipments was intercepted? Or if one of their trucks was run off the road and hijacked by anonymous men?"

She's hooked. "Things like that do happen all the time," I allow with a shrug.

"That, they do," she murmurs without so much as a twitch of her lips. There's humor in her voice, certainly, but she's taking this seriously.

"There's that warehouse of theirs, too," she muses, tapping her long, crimson nails on the arm of the chair. "The one where they store all their fenced goods."

The memory is enough to make me bristle. "I'm familiar with it."

"We could always alert the police to it. Or go in and clean it out. Or set fire to the whole damn thing. There are so many choices."

"I won't clip your wings by telling you to move one way or another. I'll leave it up to you. I'm sure you and yours could come up with a creative solution to this problem."

"I think we could come up with something if we put our minds to it. Now, what is in it for us?" And now she smiles, though there's very little warmth behind it.

"You mean to tell me the absence of Josef Alvarez wouldn't be enough?"

"Please, Mr. De Luca—"

"Call me Enzo."

"Mr. De Luca," she insists. "We're not children, and this is no fantasy. Yes, it would be very nice to pretend the absence of the Alvarez cartel would be enough, but let me ask you: would it be for you if our positions were reversed? I think we both know the answer to that."

"With all due respect, you shouldn't speak for me."

"Very well, then I'll speak for myself. That isn't enough. My family will want a piece of the pie, so to speak."

"Naturally. And we can arrange for that, you have my word. I'm not an unreasonable man, nor am I greedy. I would be happy to share a piece of the pie—but a small one," I add. "One of his transport lanes, for instance, and the merchandise that travels it. I'd be glad to hand that over to you once the smoke clears, and we've claimed the spoils."

"And I can take you at your word?"

"Ms. Martinez, if there is one thing you can be sure of, it is my dedication to my word. Yes, we'll meet again and solidify the terms of our arrangement. So long as you can accept those terms rather than demand more."

"Speaking frankly, if I end up losing men over this, I will want more. I will want repayment in kind."

"And I suppose we'll have to cross that bridge when we come to it—if we do," I add. "Because speaking frankly, as you said, there's no inherent reason you should lose men over a hijacking or the burning down of a warehouse, is there?" I glance away from her, toward her guards. In other words, if they're half as good as they should be, there shouldn't be any danger involved.

She knows it, too, and her lips twitch again. "I like to keep all possibilities open, just in case. People in our position can't afford to ignore any possibility."

"I understand that, and I respect it." Time to get down to it. I lean in, hands folded on the desk. "Do we have an agreement?"

She purses her lips, brows drawing together. I have her, I know I do, no matter how much she tries to pretend otherwise. Of course, she wouldn't jump at the offer. She'd appear too eager and might as well expose her throat if she did that.

"Very well," she murmurs, nodding slowly. "It's a deal."

"Excellent." Now it's my turn to downplay my reaction, tampering my glee. I need someone with a shrewd mind in my corner now, as Alvarez is as shrewd and cunning as they come. An animal solely interested in its own survival. He won't know what hit him. "Thank you so much for your willingness. I know this will benefit our families immensely."

"And it will grant you what you deserve. Vengeance for your grandfather." I nod in agreement, even if the truth is much larger and more complicated than she makes it sound. The less anyone outside the family understands about my marriage and how it came to be, the better.

"Shall we shake on it?" I stand, prepared to do just that, but instead of extending a hand when she stands, she glances toward the bar set up in the corner.

"I would rather drink on it. Join me?" I incline my head before crossing the room, and she murmurs her assent when I offer whiskey. I pour us both a generous amount before turning toward her, handing her one of the glasses, and lifting my own in a silent toast.

"To our mutually beneficial involvement." She touches her glass to mine, then bolts the contents back all at once without so much as flinching. A very interesting woman.

She then straightens out her suit with a soft sigh. "I hope you don't think me terribly rude, but I must be on my way. There are always so many things to manage, but then I guess you know that all too well."

"I'm beginning to get the idea, yes."

For the first time since her arrival, she offers a genuine smile. "If there's anything you need, and I mean this sincerely, don't hesitate to ask. A sudden change in leadership can be construed as an opportunity for those who'd rather steal what they want than earn it. Ask me how I know."

"Thank you. That means a lot." I hold back the rest of my thoughts on the matter rather than remind her of the grasping, greedy men in her family. Mine isn't like that—Grandfather would never allow it, for one thing. For another, my position is uncontested. Still, I have no doubt there are plenty of assholes out there who would like to take advantage. Something I only thought I understood when Grandfather was in power. I now know it's impossible to fully comprehend unless you're the one sitting behind the desk, calling the shots.

As I walk her to the door, there's one thought I can't help but give voice to. "I hope I'm not speaking out of turn by saying this, but I believe we could work together in the future. Our values seem to be in alignment."

"One thing at a time, Mr. De Luca," she reminds me with a bit of a teasing note in her voice. "Let's do the world a favor by getting rid of Alvarez first."

Nothing has ever sounded better.

11

ALICIA

I don't know what I expected to happen today. What, was I going to find Elena right off the bat and have a conversation with her? Hell, I'm still not even sure what I would say. She would probably want to know where I've been, for starters. How things went, all that. If she doesn't already know—somebody could have told her what happened, or at least the rumors they heard.

And maybe they did. Maybe she was deliberately avoiding me when our eyes met after class, and she practically ran out of the lecture hall.

She could have been in a hurry. It's not like we made a habit of connecting after class. She has her schedule, I have mine, that kind of thing. But today was different. Today she looked surprised to see me sitting toward the back of the room, and she wasted no time avoiding me.

So now it's going to be even more awkward trying to catch up with her. I have her number from when we had our project together, but I haven't used it since we did our presentation last year. It would look strange if I suddenly texted her out of nowhere.

But it might look even weirder if I ever manage to pin her down since I'm never alone. I glare at the back of Paolo's head as he drives from campus back to the townhouse. What a fucking joke. There's no way I'll ever be able to have an actual conversation with Elena, not when I have this goon following me around everywhere. It's obvious something's changed drastically from the way my life was before she sent me to the warehouse. If she's Josef Alvarez's niece, she'll be able to tell why Paolo's up my ass all the time. I'm sure she's dealt with bodyguards before.

How am I supposed to get her to trust me?

And why am I certain before I ever step foot out of the car that my husband will not give a damn, no matter how I try to reason with him on this? It's like swimming in the middle of a lake, fighting to keep my head above the surface while there's an anchor tied to my ankle, pulling me down. He's the anchor—unwilling to listen to me, making it impossible for me to succeed.

Although an anchor wouldn't hold failure against me. That's the difference.

He won't be happy to know I was unable to move forward with the plan. I have to come up with a way to keep him calm and convince him there's a way to move forward. First step: I need to stop sulking. That's not going to get me anywhere. I can't think if I'm too busy feeling sorry for myself.

I guess the best I can do is sit a little closer to the front of the room next time, try to catch her eye, and wave and smile like all I want is to catch up. The way I would if my life was anything close to normal right now. But I can't overplay it either because that would look way too obvious.

Now I know what it's like to walk through a minefield. I don't like it very much.

"Home sweet home." It's one of the few things Paolo has said all day, and there's a nasty edge to it. Like he knows how miserable I am here and how trapped. Like it's all one big joke. I have to bite my tongue, or else I might make the mistake of reminding him his entire job is to follow me around like a puppy dog. Is that something to be proud of? Is he so much better than me?

The sight of an unfamiliar car in the wide driveway puts that out of my head in an instant. My breath catches, and my heart pounds. I'm ready to run, terrified, all because of a black car I don't recognize. A man stands beside it, and he casts a cold, hard look at the car I'm sitting in as Paolo pulls up beside him.

"Who is that?" I whisper, trembling, staring out through the tinted window. Why don't I carry a weapon? It never occurred to me to carry one. I'd feel a lot better if there was a pistol in my backpack.

Paolo grunts, the way he's done all day. "It doesn't concern you."

This asshole. "Considering I live here with my husband, I think it does concern me," I mutter, glaring at the back of his head. He doesn't even bother looking back at me. I don't even deserve that much.

"It's nothing to worry about," he adds, sullen, almost unwilling.

I want to believe him, but I'd rather see for myself. I get out of the car and give the stranger a chilly look while he sizes me up silently. Finally, he nods in acknowledgment but doesn't say a word. I'm so glad I'm met with his approval, whoever he is.

I wasn't looking forward to getting home, but now I want more than anything to be inside, away from whatever is going on. Why would Enzo bother telling me we were having guests? I don't matter. I'm just an incubator for his future child.

With that in mind, all I want is to go up to my room and be alone. No matter what Enzo thinks, I do have work to do. He might not want me to go full-time, but I'm not going to give up on everything I ever wanted for him. He can't control every part of my life.

I'm at the door when it swings open, and it isn't only Enzo standing there. I fall back a step in mute surprise at the sight of an absolutely stunning woman—tall, willowy, dressed in a black suit. Her dark hair is wound into a thick bun at the nape of her neck, and her wide eyes are focused squarely on him as she leans in to kiss him on the cheek. "I'll be in touch," she murmurs in a voice full of intimacy and familiarity.

Who the hell is this bitch, and why did she just kiss my husband?

Enzo glances my way, his eyes widening a fraction like he's just noticing me, but he doesn't say anything. He doesn't even bother introducing me. I may as well not be here.

As for her, whoever she is, she doesn't so much as acknowledge me as she glides away in a pair of stilettos that click along the pathway. I follow her with my gaze the way a pair of guards follow in her footsteps, watching as she slides smoothly into the back seat of that strange car. The scent of her perfume lingers in the air long after she's gone.

"Who was that?" I whisper, staring as the car pulls away.

"Don't worry about it. She's no one you need to be interested in." Enzo steps aside. "Well? Are you coming in?"

All at once, I feel like I'm lacking. Less than. I'm nothing compared to her, whoever she is. She's graceful, classy, and confident. And she clearly has him captivated.

"You might want to get that." I rub a thumb over my cheek as I step into the house, indicating the smudge of lipstick he now wears on his.

"Thanks." He's chuckling as he pulls a handkerchief from his breast pocket and swipes it over the mark.

And that's it. That's all the explanation I get. He walks past me, heading for his study, I guess. Meanwhile, that perfume still lingers all through the downstairs. I want nothing more than to open the windows to air the place out, but it's humid and verging on rain, so I'd probably regret it. He'd want to know why I was doing it, too, and probably accuse me of trying to run away.

Now I wish I had clawed her eyes out, even though I don't know who she is, and I am very well aware of the fact that she had guards. I might have at least been able to scratch her a little before they got to me. I don't even know why I care so much—if anything, that only makes me angrier. I head straight for the kitchen and grab a cold bottle of water from the fridge, touching it to the back of my neck and my forehead before opening it and taking a long gulp. It does nothing to cool off the heat burning me up inside. Some strange woman was in my house—it might not technically be mine, but I do live here. And I'm not allowed to know who she was.

How am I supposed to get through this when I can't stop having feelings for him? I hate him, yes, but I can't forget the other feelings that were starting to develop. No, not starting; I can't lie to myself. I was deep in my feelings for him before everything went to hell. The last thing I should have done was fall in love with him, but I did, and I knew it on our wedding day.

How am I supposed to turn that off? How do I stop caring? This would all be a lot easier if I could. If I could turn my feelings on and off like a spigot. That is impossible. I can't even shake my feelings for him now when he's been cruel and dismissive. When he's used me brutally. I only want more.

What happens when this is all over? When he's wiped out Alvarez, and I've given him the son he so desperately wants? He'll get rid of me, of course. I'll be nothing but a memory. He might see me occasionally in our son's eyes or the shape of his nose, but over time, he'll learn to dismiss that, too. I doubt we'll ever set eyes on each other again.

And I'll only have myself to blame for my broken heart because this was the last man I was ever supposed to fall in love with. I knew what was at stake, I knew I was lying, and I knew there couldn't possibly be a future for us. Yet I let it happen. As angry as I am with him, I'm ten times more furious with myself. I only have myself to blame.

"Paolo?" Enzo wanders back out of his study, looking around.

His eyes land on me, and I shrug. "I don't know where he went. He's probably still outside."

"I wanted to ask him how the day went."

I blink, waiting for more and getting nothing. "You could ask me."

"I would rather hear it from him."

"Why? Are you expecting me to lie?"

I know right away it was a mistake. He snorts, looking me up and down while his mouth twitches at the corners. "Because it would be the first time you've ever lied? Don't tell me you demand trust now."

"What do you expect him to say?" Should I challenge him? Probably not, even though the tension between us makes my skin tingle and my breath come fast. I like this too much—and I deserve to speak up for myself, too, whether he likes it or not. "What, do you think I was sneaking around? Slipping messages to my lab partner? Meeting up with him in the bathroom after class?"

His jaw tightens. "You have a male lab partner?"

"What, did you expect somebody from school to check in with you beforehand in case you didn't approve?"

"Do you or don't you?" he demands in a soft voice that scares me worse than a scream.

"No, I don't," I assure him with a snicker.

He lifts an eyebrow, advancing on me slowly. "Don't play games with me. You won't like the way it turns out."

And now, a tiny bit of fear touches my heart, but it's too late. I'm not going to apologize or beg his forgiveness. I'm past that point. "So I'm not worth acknowledging in front of a guest, but I'm also not allowed to exist without eyes on me at all times? And I can't associate with men, even in class?"

"You're starting to get the idea."

"If there was anything wrong, your little watchdog would've ratted me out right away. I think we're fine." I walk past him on my way to the stairs—when he doesn't try to stop me, I know I should be glad, but my heart sinks instead. "Though it might've been easier for you if I had tried to meet up with somebody after class."

"Why is that?" he demands, now following me. Just like I shouldn't want him to.

"I wouldn't have shown up here when I did. Obviously, I'm an embarrassment if you can't even acknowledge me." I reach the top of the stairs and turn on him, making him stop halfway up. "Maybe you should fuck her instead of me. She looks like she'd be great breeding stock. Let me know the next time you have her over, so we won't cross paths."

Confusion washes over his face. "Is that what this is about?" he asks, caught between a grin and a scowl. "You're jealous?"

"Don't be ridiculous," I snap before turning on my heel. Yes. Yes, I am. I'm so jealous I can barely see straight. "We both know why I'm here and what my purpose is. But I'd like a little respect, thank you. I'm still your wife on paper."

The man is fast, and silent. I don't realize he's followed me the rest of the way to my room until he keeps me from closing the door. "You are my wife on paper and in practice," he informs me, standing in the doorway. "And if I wanted to fuck another woman, that decision would be made without your input. You say you know why you're here? You'd do well to remember it—because the alternative was death."

His mouth stretches in a cold smile that hardens his gaze. "It still could be, come to think of it. Keep pushing me, and we'll see how it goes."

"All this because I'm asking for a little consideration and respect?"

He holds my gaze a beat longer before clicking his tongue, his head shaking slightly before he turns away. "Respect is earned," he reminds me, walking down the hall. Now I'm glad he's leaving me alone since that damn perfume clings to his suit and reminds me of why this was never going to work. This is his game, his rules, and he can change the rules whenever he wants.

He's not the only one with cards up his sleeve, though. Whether he likes it or not, he's just as capable of jealousy as I am, and he can't hide it.

I wish that didn't give me so much hope that he might still want me.

12

ENZO

I now know what it feels like to eat a meal in an ice box because that's the approximate temperature in the kitchen as Alicia and I eat a rather silent, distant dinner. And here I was, hoping to enjoy the meal and the night. I managed to broker a tentative deal with the Martinez cartel, for fuck's sake.

"How is your mahi?" I venture.

"Fine." She takes a forkful as if to prove this, inserting it into her mouth and chewing, looking down at her plate all the while.

"I didn't see the point of hiring a cook when we won't be here permanently, and it seems like delivery is working out just fine."

"Yeah. It is."

This is more than simple discomfort or awkwardness. This is deliberate. She's freezing me out after our argument earlier. I don't know why I care—the meal would go much more smoothly if I could simply ignore her attitude, but that's the problem with her in a nutshell. I can't ignore her. I need to know. Perhaps there's something perverse in me that won't allow me to let it go.

"So how was your day? We didn't get much of a chance to speak when you first got home."

Alicia snorts while reaching for the breadbasket. "I thought we already went over that. I was a good girl and didn't do anything against the rules. What else is there to know?"

"I'm sorry, I thought I would at least be civil toward my wife. If you'd rather I wasn't, that's fine. Less of an effort for me."

"No, you wouldn't want to make an effort over little old me, would you?" she sneers, sliding an accusatory look my way. "You pay people to do that for you."

"Is this about Paolo? Because I am not about to entertain your irritation every single day, so we might as well have it out now. You want to go to school; there are rules you must abide by."

"It has nothing to do with Paolo, though now that you mention it..." She's scowling when she raises her head. "You realize I stick out like a sore thumb at school, right? I'm supposed to be blending in, acting normally."

"Do you honestly think anyone gives a shit that you have a bodyguard?"

"Do you honestly hear yourself? Yes, it looks a little funny for a man dressed in all black to be following me around from place to place and standing at the back of the room when I'm in a lecture."

"Would you rather he wear a clown costume?"

She rolls her eyes. "Forget it. I should know better than to try to reason with you."

"I don't much appreciate your attitude this evening. Here I am, thinking we can have at least a pleasant dinner together, and you come at me with all this nastiness."

She touches a hand to her chest, her mouth falling open in mock dismay. "Excuse me. I forgot I'm not supposed to have any thoughts or feelings about anything. I'm just a woman. I'm just supposed to sit here and be quiet and meek. And available," she adds, and bitterness drips from the words.

I shouldn't rise to the bait, but dammit, I can't let her get away with this. "Now that you mention it, yes. That is exactly how you are supposed to be."

"Of course. Anything to make your life easier."

"Considering how complicated you've made my life, I would think you'd want to make it a little easier." And now I can't pretend to enjoy my mahi. Not when she insists on being perverse and stirring me to anger. "You were the one who wanted to come back to Miami. We didn't have to leave Italy."

"No kidding."

"So don't act like I dragged you here kicking and screaming, and you're unhappy about it."

"Who said I was unhappy about coming to Miami? This was my home." Maybe she doesn't notice her choice of words, but I do. She's already thinking about her former life as just that. I'm glad because that bodes well for me. The last thing I need is a wife who won't stop crying about a life she'll never return to.

Then again, from what she's told me, there isn't much to cry about. I'm doing her a favor here, taking her away from the constant overwork and sense of deprivation that she suffered before we met. She should be on her knees sucking me off this very minute, not pouting and pushing food around on her plate with her fork.

She shifts in her chair, causing the dress she's wearing to ride up her thighs. It doesn't matter how I tell myself not to look, not that there are any boundaries between us—husband and wife—but I have a difficult time staying on subject when I'm too busy ogling her body. It's better if I keep my eyes on my food.

Yet my gaze keeps returning to those legs. Christ, what I wouldn't give this very minute to have them wrapped around me. And I could—it would take nothing to overpower her. By the time I was finished, she would be begging me for more, of that I'm absolutely certain.

But that's already gotten me into enough trouble. Letting my cock do my thinking for me. And it would be yet one more reason for her to resent me, which I've had just about enough of already.

"I take it you weren't able to connect with Elena today." I eye her over the rim of my wineglass and note the darkening of her cheeks.

"What's it matter? Even if I did have time to connect with her before she ran off, what would she say when I have somebody standing over my shoulder the whole time?" She lifts her gaze and pins me with a hard, cold stare. "Well? Got any big solutions to the problem?"

"If I didn't know better, I would think you were trying to goad me into a fight."

"Why would I ever do that? It always ends the same way, and I don't like it very much." Yet her cheeks color again, and I have to wonder how long she plans on lying to herself. We both know she doesn't hate when I manhandle her nearly as much as she pretends to.

"As for Paolo, you can complain all you want, but he's not going anywhere. I want him over your shoulder, as you put it, at all times."

"But why? That's what I don't understand. What, do you think I'm going to try to run away?"

"You? Oh no, you would never try something like that."

"Or is it to make sure I don't speak to anybody but her? Like somebody you wouldn't approve of?" She arches an eyebrow, and damn if my cock doesn't spring to life in response. Not that he wasn't already twitching, thanks to those legs of hers, now exposed more than ever after she's crossed them. It's a good thing I'm busy with my knife and fork, or else I would have no choice but to reach out and run my fingertips over them. Who am I kidding? I would do a lot more than that.

"You'll have other opportunities to connect with Elena," I remind her, ignoring the heavy-handed way she tries to stir my jealousy. "And I know better than just about anyone what a good liar you are. You can come up with a way of easing any apprehensions she has."

"Can I?"

"Can't you?" I bark, and she jumps slightly at the sudden change. Good. Let her remember I'm not fucking around. "You brought me back here for the purpose of making Elena pay for setting you up. Was that all a pretense?"

"No."

"Because from where I sit now, it certainly seems that way. Maybe I was foolish to trust you. Maybe you don't need to go to school or to reconnect with your so-called friend."

"It wasn't a pretense."

"Fine. Then figure something out." I drain my wineglass and would refill it if it wasn't for her penetrating stare. I'd rather she not read anything into my overindulging. "I told you that I don't appreciate this attitude. Do you think I'm joking? What did I do to deserve this?"

"Maybe I had a tough day."

"So tell me about it. I fucking asked you, didn't I?"

"Maybe I don't feel like talking to you about it. Did you ever think about that?"

Damn her. Why do I even give a shit? That's the true question here. I shouldn't care. She's feeling pissy and bitchy and bratty, and as far as I'm concerned, she can shove her attitude straight up her delicious little ass.

It's my fault. I've gotten overly fond of talking with her. Relating to her. Hearing her unique take on people and situations. That night we spent here in this kitchen, drinking our warm milk—that started it. There's no way of recapturing that encounter, yet here I am, doing my damnedest to get us back to that place. Unsure how we got there, to begin with.

She looks down at her plate, pushing the food around again. "Why didn't you introduce me as your wife earlier?" she mutters.

I could get whiplash, thanks to the way she changes the subject out of nowhere. "Excuse me?"

"Earlier. When that woman was here." Her nose wrinkles like she smells something unsavory. "I'm your wife, but you didn't bother introducing me as such. And I want to know why."

I shouldn't laugh—even I know that. I'm only going to end up regretting it when she throws a bigger fit and gives me a damn headache.

But it's too funny. I can't help it. "Is that what this is about? I didn't use the exact verbiage you expected in front of an associate?"

"Oh, is that who she was?" She's forgotten the pretense of eating her meal, instead folding her arms and swinging her leg back and forth. I truly wish she wouldn't since all that does is draw my attention back to her creamy skin. God, how I long for her. "Do all of your associates kiss you on the cheek before leaving a meeting?"

"Yes, for all you know."

"Give me a break, and this is about you not introducing me."

"She is who I say she is. An associate, someone with a vested interest in assisting me with the Alvarez situation. I don't appreciate having to explain myself to you."

"And I don't appreciate being treated like yesterday's leftovers in front of a stranger."

"That is your problem, not mine. And the language I choose to use in front of an associate is none of your business, so you would do well to pay no attention—or to learn how to deal with it, either way. But I won't change my communication style for your sake. Forget about it."

"Who the hell do you think I am?"

I meet her sudden outburst with bland acceptance, which clearly infuriates her. "My wife."

She snarls, even baring her teeth. "Your property, more like. You want to talk about communication style? Fine, let's talk about it. I am your wife. You do not own me. And if this little arrangement of ours is going to work out, you're going to have to stop treating me like garbage. I matter, dammit."

"When did I say you didn't? Have I not been sitting here all this time trying to make conversation? If you'd rather, we can go back to you eating alone in your room. It would be a lot more peaceful for me."

She throws her hands into the air with a bitter laugh. "Oh, well, let's not disturb your peace, Mr. De Luca. Because the whole fucking world revolves around you."

"Are you finished with your tantrum?" I ask, checking my watch. "Because I have a lot of work to get to and would like to know if I need to rearrange my schedule to accommodate your childishness."

"Go to hell."

"I'm sure I will," I murmur in acknowledgment. "But not on your schedule. Sorry if that disappoints you."

She pushes back from the table and jumps to her feet, throwing her napkin over what's left of her meal. "Maybe from now on, I will eat alone."

"Be my guest."

An entire range of emotions washes over her face all at once. Frustration, anger, dismay, all of that, and so much more. What does she want from me now? I refuse to give in, no matter what the answer is. I don't dance to anyone's tune but my own. It would be better for her to figure that out sooner rather than later.

"You're a bastard." And with that, she storms from the kitchen, marching loudly through the first floor.

I don't know why, but that's what breaks my resolve. Her childishness. She wants a reaction from me? She'll get one. I'm out of my chair and halfway up the stairs before I know what I'm doing, but now I won't stop. I can't stop. She's going to learn here and now who has the upper hand.

"Leave me alone!" she bellows upon reaching her room. That's when she makes the ultimate mistake of attempting to slam the door in my face. I catch it before it closes and shove hard enough that it bounces back and slams into the wall beside it.

"Oh no, wife of mine," I growl as I enter the room. "That's not how this goes."

VOW

13

ALICIA

"I told you to leave me alone."

That isn't what I want. If it was, I wouldn't have started an argument in the first place. It wouldn't still stick in my craw that I watched another woman kiss my husband. A woman he couldn't be bothered to introduce me to. A woman who makes me feel small and insignificant and not enough.

His narrowed eyes move over my face. "All this childish foot stomping, only to be told I should leave you alone? You need to make up your mind."

I back up against the bed, then slide along its length until I'm against the wall. I would have to go and corner myself like this, wouldn't I? And I don't have anything to defend myself with, not that he wouldn't make me regret pulling a weapon.

The only weapon I have is my words. They're all I can use. "You don't think anything was wrong with what happened earlier today? Seriously?"

"Seriously. My business is my business. I won't be told what to do or how to do it, not by you or anyone, for that matter."

"Okay." I fold my arms, glaring at him while I try to keep from shaking. It isn't only fear making me do it. There's still a red-hot river of anger rolling through my body. "And it was totally innocent, I guess."

He blows out a sigh. "If it matters to you so much, yes. It was innocent—at least, in the way you mean it."

It's the laughter in his voice that hurts the most. This is all so amusing. My frustration and confusion are funny. "Then it would be okay if you came home one day, and I was showing some guy from school to the door?"

His nostrils flare, and I know the question hit him like I wanted it to. "What?"

"Some guy from class. A study partner. If you came home one day, and I was showing him to the door, and he kissed my cheek. That would be fine? Because it would all be innocent?" I'm goading him, wanting him to feel the same way I do right now.

"Not the same," he mutters, his brow lowered. I'd swear his eyes are burning.

"How? Why wouldn't it be the same? Totally innocent, working together on a class project or something. Even without the kiss," I offer. "Just studying together, alone. You'd be okay with that the way I'm supposed to be okay with you having some strange woman here with me not knowing who she is?"

He's like a bull ready to charge. Face flushed, breathing harder, faster. Like even the thought is enough to set him off. "Not. The same."

"Says who?"

The fire in his eyes hardens into something vicious. Something feral. And I know before he even lunges at me that I pushed too far.

But I know something else, too. I know the idea of me being with anyone else—even studying, even something as simple as that—makes him crazy. That alone lights me up inside, even as he pins me to the wall, knocking the breath out of my lungs. He wants me. Pretend all he wants, there's no changing the fact.

"We would have a serious problem on our hands if you ever spent time alone with another man." He's breathing heavily, unhinged, and my pulse races at the knowledge of how close he is to losing control.

"Would we?" I whisper, as defiant as I can be, when what's happening to my body is another story. My pussy is already wet and getting wetter. This is the only way I can make him touch me and show he cares. Even though I could be in danger, the payoff is worth it. "How so?"

"Don't play dumb." His hand encircles my throat, and my nipples tighten in response. "If another man so much as touched you without permission, I would have no choice but to cut off his hands."

He leans in, his grip tightening. "You are mine," he whispers through gritted teeth.

Yes, I am. God help me.

I need him. I know that now. There's a part of me that lights up in moments like this when I'm equal parts turned on and terrified. The anticipation is excruciating. He's going to take me, he's going to fuck me, and I'm going to love it the way I always do. Even when he hurts me, I love it because it's his touch I need the most. I need the pleasure only he can bring me. It's fucked up and twisted, and I know it, but I don't care. Not right now. Not when he's looking at me like he wants to tear me to pieces.

"Let's get something straight," he growls, and I shiver at the sound of it. "I am not the man you storm off on. I will not accept you behaving like a fucking child. And you do not spend time alone with any man, for any reason, unless I've given you permission. Do you understand me?"

I don't understand anything right now. I certainly can't get a grip on the way my entire body reacts to him. Head to toe, I'm on fire, tingling, throbbing, hungry. So hungry for him, for the oblivion he brings me.

"Answer!" he barks, making me jump.

"Yes!" I gasp. "And I will not accept you treating me like shit, like I don't matter. I'm your wife. I deserve to be introduced to people. I deserve a little respect."

"Respect?" His hand tightens until I can hardly take a sip of air. I gasp, eyes bulging, but he won't let up.

His face is close enough to almost touch mine, and I have to fight off the impulse to touch my lips to his. It would be so easy, and I want to kiss him so much. No more talking, no more yelling. All I want is to feel him —on me, in me, all over me. I'm so tired of craving him, craving this even when I know it's no good for me. The harder I try to fight it, the worse the addiction becomes.

"I have more respect for stray dogs than I do for you," he mutters, eyes locked with mine. "A stray dog does what it needs to survive. You?"

"I did the same thing."

"Like hell you did. You had every chance to make things right, but you deliberately refused. You weren't surviving. You were a coward and a liar, and you have blood on your hands."

His hand, meanwhile, tightens further. I see stars swimming in front of me, and I blink them away. Now isn't the time to pass out. "And you stomp around here, throw fits, and have the balls to demand respect. What a fucking joke."

I gasp when he thrusts a hand between my legs, taking hold of my pussy and rubbing hard. "This is all you deserve. Having your body used. It's the one good thing about you, your body." He rolls his hips, driving his dick against me. It's hard, telling me he's enjoying this the way I am. That he wants this. Wants me.

He works his fingers under my panties and lets out a nasty laugh when he feels my wetness. "You love this, don't you?" he demands, breath quickening. "Tell me. You love it when I use you. You want this. You crave this. Tell me."

"Yes!" I admit, hanging between shame and elation. I can't help but rock my hips and bear down on his hand.

He's glaring at me. I can't look away. I won't. "And what do you want now?" My tongue darts out, and I moisten my lips. His soft groan hints at his helplessness. He's not as in control as he pretends.

He yanks my panties down around my knees, then uses his foot to push them down to the floor while frantically working his belt and zipper. He doesn't say a word, staring at me the whole time. There's darkness swirling behind his eyes, danger. I should be afraid. I should be crying, begging, and maybe that's what he wants from me.

But I can't pretend. I want this. I crave it like a drug. It's no good for me, and I know I have to find a way to live without it, but now is not that time.

Inside, I'm practically rejoicing, so happy to get what I want. There must be something wrong with me.

Whatever it is, the same thing is wrong with him. Maybe that's what it's all about. Two fucked-up souls finding each other.

He drives himself into me with a grunt, and I shudder with pleasure and relief at the connection. His hand never leaves my throat, his body crushing me against the wall. His teeth are gritted, and his breath is coming in short gasps that match mine.

Harder, harder. He takes my leg and wraps it around his hip, and now he can go deeper, and yes, yes, I love that. He's hitting all the right spots, and I grind against him, rocking my hips, meeting his strokes. The friction against my clit is unbelievable, making me see stars, or maybe that's the hand around my throat cutting off my air, but oh, God, yes, yes, it's good, it's right, it's perfect.

He doesn't say a word, only bares his teeth in a snarl, grunting every time our bodies slap together.

He's a monster. He's the devil. He's the entire world, and he goes harder. Deeper. Pinning me in place and using me like I want to be used.

I lift my other leg, wrapping it around him, crossing my ankles, and locking them. I now bounce between him and the wall, riding him while he rides me. There's no sound in the room but our panting and the wet, sloppy sounds of our bodies slapping together. I'm wetter with every stroke, coating his balls and his dick, and I ride him, yes, I ride him. I ride him as hard as I can while he fucks me, and my rasping breaths become a high-pitched whine that gets louder every time we crash together.

"Fuck... fuck..." he grunts in time with his strokes, and that's all I hear besides the pounding of my heart and the whining I can't hold back, and then oh God, yes, I'm coming. It hits me all at once, and I scream because, oh God, it's so much, so much I can't handle it. I'm going to fall apart, and I'm going to die from it.

He slams into me one last time before going stiff, roaring through clenched teeth, bathing my insides with his seed. All I can do is slump against him, still held in place by his body and his hand. The world is spinning, but the color returns to it when he loosens the pressure so I can breathe again. I shouldn't like that as much as I do, should I? But it's so fucking intense.

He finally stands up straight, and I take that as my cue to unlock my legs and unwrap them. He leaves me that way, slumped against the wall, fighting to regain my breath while he tucks himself back into his shorts, then zips his pants. He's breathing like an animal, and there's sweat shining on his face and neck, dampening his hair.

But he doesn't say a word. He only stares at me in what looks like disgust and disappointment before walking away and closing the door softly.

I can't bring myself to hate the way he dismisses me without a single word. Not when the aftershocks of pleasure still make me shiver.

Not when I'm this satisfied.

And maybe that's the problem. The way I like it—love it. Maybe he's finally clueing in and figuring out how easy it is for me to lure him into giving me what I need. If I can't get it any other way, I don't have a choice.

14

ENZO

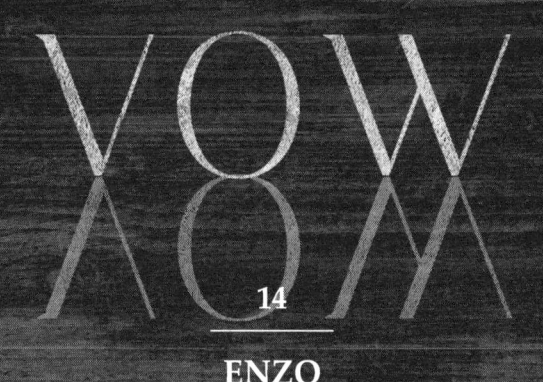

I've been putting off going through my grandfather's things. The task looms over me like a storm cloud I can't escape.

At first, I couldn't shake the idea of it being an invasion of his privacy. Even back in Italy, after the funeral, there was no avoiding the sense of searching through things I had no right to look at. Like I was a sneak, a thief. That sort of thinking is childish, and I'm not proud of it, but there was no helping it.

It was cover for what was truly going on in my head. I had already stepped into his shoes, somewhat, at least. I had returned to the house as the owner, the head of the family. That was already enough for me to handle all at once—more than enough. Overwhelming, that feeling of suddenly being called upon to do more than I ever had. To be more than I had ever been. One minute, I was standing in front of a minister, reciting my marriage vows. Then everything changed. I still haven't gotten myself used to the idea.

I have to wonder how long it will be before I do.

Looking through his books, his calendars, his papers... It would mean admitting this was real and forever. That he was gone. That he had no use for any of it anymore.

I can't leave it sitting forever. I need to get myself up to speed—what was he doing, who did he make arrangements with? What is our financial situation? It isn't enough for me to simply know we are in good shape. I need specifics. While I would hardly call myself a micromanager, I may need to be. It will all come down to what I find in the books.

And if there's anything I don't need, I'll burn it. I think he would understand. I don't want endless reminders of him sitting around, waiting to surprise me at the worst possible time, which it seems is always when things like that happen to pop up. I can't imagine a good time to be reminded of the man, is the problem. The pain is too acute. Perhaps in time, it will get easier.

I doubt he would think highly of me blubbering over him or even of me avoiding his books and papers. That helps, as well.

"How's it going?"

I look up at the sound of Prince's voice and wave him into the room. He's been busy digging into the debacle that was my wedding day, and I hope his presence means he's found something worth reporting. Yet all he does is pick up one of the ledgers and flop down in a chair near my desk.

"You're looking at it," I explain. "Making sure there's nothing in any of these ledgers I need to be aware of. You know him. He never trusted computers."

"Can you imagine how much paper got wasted back in the day?" Prince opens the book and crosses one ankle over the other knee to balance it in his lap. "And those old-fashioned Rolodex things that would sit beside a phone to keep track of a person's contacts. How archaic. What were you supposed to do? Take it with you when you travel?"

"No, that was why everyone needed a secretary. You called her, and she looked up the number for you."

"Sounds very efficient." He glances up at me from the page in front of him. "How are you managing things?"

"I would be doing better if you'd find something. Then you could go through these books for me, and I could... handle one of the many other tasks in front of me." There's too much for me to choose just one thing, though Alicia's face was what came to mind first. She needs my attention, but so does everything else. If anything, work is a good distraction from her. I'm finding it harder and harder not to give into my needs, not to go back to the way things were before.

"You always could avoid a topic you were determined not to talk about."

I would rather not take the bait, but my patience is running thin. "What is this? A therapy session?" I forget about the bank statements, for the time being, glaring at him instead. "Because I'm not in the mood."

"Yes, I've turned over a new leaf. I'm all about discussing feelings now."

"It seems that way from where I'm sitting."

"I suppose I'm the first person to ever tell you this, but sometimes, it's all right to admit you want to talk. I doubt you share many of your thoughts and feelings with Alicia."

"Don't talk about her." It's one thing for me to feel conflicted when it comes to her, but I won't have him dropping her name so casually. That's my business, not his. She's my wife.

He takes it well enough, letting the subject drop and returning to the ledger. "He had very neat handwriting, didn't he?"

"I can't believe he didn't go blind, staring at these small numbers for so long. You know how he would sometimes hole up in his study for hours, going over the books."

"Why would I pay someone to do something I can do myself?" he asks, and I'd swear my grandfather is in the room with me. Prince's impersonation is that spot-on.

"That's the trouble with you children," I continued, waving a dismissive hand the way he so often did. It isn't quite the same without a cigar between my fingers, but it's close enough. "Always wishing to outsource the most important tasks. Unwilling to put a little bit of effort into making certain no one is cheating you."

He laughs, but his laughter trails off as he lifts the book, squinting down at the numbers. "This is very recent. The most recent transactions took place in the weeks before he—before the wedding," he quickly amends, but not quickly enough. In the weeks before he died. I wish he would come out and say it and stop being so irritatingly concerned.

"What about it?"

"A lot of payments are going out."

"There are always a lot of payments going out."

"But I see three here, identical amounts paid within a week of each other. Doesn't that seem strange to you?" He brings me the ledger and lays it out across the desk. "See? The first payment is to a D.S., while the other two went to F.M."

"Initials," I muse, "but to whom did they refer? And why?" We both start flipping through pages, searching for those initials elsewhere. I might be able to link a line to an entry in a bank statement, but after an hour, we're no closer to answers, and my vision is starting to blur.

D.S. and F.M. The second set stirs something in the back of my mind that's probably unrelated, but the man's been in my thoughts lately—rather, his absence has been in my thoughts.

"One of the guards who was here during the wedding went MIA," I murmur, sitting back in my chair and closing my eyes after an hour spent poring over pages of small, tight handwriting. "At least, I haven't seen him. Frankie Morris, I think it was. Someone Grandfather hired to have his back here in Miami."

"Do you think that's what F.M. stands for? If the old man hired him as protection, it makes sense there would be payments to him."

"That's not how he did things. The money went to the head of security, then was dispersed." I'm already on the phone with my grandfather's longtime security chief. He would have made any such arrangements in advance of Grandfather's arrival.

"Can you put me in contact with Frankie Morris?" I ask. "I need to speak with him about the arrangements he made with my grandfather."

"I haven't been able to reach him—in fact, I was going to ask about him to find out whether he'd joined your crew there in Miami."

"He hasn't."

"He did beg off sick immediately after the wedding."

My free hand curls into a fist. "You thought nothing of that? Have you checked with him since? Or sent someone over to see him? Anything?" I don't wait for an answer, instead pulling out a pen. "What's his address? I want to speak with him personally." Prince is already prepared to leave, waiting in the doorway for me to jot down the address.

When the call is over, I'm barely able to stop short of throwing the phone across the room. "The man is lucky there's an ocean between us," I growl. "He acts like there's nothing unusual about a personal guard vanishing out of nowhere."

"What are you thinking?"

That's the problem. I don't know what to think. "It only seems strange. Too convenient." And I would like to know what the man was doing while my grandfather was in an assassin's crosshairs. I didn't cross paths with him much, but I would know him on sight. He stayed very close to Grandfather when he visited the townhouse. Looking back, I remember appreciating his solicitousness and how seriously he seemed to take his job.

And now he's disappeared?

We're in the car before Prince speaks again. "It could be he feels guilty. He fell short of his job."

"He could also be an enormous pussy, afraid to face me after getting my grandfather killed."

"Also possible, yes."

"Either way, I would like to hear about what he's been doing with himself since then." And why my grandfather would have reason to pay him personally. What sort of private arrangement did they have? The questions mount.

I'm not surprised when we pull up in front of a modest-looking apartment complex block away from the downtown area. Our men are paid well enough that they won't be easily lured over to the other side, a mistake other families have made. They barely pay their men enough that they can afford to eat, and they wonder why the guys break ranks. Another of Grandfather's lessons. It's amazing how many of them come back to me now without me trying to bring them up."

"Apartment 4B," I announce as we cross the street. We head straight to the fourth floor, passing under an arched entrance and crossing a paved courtyard along the way. A pair of old women sit on a bench and watch our every move from behind enormous sunglasses, but they're wise enough to keep their mouths shut. I'm sure they've seen plenty from their perch, the apartments looking down upon where they sit.

Prince keeps an eye out while I knock on the door to 4B. When there's no answer after the third round of banging, I cup my hands around my eyes and peer through an opening in the curtains over the front window.

"Do you see anything?" Prince asks.

"Furniture. But that's it." I signal for him to follow me, and we return to the entrance, this time stepping into the front office. Along one wall are rows of mailboxes, and the box for 4B is stuffed to the point where the door hangs open. Junk mail—flyers, envelopes addressed to Resident. Nothing personal. He hasn't picked it up in days, probably weeks. I wonder why no one has emptied it before now.

"Can I help you boys with something?" I turn to find myself observed by an old woman who reminds me a lot of those we crossed paths with outside, except for the lack of sunglasses.

"I would like to see the owner."

"You looking to rent?" Her mouth is set in a thin line full of disbelief and skepticism.

I barely manage not to laugh out loud at the absurdity of the idea. "No, we're not interested in renting."

"Good thing since we don't have any units for rent at the moment. Just filled the last vacancy yesterday."

"Would it be 4B?"

"How did you know?"

"Just a hunch." When her shrewd eyes narrow, I gesture to the mailbox. "It doesn't look as though anyone has checked the mail in some time." I lean my elbows against the counter between us and give her my warmest smile. "It would be a big help if I could speak with the owner of the complex. A close friend of mine lived here, and none of us can track him down. We're concerned. I'm hoping he might have left a forwarding address or some sort of idea of where he could be found."

"He's very busy."

"I'm sure he is, but it will only take a minute." I give her a wink. "What do you say?"

Now she looks like a grandmother torn between chiding her grandchild and admiring their persistence. The look in her eyes reminds me of the man whose death brought me here. "All right. But just a minute. You can go right in—he's not really that busy," she adds in a whisper.

No, I didn't think he was. He can't even be bothered to empty the mailbox of a unit that's been unoccupied for a while.

Prince precedes me, opening the door. The paunchy man behind the desk sits upright all at once—and unless I'm mistaken, he's holding something, which he quickly tucks back into his shorts. Busy, indeed. "What do you boys want? I don't want any trouble here."

I cast a pointed look at his crotch. "If you don't mind, I won't shake hands. I'm only here for information." Prince stands to my right, arms folded. I know the two of us make a formidable pair.

"Information on what?"

"What happened to Frankie Morris? 4B," I prompt in case he's not so good with names. "Where did he go? We've been looking for him, and from what I gather, you rented out his unit recently. What happened to him?"

The man's bloodshot eyes bounce between Prince and me. I don't think the sweat on his brow has anything to do with the activity we caught him in the middle of. "I don't know. I don't know where he went."

"Did he move out? Or did he simply disappear?"

"He moved out. Collected his deposit and all that. He was real neat, no damage. It isn't every day you have a tenant like that."

As if I care. "Did he tell you where he was going?"

His head swings back and forth. "No, he didn't. Never said a word. Then again, it's none of my business, is it?"

"There's no forwarding address?"

"No, I swear, he didn't leave one. He moved out..." He shuffles through papers on his desk before coming to a lease agreement with notes scrawled in the margins. "Three weeks ago. The eighteenth."

My throat is suddenly too tight. Prince steps in when I fall silent. "You're absolutely sure of that?"

"Positive. It was Saturday the eighteenth, later in the day. I remember that part since it seemed odd to leave out of nowhere at that time of day."

I know without looking at him that Prince understands what I now do. "Thank you. We were never here, got it?" His head bobs up and down, eyes bulging, and I decide to leave it at that.

It isn't until we're outside that Prince speaks. "The eighteenth. Wasn't that—"

"Yeah," I grunt. "My wedding day."

15

ALICIA

I planned to get up early today, but I'm up even before my alarm. The sun has barely risen, and I sort of wish I was still asleep. When I'm asleep, I'm not here. Sure, sometimes I dream about my life, but usually, they're nightmares, not nice dreams. It's still better than reality.

My period must be coming up because I am so freaking emotional and hormonal. I have to shake it off—there's a lot of studying I need to catch up on, which was the entire reason I wanted to get up early this morning. Lying here and wallowing in misery isn't going to help anything.

At least I don't have to worry about waking Enzo. He never stays with me in my room. Once we're finished, he leaves me alone. Like I need another reminder of how much I don't matter to him. I'm getting used to that, though. What's the point of wishing for what I can't have? Whatever there was between us broke the day of our wedding, and I'm not going to get it back. I need to accept that. Maybe I'm finally starting to since every time he fucks me and leaves me, it hurts a little less.

I force myself to sit up with a sigh and throw black the blankets.

A moment later, I'm scrambling out of bed and running for the bathroom. I barely make it, sliding the last few feet on my knees, but at least my face is hovering over the toilet bowl before the first rush of vomit makes its way out of my mouth. Again and again, my stomach heaves, and I grip the sides of the bowl, straining until the last few drops fall from my lips.

Holy shit. That came on so fast. I'm afraid to get up in case it happens again, but after a minute or so, I'm reasonably confident enough to flush the toilet, then get on my feet to brush my teeth. A part of me wonders if this is a waste of time—if I have a stomach virus or food poisoning, that won't be the last time I'm sick today. I might end up having to do this again in a few minutes.

I feel awful. All I want to do is crawl back into bed and shut out the world until this passes. What the hell did I eat last night? Even thinking about food makes my stomach churn, but I want to remember. We had grilled salmon, that's right. Maybe it was off? I don't remember it tasting bad. But then it doesn't have to taste bad, does it?

Wait a second.

I drop the toothbrush into the sink and stare at myself in the mirror. Oh shit. There I was, thinking I was feeling hormonal because my period's coming on, but when was the last time I had my period, anyway? I totally lost track of time. That's the one thing I should have been paying closer attention to in all of this, but I haven't.

Am I pregnant?

I probably am. I mean, hardly a night goes by when Enzo isn't doing his best to knock me up. And it's not like he ever used protection before we were married, either.

A baby. I put a hand over my belly and look down, but of course, it doesn't look any different than usual. That won't come for a little while yet. Right now, to the rest of the world, I look like any average woman my age. My boobs are a little bigger, now that I think about it, but it's not like that's a telltale sign. Only when my bump starts to show will anybody be able to tell.

Like my husband, for instance.

A rush of cold fear washes over me, and for a second, I think I'm going to throw up again. But morning sickness isn't why I'm feeling this way. I know it. It's the thought of Enzo finding out.

Why can't this just be normal? What's so wrong with me that I don't deserve the happiness, the joy of telling my husband we're going to have a baby? Other people get to experience that kind of joy. Why can't I? Why does every aspect of my life have to be so much harder than everybody else's?

What happens when he finds out and doesn't want anything to do with me anymore?

I'm ashamed of that thought, so ashamed I can't look at myself in the mirror anymore. I turn my back on it, leaning against the vanity, folding my arms over my stomach and trembling. What am I supposed to do? How do I handle this? He's frustrated that I'm not pregnant yet after all these weeks. I know that much from the almost mechanical way he takes me now. There's not even lust involved anymore. It's another task to get out of the way before he moves on to the next thing, and the thing after that.

But it will be even worse once he knows we've been successful. Even lonelier. What use will he have for me now when all that's left for me to do is grow our baby, then hand it over to him after it's born?

At least if it's a boy. I'm not sure if I want it to be or not. I dread the idea of Enzo raising our child just as much as I ever did. This life growing inside me, if it is really there—and I'm pretty sure it is— deserves a chance. Not just his money, not just his name or his influence. They deserve a chance at a real life of being nurtured and loved. What could he possibly know about that?

How would I live with myself day after day, year after year, knowing I left my son with a man who will only screw him up?

And if it's a girl? Will he even want to have anything to do with her? I've asked myself that question before so many times, but now it's not hypothetical anymore. Everything feels a lot more real, and the stakes are higher than they've ever been.

I almost loathe the life growing in me. On the other hand, I love it. My baby, a piece of me. I wipe away a tear as it rolls down my cheek, still staring down at my flat stomach and knowing it won't be that way for very long.

He's going to get up eventually. I don't want there being any evidence of my morning sickness for him to find later. I carefully clean the toilet before getting in the shower, and by the time I'm out and on my way back to my room, his bedroom door is open. He must have used another bathroom when he found me already using this one.

What am I supposed to do? The question plagues me as I go through the motions of getting ready for my day. I'm not even thinking about it, simply going from one step to the next. My mind may as well be a million miles away.

A baby. What am I supposed to do? What's my move? If I tell him I'm pregnant, I doubt he'll let me go to school. He probably won't even let me out of the house, period. He'll be too worried about something happening to me, keeping me safe, whatever he needs to tell himself as an excuse to control me. I don't want that any more than I want him to ignore me sexually.

I don't want to be without that. Even when he uses me and leaves me, it's better than nothing. How am I supposed to live under the same roof with him knowing he'll never touch me again?

I'm no closer to an answer by the time I walk slowly down the stairs. My feet are as heavy as my heart, which is filled with dread and doubt. What do I do? What's the best thing for me, for my baby?

"Good morning."

I almost drop my backpack on the floor at the sound of Enzo's voice coming from the kitchen. He's watching me, standing by the coffee maker. "Do you want a cup?"

Shit. I'm not supposed to have caffeine, am I? Or is it okay in moderation? I'm not a hundred percent sure I'm pregnant yet, but I already have to think about this. He's waiting for an answer, his brows lifting higher the longer I make him wait.

"Sure," I decide. I don't have to drink all of it, anyway, but if I refuse it, he'll know something's up.

"How was your night?" He would pick today to decide he cares about my life, wouldn't he? If I didn't know better, I would swear he's aware of something being different.

"Too short," I admit, snickering a little as I pull a travel cup down from the cabinet.

He's standing too close, leaning on the counter while I pour my coffee. What's with the lack of boundaries today? Why now, of all times? "I noticed you were up earlier than usual this morning. Everything okay?"

My hand shakes, and I splash a little. "Oh sure. I had to get a little extra homework done before class."

"I'll give you credit. I don't know that I would be so dedicated to my work if I knew I didn't really need to do it."

This again. "I've always been a serious student. Kind of nerdy, I guess."

"Like I said, I give you credit." As he passes, he places a hand on my back. I can't believe how good it feels, how a ripple of pleasure moves through me. At the same time, I wish he wouldn't touch me because all it does is make me suspicious. He's too interested in me this morning.

I'm being paranoid. I know it. And I can't afford to tip my hand by acting all weird and fidgety.

"I need something to do, anyway. Something to keep my brain busy." I fix up my coffee, and take a sip, hoping I don't end up screwing my baby up somehow. I need to get a test. How am I supposed to get a test without him knowing about it? Maybe they have some at the convenience store close to campus, but that would mean getting rid of Paolo somehow. Could I order one online? Again, how can I guarantee I'd be able to get it here without somebody opening the package to see what I ordered? I wouldn't put it past Enzo to do that.

"Do you want something to eat?" he asks. "We haven't sat down to have breakfast together in a while. I thought since I had a little time this morning..."

This is torture. It's absolute torture. Here he is, actually being nice, and all I want to do is get the hell out of this house before he knows for sure there's something up. "Actually, I was just going to grab a banana and a protein bar or something like that and eat once I get to school. I'm kind of distracted—I have an exam today." I don't, but it's not like he would know either way. I doubt he gets reports from my instructors, no matter whether his name is on my file.

"Okay. Are you feeling all right?"

"Just distracted. Like I said, for some reason, it still matters how I do in school."

I feel better when he rolls his eyes. "Fine. Have a good day, I guess."

"You, too." Paolo is always waiting for me out in the car, and this morning is no exception. I'm glad for that since I wouldn't want to have to wait around for him and deal with Enzo's penetrating stare.

He's going to find out eventually. I need to accept that, just like I need to accept how my life is going to change once he does.

16

ENZO

"We're close to finding him. Trust me on that." Prince stands before me, hands clasped behind his back, his chin held high. Defensive, and with good reason, since I'm ready to tear his head off for letting me down.

"Believe you? It's been weeks since we walked in on that perverted slob jacking off behind his desk. Did Frankie vanish off the face of the earth? How is it possible for someone to disappear the way he has?"

I get up from my desk since anger won't allow me to sit still. "Are you sure he's alive?"

"He's been spotted by various contacts as recently as three days ago. I have eyes in all his usual locations. The minute he shows his face, we'll be on him. Trust me."

Again, with the *trust me* bullshit. Famous last words. "The minute, and I mean the very minute, he shows up, you tell me. I'm not letting him get away with this." Whatever this happens to be. I still have no proof of wrongdoing. Only a hunch brought forth by a very convenient set of circumstances.

"No one thinks you will. No doubt he's watching his back. He can't hide forever."

No, but he's done a pretty damn good job of it so far. What could have happened to change his mind and shift his loyalties? I won't admit to Prince how much sleep I've lost over this. I don't even want to admit it to myself. If a man as highly respected as my grandfather could be double-crossed by someone he trusted, what chance do I have?

No, there had to be more to it. I refuse to believe Frankie didn't act without a backer—namely, Alvarez. He can lie all he wants about how that bullet ended up lodged in my grandfather's body, but I won't believe it until I see proof. Since I doubt such proof exists, something tells me I'm not going to have my mind changed anytime soon.

He could've run out of guilt and the certainty that I'd come calling. Anyone with half a brain would do the same thing. But the fact that he moved out the night of the wedding—unannounced beforehand, ready to go—tells me there was planning involved. He was ready to run. The money Grandfather paid him could easily afford a new place. The only question is, why did he allow that shot to be fired without protecting his boss?

And who's protecting him now?

I turn toward Prince, but it's the person walking past the open door to the study who catches my attention. If I didn't know better, I would think she was sneaking past me. "Alicia. What are you doing?"

She pauses, then doubles back. Her cheeks are flushed, and she won't meet my gaze. "I'm going to school. I have class in twenty minutes." She checks the time and frowns. "Eighteen minutes."

Prince's curious stare isn't lost on me, but I make a point of ignoring him. "All right. Is Paolo waiting for you?"

"Where else would he be?" Her voice is tight, as is her half-hearted laughter. "I really better go."

"Go on, then. Don't let me keep you." The word scurry comes to mind as I watch her rush off, her head low, both hands gripping the strap of her backpack tight enough to make her knuckles stand out bone white.

"How's that going?" I ignore Prince's question in favor of going to the doorway and following my wife's progress. I'm just in time to watch her duck out the front door, and if I didn't know better, I would think she stole something and doesn't want me to know it. But that's absurd.

There's nothing for her to steal, for one thing. I've given her access to very little.

Prince is still watching me, and I have to grit my teeth against a demand for him to mind his own business. "Isn't there something else you should be doing right now?" I mutter.

"You could just tell me to mind my own business."

"Go and mind your own fucking business. Find Frankie. That's all that matters right now."

"Whatever you say, boss." I hate the way he says it, the humor in his voice that I know is meant to conceal irritation. Some other time, when I have the mental bandwidth to manage it, the two of us will have a discussion about respect and boundaries and such.

At the moment, I'm more interested in what the hell is going on inside Alicia's head. She's been so strange lately, at least the past few days. When I look back to pinpoint when it all began, that's the best approximation I can come up with.

It's nothing obvious, nothing glaring. There haven't been any temper tantrums. No arguments, no stubbornness.

And that's the problem, I realize as I pour coffee in the kitchen. It's bright and sunny in here, almost glaringly so. I almost resent the sunshine since it's in such contrast with my mood.

I've told myself countless times the past few days to be grateful she's calmed down some. I have more than enough on my plate without a nagging, resentful wife fucking things up. I should be grateful, just as I'm grateful for the coffee, which helps cut through some of the worst of my head fog.

It also brings my concerns into focus. That little performance just now is more than enough reason to suspect her. She acts like this meek little lamb when I know she's anything but. It's as if she's compensating for something, wanting to stay out of my way in hopes I don't notice whatever she's trying to hide. Is that paranoia? It could be, but I would rather know for sure than dismiss something that might turn out to be a problem. If anything, I tell myself as I carry my coffee upstairs, this is a good habit to get into. I can't allow myself to dismiss my instincts, not if

I'm going to lead this family in any meaningful way. Sometimes, instinct is all we have.

I wonder what Grandfather's instincts told him about Frankie.

Her room is neat as a pin. I appreciate that about her. Not much disgusts me worse than an undisciplined slob. I do a cursory search of the rest of the dresser before turning away from it and going to the bed. There's nothing hidden underneath, so I begin searching between the mattress and the box spring beneath it.

"What's this? Looking for contraband? Or are you so obsessed with her that you can't help but go through her stuff when she's gone?" Prince barely ducks in time to avoid getting hit with a shoe that ends up in the hallway.

"Mind your own fucking business for once." I stand and take care with straightening the bed, so it won't look like I was going through it.

"I'm just saying, you've fallen far if you've resorted to tearing her room apart."

"I could shoot you where you stand."

He nods as if accepting this. "What are you doing? All joking aside." He returns the shoe under the bed next to its mate before turning to me, and all traces of humor are gone.

"As I said, mind your own business. This is a domestic situation. You wouldn't understand."

"Oh, so that's how it's going to be? Just because I wasn't forced to marry a stranger, I couldn't possibly understand."

"Something like that." Her nightstand only contains a couple of paperback books. She lives a sparse life, but then a lot of that is by design. She doesn't deserve much more. If anything, this is much better than she ought to have. Why would I reward a liar like her?

"Should I leave the room before you sniff her panties?" I shove him out of the way and go out into the hall, then into the bathroom. Yes, I'm sinking low by doing this, but there has to be a reason for her sudden change. I never thought I'd find myself missing that fiery spirit of hers.

Before Prince can make another snide comment, I close the door, then turn on the water in the sink to drown out the sound of my search. This is not exactly my proudest moment, digging around under the sink, in the drawers. Nothing seems out of the ordinary. I also check under the drawers like I did in the bedroom but don't find anything taped to the underside. It's enough to make me laugh at myself. Who is she, a spy? But I wouldn't put anything past her, just the same.

I'm about to leave the room when my gaze lands on the wastebasket. Am I truly this obsessed? I already know the answer before I overturn the thing, which was thankfully only half full to begin with. Balled-up tissue, a few Q-tips.

And something else, something wrapped in toilet paper. It's obviously a box. I can almost make out the print on it as I unravel the cocoon of paper surrounding it.

There's a final layer to remove by the time I'm able to make out the print. Reliable Pregnancy Test.

I flip down the toilet lid and sit on it, staring at the box. The slightest movement leaves something rattling around inside. I tear it open and spill out the contents into my palm. Two tests. Like she wanted to be sure.

And I don't know much about these things, but the presence of two lines on both tests sends a very definite message.

I flip the box over and scan the back. Sure enough, two lines means pregnant. They're faint—they must be old, maybe a few days, but how would I know for sure? This is my first time ever holding a pregnancy test, much less trying to analyze one.

She's pregnant. And she fucking knows it. She's fucking known it for days.

And there I was, thinking she might try to sell the diamonds. I'm disappointed in myself for not having come to this conclusion on my own.

What did she do with the evidence? She wrapped it in layers of toilet paper and hid it in the bottom of the wastebasket. Like a guilty child. As if she could truly hide anything from me.

I crumple the box in my fist and throw it into the can along with the tests. Washing my hands, I look at myself in the mirror. I'm going to be a father. That is if she hasn't done anything to fuck the pregnancy up already.

Why didn't she tell me? What is she thinking? What is she planning? She wouldn't do anything to hurt herself or the baby, would she? At least I know she has Paolo with her. He wouldn't let her do anything irrational, but then again, she got her hand on those tests somehow, didn't she? He must have turned a blind eye at some point. What else has he missed?

One thing's for sure: I'm not about to sit around and wait for her to come back. When I blow past Prince in the hallway, he calls out behind me, "What is it? Did you find something in the toilet tank?"

"Do us both a favor and do your fucking job," I growl over my shoulder, heading straight for the front door. "I have somewhere to be." The slamming of the door is a final punctuation mark. He needs to spend less time concerned with what I'm doing and more time finding Frankie.

I wave off the offer of a driver and get behind the wheel myself, the tires squealing as I back out of the driveway, then swing around and peel down the street. She's going to regret lying to me. Again.

VOW

17
ALICIA

Where is she? Dammit, is she deliberately ducking me? I look around the room as we all stand, ready to go the second the instructor ends the lecture. Maybe Elena slipped in when I didn't notice. But no, she's not here. It's like she knows I have it out for her.

Normally, I would brush off a thought like that and call it paranoia. But I don't think I'm being paranoid now. It's been a few weeks, and I still haven't managed to pull Elena aside and talk to her. This is our only class together. How am I supposed to reach out to her without looking obvious?

What if I text her and ask why she's been a stranger? It's as good an idea as any. One friend being worried about another friend is totally normal. I have to figure out the right way to say it is all.

I can't help but drag my feet out of the room. I'm the last person to leave, in fact, and by the time I reach the door, even the instructor is gone. It's just me in this otherwise empty lecture hall, trying to come up with a way to sound natural when I ask Elena why she's ducking me.

Until someone joins me, grabbing me by the arm before I can step through the door and shoving me back into the room. He's slammed and locked the door before my brain can catch up to what's happening. Then he whirls on me, and everything comes into sharp, terrifying focus.

I've seen Enzo like this before. On our wedding day, for example, after his grandfather died and Alvarez dropped the truth. When I knew he wanted to kill me and was afraid it would happen at any second. He looked this enraged then. Wild. Like he was holding his self-control by a thread.

"What are you doing?" I ask him in a choked whisper. My heart is going a million miles a minute, and a cold sweat breaks out because I know exactly what he's doing. I can read it in his eyes, the way they blaze. I'm surprised I don't burst into flames on the spot.

"Is there something you need to tell me?" he demands. "And I need you to think very seriously about the next words that come out of your mouth, Alicia. I need you to consider them carefully. Don't even think about lying to me or coming up with some bullshit story. It's time for the truth."

"The truth about what?" I ask. It's obvious I'm stalling. What do I do? How does he know?

His laughter makes the hair stand up on the back of my neck. "Wrong answer."

"I don't understand. Where is this coming from? You can't just barge in here and lock us in an empty room, Enzo. We're going to get in trouble."

"Right," he sneers, pacing in front of me and blocking the door. "Because that's all you care about, isn't it? Doing the right thing. Being a good girl. Obeying the rules."

"If obeying the rules means security not throwing us off campus and telling me to never come back, then yes, I would like to obey them."

"I guess none of that mattered the night you sneaked into that warehouse, did it?"

"I already told you why I did that. Why are you throwing that in my face now?"

He comes to a stop before lunging at me. "What are you hiding from me?" he bellows. His voice echoes in the large room, and I recoil from it, both hoping somebody hears and wants to help and dreading the idea. This will get so much worse if anybody else becomes involved.

"Okay, okay," I whisper as I back away, lowering my backpack to the floor and holding up my hands. "This doesn't have to be a big thing. We're in public."

"Fuck the public!" He bends down, picks up my backpack, and hurls it across the room. I jump when it hits the wall; glad my phone is in my pocket. He would have crushed it otherwise. "Do you think I give a fuck what anybody else thinks? I don't have to. I'm not some pathetic nobody. I am Enzo De Luca, and I want the truth from my wife. For once. Just tell me the fucking truth!" He takes the random textbook lying on the table at the front of the room and throws it up into the seats, where the bang it makes reminds me of a gunshot.

He's not going to stop. I know that much. It's useless to stall. "You want the truth?"

His breath comes in big, heaving gasps. "What the fuck have I just said? Yes."

He never did say what he was talking about, this big truth he requires, but he doesn't have to. I know exactly what this is all about, and I'm too tired and too scared to keep pretending.

So I take a deep breath and brace myself. "I guess you already know, don't you? I'm pregnant. I thought you would be happy about it."

"Happy? Happy?" he screams, spittle flying from his mouth, his face deep red. "Happy about what? Happy to find out you lied to me again?"

"Lied to you? When did I lie?"

"You hid this from me, which is the same as lying."

"But it's not. I was waiting for the right time to tell you."

"The right time? Exactly when the fuck would that be?"

"For one thing, it's only been a couple of days since I took the test."

"You should have told me immediately."

I knew I was taking a risk by keeping this to myself. Somehow, though, it never occurred to me that he'd reach this level of insanity once he got the news.

I should apologize and try to explain myself. So why do I fold my arms instead? Why do I glare back at him? "Right. I forgot you own every part of me. I don't even get to decide how to tell you we're going to have a baby. Because you're like my boss. I was supposed to walk straight up to you and hand you the test and hope I get a bonus this year or something, right? Job well done, pat on the top of my head?"

His lip curls in disgust, like the situation is very different from what I described. "Don't do that. Don't make this about you."

"Right. Because everything is about you!" Now I'm the one threatening to make a big scene. Maybe it's the fact that we are in public, technically. I'm not as afraid. And he knows I'm carrying his child now, so he's less likely to hurt me over this. Thinking about that lights a fire in me. "You wouldn't want to maybe think I needed a day or two to process this for myself."

He points at my stomach. "That is my child you're carrying. Mine."

"And mine."

"That is not the agreement we made."

"Of course. Our agreement." It's my turn to let out an unhinged laugh. "Maybe you need to get a few things straight. One, I have no control over whether this baby is a boy or a girl, so if it is a girl, I still owe you a son. But this child would still exist—and it would still be yours, whether you wanted to acknowledge it or not. Maybe you'd better wrap your head around that before the kid is born. Second, you are not the one carrying the child. I am. And I wanted a couple of days for it to just be me knowing about it, like a special little secret. I have nothing of my own anymore. Couldn't I have this for just a couple of days?"

Silence falls between us for a few seconds, and I know I said too much, but it had to be said. He needed to hear it. Was it the complete truth? No, but it was a start.

"Are you finished?" he murmurs. "Because that is the biggest load of bullshit I have ever heard. We both know what this is about. You don't want my child, and you never have."

"That's not what our agreement was about, is it?" I ask, and it's almost fun to see him squirm for once. "This is life or death for me, and those are the terms you set. So I think it actually behooves me to get pregnant as quickly as possible and to get this the hell over with or else risk you killing me. I don't have any reason to hide this from you—and it would be stupid to try."

"Yet you still tried."

"Burying a pregnancy test in the trash isn't exactly the same as trying to hide a pregnancy. If I was that determined, I wouldn't have thrown it out at home."

"I deserved to know right away."

"I'm sorry, that wasn't one of the terms of our agreement, was it?"

"Did it have to be?" he bellows, throwing his arms into the air.

"Obviously, it did."

All I want is to tell him the truth. All I want is for him to want me. To still want me even now. That's what's bothering me the most; that's what has my stomach in knots and my chest hurting. Not getting caught—he was going to find out eventually. It's knowing our relationship as I know it is really over now. And even if the baby is a girl, all he'll do is rush to impregnate me again. It'll never be like it was before, like it could have been.

With him acting the way he is, that shouldn't hurt. I should be glad, but I'm not. I'm about as far from it as possible. It would be so easy just to admit it all, to lay myself bare in front of him here and now. He might be surprised out of his anger.

He might also get angrier. Or, even worse, dismissive. Cold and cruel, both of which seem to be his specialty. I don't think I could handle that. I think that might be what finally breaks me once and for all.

"You've betrayed me once again." His voice is quieter now, but somehow, it's even more frightening. Cold, flat, and totally absent of emotion. I can't help but shrink a little at the sound of it. "Just when I thought we were getting somewhere, you remind me that I can never be too comfortable with you. I suppose I ought to thank you for that."

"You're wrong about this."

"No, I don't think I am. You're lying to me even now. Is that all you know how to do? Lie? Saying anything, so long as it means you are saving your ass?"

"I'm not lying. You're wrong."

"Am I? Then please, enlighten me on why you hid that test instead of telling me right away because your special little secret excuse is bullshit. What's the truth, Alicia? Do you know what the word means anymore?"

I should tell him. Wouldn't that shock him into silence? "I wasn't planning on hiding this from you. I would have told you soon. Now, you've even taken that from me. The opportunity to tell my husband I'm pregnant, that we're going to have a baby. Congratulations. You've taken away just about everything I was ever looking forward to."

"Do not make yourself out to be a victim here."

"I was only telling the truth. Isn't that what you want? Or would you rather only hear what makes you happy? That's not how it works."

"Enough of this." He's practically on top of me in an instant, and I press myself against the wall near the door when he leans in close. "From now on, I want to know everything. Immediately. You keep nothing from me, not for any bullshit reason that twisted little mind of yours comes up with."

Twisted mind? I have to bite my tongue against what threatens to come out of me the moment I hear that. As if he has any room to talk about being twisted.

"Do you understand?"

"Yes," I grit out, forcing myself to hold his gaze. I'm not going to look away. I will not back down.

"Good. I expect you home right away since I know you don't have any other classes after this today. Paolo will take you straight there, and it would be for the best if we don't cross paths. I don't want to look at you anymore today."

He thrusts a finger in my face, and his hand is trembling. "Take care of yourself. Don't even think about doing anything that will hurt my son." With that, he leaves me, swinging the door open so hard it smashes into the wall.

And all I can do is stand here, shaking, staring straight ahead but seeing nothing in front of me. No, all I see is my future, which has never looked as bleak and empty as it does right now.

VOW

18

ENZO

"From now on, you report everything to me and I mean everything."

"Yes, sir." Paolo stands straight and tall, but there's no disguising his discomfort. He's lucky it's only discomfort he's dealing with. I might have decided he'd look a lot better without the back of his head. I might have decided to paint the walls of my study with his blood and brains. It's still a possibility, in fact.

"If she steps into a store, I want you following her around that store," I continue. "And once she's finished making her purchases, I want you looking through that bag. Got it?"

"Got it. It's just that..." His brows knit together, and I can barely keep a hold on my rage.

"It's just that what?" I bark when he falls silent.

"She said it was... feminine stuff she had to buy."

"And you're that afraid of maybe touching a box of tampons? Jesus Christ. You're lucky I don't blow your fucking head off here and now. Do you like living, Paolo?"

"Sir?" he asks, confused.

"Living. Do you enjoy being alive?"

"Of course, yes."

"Then I suggest you suck the fuck up and remember who's paying you. And who's allowing you to get out of this situation with your life. I promise you, you will not get a second chance."

"Understood, Mr. De Luca."

"Get out of my sight." To his credit, he stops short of running from the room—but not very far short. How the fuck did I end up with these assholes in my crew? And she's a clever one, too. Telling him she was buying feminine products, knowing he wouldn't search too hard. If it wasn't my heir's life hanging in the balance, I might have to congratulate her for being smart.

As it is, she's lucky she's carrying my child, or else she would be in a world of pain. There is such a thing as being too clever, it turns out.

I hardly have time to breathe before there's a brief knock on my door. "What?" I bark.

Prince opens the door enough to peer into the room. "Is it safe? Or will I get another shoe thrown at my head?"

"It depends upon your reason for interrupting me."

"Oh, then I'm safe." He enters the room, and his smile drops away. "We found him."

"Frankie?" I'm already out of my chair, prepared to go. "Where?"

He winces, and I'm reminded of how unusual it is for a piece of news to be truly good with no strings attached. "That part you're not going to like so much."

"Out with it, for fuck's sake. I've had enough games today."

"He was seen coming and going from the Alvarez compound."

I knew it. For once, I didn't want to be right. "That motherfucker!" I sweep an arm over my desk, sending papers, books, and even my phone flying. Prince merely takes a large backward step to get out of the way. "And you're sure it's him?"

"Positive. I've seen him enough times. As soon as you see him, you'll know it's true."

"Yes, I'm sure I will." Prince has never come to me with bad intel, and I highly doubt he would have made this announcement were he not completely sure.

Why did it have to be Alvarez? It's almost sad how very clear everything is. Alvarez obviously lured him in with some promise or another, though I can't imagine how much the man must have promised to sway Frankie's loyalties. The man made a hundred-thousand dollars off my grandfather in the days before his death. What more could Alvarez promise?

I'm kidding myself, asking questions like this. There is no limit to the depths some will sink to when it comes to money. There's no such thing as enough.

"That fucking bastard. I'll kill him. He's fucking dead." I can barely think for the pounding in my head, the rushing of blood in my ears. I want him in front of me, here and now. I want to hear him scream. I want to rip out his beating heart and hold it in front of his face so he can look upon it in his final moments.

My hands shake with anticipation as I pour myself a drink and gulp it down all at once. That lying, traitorous piece of shit. Grandfather trusted him, and look where that trust got us all. The whiskey does little to blunt my fury, so I have a second before slamming the glass down. "I want to see him. I need to see the bastard for myself."

"I was going to suggest we run surveillance." Prince glances toward the window, where darkness is about to fall on the other side. "And I have a new toy I'd like to test out."

"This isn't the time—"

"Believe me. You'll understand once you see it."

"Fine. So long as that toy doesn't give us away somehow."

"It won't, trust me." I don't have much of a choice, do I? He's one of the few people I can trust in all of this, a point that becomes clearer by the day. Even Paolo, someone I believed I could entrust with the care of my wife, failed me in the end. Pathetic.

We can't leave right away, no matter how eager I am to set my eyes on that piece of shit traitor. "Paolo!" I call out, knowing he can't be far. And he isn't, appearing mere moments after my echoing voice fades to silence. Of course, now he's eager to please, asking how high when I tell him to jump. He wants to get back in my good graces.

"I'm going out. I can't say for how long. I need guards throughout the house—front and rear doors, here in my study, and walking the perimeter. Four-hour shifts. I'm trusting you with this."

"You can count on me."

We'll see about that. Before he can leave, I ask, "Is she upstairs?"

He nods. "She hasn't left her room since we returned from the school."

"Good." She can't get into any trouble up there—after all, I already went through everything.

"What should I say if she asks where you've gone?"

"Since when does she need to know where I go?" He accepts this with a firm nod, then pulls out his phone before leaving the room. I hear him requesting extra bodies and leave him with a reminder to reach out immediately at the slightest hint of trouble.

"What's his story? I heard you tearing into him." Prince gets behind the wheel while I slide into the passenger seat.

"Don't worry about it. Just get us there." His sigh only makes me bristle. "What business do you have eavesdropping on what happens in my study, anyway?"

"Eavesdropping? I could've been around the corner, and I would have heard most of what you were saying. You didn't exactly take great pains to be quiet, you know."

"I was angry."

"No shit. Tell me something else I don't know."

"I am not in the mood for banter."

He falls silent, and I couldn't be more grateful.

Is this what it will always be like? Countless people and problems constantly vying for my attention? Will there ever come a time when I can sit back and breathe for a minute without another catastrophe looming?

I've already received intel as to the location of the Alvarez compound, which is why I'm surprised when Prince comes to a stop and parks a mile or two away after driving forty-five minutes. "Why are we stopping here?" In the middle of nowhere, no less, without so much as a streetlight to give us away.

"Wait and see." He gets out of the car, leaving me alone. I've never been someone who enjoys being the last to know, and this situation is no exception. I'm already irritated enough as it is. This delay isn't doing much to help my mood.

He opens my door, and I have the benefit of the car's interior light, giving me just enough that I can make out what he's holding. "Son of a bitch. I didn't know you had one of these."

He holds up the drone, clearly pleased with himself. "I bought it not long ago. After a certain unfortunate incident at an abandoned hangar."

"So what, the idea is to send this ahead of us?" I can see how that might have come in handy, certainly. He might have avoided nearly bleeding to death if we'd been able to examine the area from a distance.

"I was hoping to use this to get a look at the compound and find that bastard if he's still around. Why risk getting too close if we can send this in our place?"

"Where else could he be? It makes sense, considering he can't be found elsewhere. Alvarez would want to keep a close hold on him because, naturally, I'd want him dead, either for pulling the trigger or for not doing his job." I can imagine him in there, thinking he's safe, protected by Alvarez. Perhaps he's gloating over getting away with double-crossing us.

Prince finishes checking over his toy with a satisfied grin. "The camera has night vision and can pick up a clear image from two hundred feet away. We can watch from here on my tablet."

"I have to give you credit. Good idea."

"Wait a minute. Let me make a note of that somewhere. Enzo De Luca told me I had a good idea." He's chuckling as he sets the drone on the ground, then uses a controller to send it flying. "The tablet's in the back seat. Take a look."

Eventually, he joins me in the car, and we watch while he controls the drone's progress. "How far can this thing go?" I ask, eyes trained on the screen.

"A few miles." He points at the screen. "There it is. The compound." Yes, and it's sprawling and overdone. Exactly what I would expect from the man. At least the estate back in Italy is tasteful.

"Take it easy. Stay close to the outer walls." Prince only grunts softly in reply, focused on the job. "What are those glowing points?"

"Cigarette tips." Of course. A cluster of men is having a smoke near the front of the house. The group moves toward the courtyard, and the lights mounted near the door provide a look at who's who.

"Son of a bitch," I whisper, jabbing a finger at the tablet. "There he is."

"Yeah, that's him." Prince maintains his position, hovering near the wall bordering the property. "I told you, didn't I?"

"He seems comfortable with them, doesn't he?"

"They're not keeping him against his will if that's what you're getting at."

"The prick. Enjoying a smoke with his buddies." My chest is burning, and my stomach clenching at the sight of him. The bastard. "I can't wait to chat with him the minute he's off the property."

"That could take a while. He might not leave tonight or even this week. Not if he's hiding out there."

"He has to leave at some point. I'll come back here every day if I have to. I'll assign men to watch."

"With my drone? I don't think so." Our eyes meet, and he scowls. "I'd better be reimbursed if there's any damage."

"What is it you say all the time? Trust me?" I settle back in my seat, watching Frankie enjoy himself with his new friends. It'll be a long night, but I have all the time in the world.

If he leaves, I plan to follow.

He can't run from me forever.

"Hey, I meant to ask you..."

"Hmm?" I murmur.

"I heard a little more than I should have earlier when you were shouting at Paolo. What happened with Alicia? Really."

With the tablet to stare at, it feels easier to talk about things like this. "She's pregnant. I found the tests in the bathroom trash."

"She's pregnant? That's great news!" He nudges me with his elbow. "Congratulations! That took no time at all. Good work."

I can't bring myself to share his excitement. Not with the reminder of how quickly everything can go to shit here in front of me, smoking, laughing at somebody's joke. Only once he's taken care of—and his benevolent host along with him—will I be able to enjoy the notion of being a father.

As it turns out, this isn't the night for his reckoning. Four hours pass, five, and still neither Frankie nor anyone inside those stone walls steps foot beyond them. "There's only so much longer it'll work without being recharged," Prince finally points out in a quiet voice tinged with disappointment.

"Very well." I'm stiff from sitting in this position anyway and could use a piss and something to eat. "We'll be back. At least I know where to find him now."

And he can't stay in there forever.

VOW

19

ALICIA

The house is usually quiet at this time of night. Not that it's exactly noisy now, but a different kind of energy is in the air. It's unsettled—tense. Like static electricity is in the air and if I touch the wrong thing, I'll get zapped.

It's probably because there are so many guards patrolling. More than I've ever seen here at once, even more than we had at the wedding. The house is crawling with them, and that's not counting the men I sometimes hear exchanging words outside.

I can't help noticing them on my way downstairs to grab water to keep in my room. None of them pay me much attention beyond a quick, cursory glance. Nothing about it gives me any insight into what they're thinking.

And none of them are Enzo.

That shouldn't worry me. After the way he flipped out on me, he's the last person I should give a damn about. Let him go off and do something stupid and get himself in trouble. That's not my problem.

But I am carrying his child, and he is my husband. With that excuse in mind, I approach one of the men standing just outside the kitchen door, keeping watch on the backyard. I slide the door open, and he turns at once, almost like he's expecting trouble.

"It's only me," I offer with a faint smile. He doesn't return it, but then

I don't expect him to. "What's going on, exactly? What's with all the faces and bodies around here?"

I should have known better. He smirks before turning his back on me. "Nothing you need to worry about."

That sounds much too familiar. I'm getting sick and tired of being told what I do and don't need to know about.

I straighten my spine and lift my chin, reminding myself he isn't Enzo. He has no hold over me, this nobody. Some goon with a gun who Enzo would castrate if he ever hurt me. "I am Mrs. De Luca," I remind him. "And I would like to know."

"If you needed to know, the boss would have told me so. He's the one who pays me, not you."

None of these men are exactly what I would call geniuses. I wouldn't want any of them performing surgery on me. But they know how to put a person in their place. I close the door quietly, feeling small and insignificant—especially after trying to put on an act like I was all big and bad.

And I'm angry. So damn angry. I don't know if it has to do with the baby affecting my hormones or what, but something that would normally make me roll my eyes before trudging upstairs has me steamed. Fuck these guys. Who do they think they are, talking to me this way? Is this the kind of life I would have to look forward to if I stayed married to Enzo?

I forget all about my water, instead choosing to go through the house into the living room, where a man is posted by the front door. "Excuse me. Do you know where my husband is?" It's past midnight, and he still hasn't come back from wherever he went with Prince. Not that I was clued in or anything. I happened to overhear him making plans on the phone.

"If you don't know where he is, why would I?" He snickers as I turn away, my face flushing with both embarrassment and rage. This is ridiculous. Do these men take courses on how to be cold and dismissive?

At least he said something to me. When I ask the guy posted in Enzo's empty study, he doesn't bother saying a word. He only stares out the window, his back to me, like a statue. A statue who would probably blow the head off an intruder.

There has to be a reason they won't at least tell me where he went, like a meeting or something. They won't even bother telling me they don't know—maybe they don't. Why would he keep them informed? But their egos probably won't let them admit that.

I drag myself back upstairs, my heart as heavy as my feet. Where is he? He's never out this late for any reason. If he's working, it's here in the house. If he has a meeting, which he hasn't really had many of since we got back here, he's still home at a decent time—unless the meeting is here, like it was a few weeks ago when I crossed paths with the beautiful woman whose name I'm still not allowed to know.

That woman. I pause at the top of the stairs, gripping the banister tight, staring down the hall but seeing her instead. She was so sophisticated, the kind of person who's intimidating without having to say a word. Her presence alone was enough.

Her lipstick on his cheek. She kissed him on the cheek. That's not professional. Am I supposed to believe the two of them don't know each other in some other way?

I can't believe I'm actually thinking like this, but it's so clear now. He's with her, I bet. Or some other woman. What difference does it make? He's not with me. Why would he be? All I am is a means of getting himself an heir.

I'm pregnant, so that's settled. But his needs still have to be met, don't they? And I am a traitor, the person he blames for his grandfather's death. Why would he turn to me? I'm only his wife.

Rather than close the door, I leave it cracked a little so I can hear if he comes in downstairs. It's not like I'm going to be falling asleep anytime soon, not when I'm so freaked out. I pace the room, trying and failing to keep ugly images from flashing in my mind. The two of them together, having a great time. At a club, maybe, or a high-end restaurant. Cruising around, going back to her place or to some hotel somewhere. Fucking like a couple of animals while I sit here and wait for him to come home.

I guess it only makes sense if he doesn't feel anything for me but hatred. Looking at it from his perspective, I can't even blame him. He's young, powerful, and, God knows, he's hot as hell. There's no reason for him to lock himself in this house with his pregnant wife, who he hates, when there are so many other women out there, women from his world, women who know the score. Not naïve little nobodies like me who only stumbled into this by mistake.

That woman, whatever her name is, she's the kind of woman he should be with. I bet dear old grandad would love her. He probably wouldn't be able to stop himself from hitting on her long enough to broker a marriage deal. Even now, when the man is dead, I find myself grimacing at the thought of him. I'm sorry he went the way he did, but that's more for Enzo's sake. I guess I don't have it in me to quickly forgive somebody who threatened to have me murdered for not giving his grandson an heir on his schedule.

One o'clock comes and goes. Two o'clock. I sit down on the bed and try to concentrate on catching up with my reading, but it's no use. I can get through a whole chapter and not actually absorb any of the information. Not with Enzo at the forefront of my mind. Not when I can't help but imagine him rolling around in bed with that woman.

The house is quieter now. I tiptoe to the door and listen hard—there's no pacing downstairs, no muttered conversations.

In fact... at first, I think I'm imagining the sound, so I creep out into the hall and peer down the stairs. Sure enough, the soft snoring I thought I heard is for real, coming from the guard posted by the door. He's now seated on the couch, his head hanging low. I bet he wouldn't be so dismissive if I threatened to tell the boss he fell asleep on the job. He's supposed to be guarding me. Well, the baby, and I just happen to be the person carrying the baby, so I'm included.

He couldn't even bother to stay awake. Yeah, he might soon regret talking to me the way he did.

That's childish—worse than that, it's a distraction from what I need to be thinking about. Here I am, wanting to get these guys in trouble when I should be concentrating on how to use this to my advantage.

I could leave. I could sneak right past that guy. He's out cold, the way I'm sure most of the other guys are by now. It must be boring, just standing or sitting there with nothing to do but wait for something that probably won't ever happen. The house is quiet as a tomb. I would probably fall asleep, too, if I wasn't so busy imagining the various positions my husband is twisting that strange woman into right this very minute.

I need to get out of here. This is my chance. I sure as hell don't want to look at Enzo, not if he's been with somebody else. Even if it wasn't her in particular, what else would he be doing right now? At this time of night? I back away from the top of the stairs as silently as possible, then just as silently close the bedroom door before turning on the lights and pulling my tote bag out from under the bed.

I shouldn't be crying. It must be the hormones. Enzo does not deserve my tears; I've known that all along. So why can't I stop myself from weeping as I throw things into the bag?

Especially the bracelets I take from the top drawer in my dresser, under my socks. I asked to look at them the other day, and he never took them back which just happened to work out in my favor. I don't have anywhere else to put them—there's no safe or anything that I'm aware of, and I don't even have a jewelry box. I don't have anything really, nothing to make this room or this house my own. I had to put them somewhere. I'm surprised Enzo even let me keep hold of them rather than holding on to them himself.

I wrap the box in layers of clothing until it's cocooned and very carefully tuck it into the bag before stacking more clothes, then toiletries on top. It's not lost on me that I'm carrying many thousands of dollars by the time I zip up the bag, and it's a little nerve-wracking. Those bracelets alone could probably have put me through school, and then some. I wouldn't have had to worry about anything. I could sell them now, I guess, and have enough money to live off while I think about what to do next.

He's never going to let you go. Are you crazy? What do you think you're going to do once you're out of this house? I don't know the answer to that, and I'm sure he's not going to let this go. But damn him, I'm not going to sit around here and wait with my heart in my throat all the time. And I'm not going to let him smirk in my face when I ask where he was tonight. I'm not going to let him do that to me. I've already let him do too much as it is.

I let him make me fall in love, for starters. And I hate him for it almost as much as I hate myself.

With my tote bag in one hand and my backpack over the other shoulder, I creep out into the hallway again. It's going on two-thirty now, and what was soft snoring at first has become considerably louder. I have to wonder if everybody in the house is asleep, or at least halfway there, because why wouldn't they go wake him up?

Either way, that works for me. I check my phone to make sure there are cars in the area—it's not a surprise that there are since the bars are still serving for another couple of hours. I'm sure plenty of people need a ride at this time of night.

Where am I going to go? I'm not sure. That's the one thing I haven't figured out by the time I'm tiptoeing down the stairs, holding my breath, and watching the guard for any signs of movement. The only thing that moves is his chest as he snores. Once I reach the bottom of the stairs, I look around, through to the kitchen, just in case somebody's walking around in there. It's just as dark and quiet as everywhere else in the house.

I feel like I'm right back in the beginning, trying to sneak out while Enzo was asleep on the couch. This time, I'm fully dressed, and I'm not practically empty-handed like I was before. But I'm just as scared—even more scared than before because this isn't just about me. I have the baby to think about, too. I need to believe this is for their sake just as much as it is mine.

It's the only thing that keeps me going as I open the door slowly, making sure there's nobody out front. There isn't; the area is free and clear. Maybe somebody was supposed to be out here but went inside. It doesn't matter. I hustle down the driveway before requesting an Uber, then walk through the development and out to the main road to wait for them to pick me up.

I'll figure something out. For now, it's enough to know I won't have to face him tonight. I couldn't do it without breaking down.

"It's okay, baby," I whisper. "We're going to be okay." Even if I don't know how.

20

ENZO

"They'd better be fucking careful with that thing." Prince is none too happy, glaring out the windshield at the pair of men assigned to watch the Alvarez compound this morning. They weren't able to conceal their childlike glee at having such an expensive toy to play with, though they promised to take care of it. "I've kind of become attached."

This again. He acts like the damn thing is an extension of his body. "I'll buy you ten new drones, for God's sake. What's the big deal about a drone?"

"It's mine." He leaves it there, as simple as that. And the fact is, I can't pretend I don't relate. What's mine is mine. All the substitutes in the world won't make up for it.

It's no surprise when my thoughts turn to Alicia. "Christ, I didn't think we would be out this long." The sun is on the rise as we make the drive back to the townhouse, and already traffic is getting heavier. So many worker bees on their way to the hive. As always, I'm grateful to have avoided that drudgery.

"I'm not the one who refused to tear himself away." Prince cuts himself off with a yawn before adding, "I was ready to go home."

"You sure I shouldn't be the one driving?" I ask when he rubs a fist over one eye.

"I'm fine. Though I could use some coffee." He flips on the signal like he wants to take the upcoming exit, where there's a mall surrounded by fast-food shops.

"There's coffee at the house."

"It's never as good, and I'm hungry now. With this traffic—"

"Which is more reason to keep going. I don't feel like sitting twenty minutes in a drive-thru, then hitting even heavier traffic after that."

"Fine, fine. But I would like to state again for the record that you're the one who couldn't bring himself to leave hours ago."

"And you were the one who was so excited when I suggested we charge the drone in the car." I pick up the cable, still plugged into the dashboard. "You didn't want to stop playing with your toy. And it isn't like we didn't stop off for a break." The car still smells like cheeseburgers and fries, an aroma I enjoyed at the time but now turns my stomach slightly.

He grumbles but remains on the road. I can only be grateful he isn't offering more of an argument. I'm not in the mood, not that I would be normally, but especially not after hours spent in the car, just the two of us.

He's right. I didn't want to leave, and as soon as I looked up the drone's model number and found how easy it would be to charge it in the car, I leaped at the idea of extending our stakeout. We're no further along than we were hours ago. It was a waste of time.

Though thanks to the drone, I now have a clear image in my head of the compound. Entrances, surrounding structures, and roughly how many guards Josef has out there at night. That information could come in handy at some point. In our world, information is priceless.

"What's the hurry to get home?" Prince mutters. Clearly, he isn't over being denied his latte or whatever the fuck he wanted.

"For starters, it's home?" I offer. "Where I can take a shower, change my clothes, and not feel so rumpled and soiled? Isn't that enough? And since when do you question my decisions?"

"I was only asking."

"Don't do that. Don't sulk. If it makes you feel better, go get whatever you want after you drop me off. What I want more than anything now is my bed, after showering."

All it takes is the slightest snort from him—so soft as to be nearly inaudible.

"What?" I snap.

"Nothing."

I'm going to let it go. It's what a leader does, and that's who I am now. I can't let him get under my skin. I have to be above that. No matter how much I want to shoot him sometimes.

The sight of the familiar development is a relief after more than an hour on the road and ten hours spent staking out Alvarez. But it isn't a shower or my bed at the forefront of my mind. It's her. I hate how much I long to be with her now. After all these hours, I want nothing more than to touch her. To smell her—she's a far cry from old cheeseburger wrappers. If things were different, I would crawl into bed beside her and order her not to get up, even if it was time to get her day started. I would hold her and forget everything else because that's the sort of relief she would provide. It's what I need more than anything to forget for a little while.

It takes conscious effort to keep from rushing out of the car and into the house. Prince takes the car, determined to spend too much money on an overpriced coffee that isn't nearly as good as anything we could get back home. I leave him to it, focused on one thing only.

"Sir." I nod in recognition of the guard on the door. His name escapes me—I've only worked with these men since arriving in Miami, and sometimes their faces blend.

"Everything under control here?" It seems to be. The house is quiet, as I would expect it to be at only seven o'clock in the morning.

"It is, sir. It was a quiet night." I'm grateful for that, grateful for the chance to be a mere human for once, to climb the stairs with my heart hammering in anticipation of seeing my wife after a long night. Right or wrong, she's the one I want to come home to. She's the one whose touch lingers in my memory, who makes me yearn. She's the only woman I've ever yearned for.

Yet when I open her bedroom door, I find the bed empty. She's been in it, though—the blankets are thrown back, the pillows arranged in such a way that I can tell she was sitting up at some point. Reading, I imagine. Did she have a sleepless night, too? I won't bother entertaining the idea of her missing me.

Instantly, my thoughts go to the baby. I dart across the hall, my heart in my throat, expecting to find her in the bathroom. Sick or worse. Yet that room is empty, as well. I place a hand over my chest, breathing hard.

The rest of the upstairs is empty. I search it anyway, going through my room, the closet even. Nothing. My irritation grows as I jog down the stairs. Several of the men are in the kitchen, where it looks like one of them delivered breakfast for the rest. They ignore their half-eaten sandwiches upon my entrance. "Where is Mrs. De Luca?" I ask, scanning the group.

All I get in return is a bunch of blank stares.

"Well?" I prompt. And now they're looking at each other as dread forms in my chest. "Dammit, where the fuck is she?" When no one answers beyond wordless stammering, I head to my study and open my laptop. My hands are almost shaking, thanks to the rage burning a hole in me.

I manage to pull up the security footage and start clicking through the different feeds until I reach the front door. Dammit, I should never have taken the system off 24/7 monitoring—I would have been alerted to any movement outside the house via text and could have logged into the system from my phone to monitor things. There I was, assuming a group of men could handle that for me.

I scroll back through the footage until I reach the point where Prince and I left for surveillance. With the speed turned up to its maximum setting, I hover in front of the screen, watching. Waiting.

And at around two thirty, I see her. I stop the replay, turn the speed down to its normal setting, then go back to watch her sneaking out of the house. She's carrying her backpack over one shoulder and a large duffel in the other hand. She doesn't hesitate either, heading straight down the walkway, then nearly jogging down the driveway until she reaches the sidewalk. That's the last I can see of her, thanks to the angle of the camera.

Motherfucker. She's gone, and no one even noticed she left. No one stopped her. They must have all been asleep.

"What the hell is going on?" Prince saunters into my study, a cardboard cup in each hand. "I thought I'd bring you back something, but it looks like a funeral in the kitchen."

"It will be one soon enough. I need you to gather up the guys who were here around two-thirty this morning. Whoever had that shift, I want them in front of me in the garage immediately." Either he knows better than to ask why, or he doesn't need to. There's only one reason for me to make such a demand.

She fucking left. She left! And there I was, practically falling over myself with eagerness to see her. She wasn't here. She hasn't been here for hours. And anything could have happened.

While these sons of bitches slept.

Within fifteen minutes, I'm face-to-face with half a dozen men, all of whom look as though they were pulled from sleep. "I would've thought you got plenty of sleep last night while you were supposed to be on the job," I muse. My trigger finger is itching to be used, but I have the men line up first. They're nervous, shuffling their feet, eyes darting around the garage. Losers, all of them, brought in when it was clear we needed to beef up security, thanks to Alvarez. Look where they got me.

I walk slowly up and down the line without saying a word, heightening the fear and tension when what I need more than anything is to put my hands on her again to prove to myself my child is well. I'll find a way to make her wish she hadn't stepped foot off the property.

First, this.

I come to a stop at the end of the line, facing a man who was bleary-eyed when he first appeared but is now alert with fear. "Where is Mrs. De Luca?" I ask in a flat voice, staring at him.

He moistens his lips with the tip of his tongue. "I..."

"Speak up. Where is she?"

His brow furrows. He knows the answer and knows I won't like it. Finally, he mans up. "I thought she was in bed. If not, I don't know when she got past me, and I'm sorry."

"I appreciate your candor." In the next breath, I put a bullet in his head. He drops to the floor.

"Your turn." I move on to the next man, who looks like he wishes he were anywhere else. He can't stop looking at the corpse beside him. "Where is Mrs. De Luca?"

"I... I don't know." A second gunshot cracks through the air, and now there are two dead bodies at my feet.

Four more to go.

"Next." I step to the left and fire another shot when I get the same answer. And again. And again. Finally, the sixth useless piece of shit is dead, the garage is full of bodies, and I'm no closer to finding my wife.

Prince's high-pitched whistle stirs me out of my rage. "What next?" he asks. I appreciate his lack of surprise at the bodies, their blood now mingling and congealing on the concrete floor.

"Get the car," I mutter, staring down at the carnage Alicia caused. "There's only one place she could go."

VOW

21

ALICIA

It seemed like a good idea at the time. Maybe they'll put that on my headstone one day.

Here I am, the only place I could think to go. At first, I figured I would come to school where I knew there were security guards, someplace I didn't have to feel completely exposed and endangered. I thought once I got here, I'd be able to sit down and think about what to do next. All that mattered was getting away from the house, or so I told myself.

Seven hours later, I have no more of a clue than I did when I first got here. I'm too tired to think, exhausted, practically swaying on my feet. My hand has been wrapped around the straps of this tote bag so tight I wonder if I'll be able to loosen my fingers and let it go when the time comes. I wonder what people would think if they knew what I'm carrying around. Hey, see that strange, bleary-eyed girl wandering around? She's got thousands of bucks in diamonds in that bag!

I need to figure something out; that much is obvious. I can't hang around here forever, going from one building to the other, trying to sneak in a nap before being asked to leave. I don't have any friends, nobody I am really acquainted with except for Elena. I can't even call somebody up and ask to stay in their dorm room for a night.

I only thought I understood how isolated my life was before now. It's almost embarrassing how alone I am as I sit on a bench outside the

Activities Center. I was hoping to go in and grab a snack, but of course, my stomach is churning thanks to morning sickness. All I can do is hope I don't have to throw up. That would make this already miserable experience even more painful. There's a trashcan next to the bench, so at least I'm covered if nausea wins out.

I wish I had never left the house. Enzo is bound to know by now that I'm gone, and I have no doubt he'll come looking for me here. After all, it was the only place I could think to go for a reason. I don't have a home anymore. I don't have family to turn to. There are only so many options here.

So now, he'll find me and drag me back to the house, and life will be just a little worse than it was before. He might go back to locking me in my room after this.

And once again, I know I can't tell him the truth. That I left because my heart was broken. That he hurt me so much last night by not coming home. That I was disgusted and insulted and in tears at the thought of him being with another woman. I'm sure he would think it was hilarious, the idea of him meaning anything to me—either that or he would figure it was all a lie because that's all he thinks of me now. I'm a liar, a traitor, all of that. He's determined not to believe anything I say, so it would be a waste of time. I'd only end up hurting worse than before after he dismissed me or laughed at me.

And here's everybody walking around me, living their normal lives. To think, I used to resent them before. I used to wonder why my life couldn't be normal like theirs. Why I had to struggle while they got off easy. I only thought I had problems back then, and it's enough to make me laugh at myself. I do, too, softly. I don't need anybody noticing and thinking a crazy homeless girl is hanging around campus, clutching a tote bag to her like her life depends on it and laughing at nothing but the voices in her head.

I should go someplace else, somewhere less visible. Somewhere Enzo won't be able to find me right away. Or should I make it easier, so he won't be as pissed off when he finally catches up to me? I'm frozen with indecision.

And then I see her when I look up at the students walking in and out of the building. She's coming out, holding an iced coffee from the café inside. "Elena," I breathe as my pulse quickens. She looks like she's on top of the world, and why shouldn't she be? She's always had everything going for her, from her looks to her family connections.

But when she sees me, her face falls, even if she tries to cover it at the last second. She's not fast enough. I saw it, but that's not going to stop me when she might be my ticket to getting out of this without Enzo breaking my neck for running away.

"Elena!" I'm off the bench in a second, fatigue and morning sickness forgotten. "I've been wondering about you!"

"Hey, girl." She tries to sound sunny and enthused, but it falls flat. "I've been meaning to text you."

Yeah, right. I'm sure she has. I keep smiling like there's nothing wrong. "Where have you been? I was hoping I could catch up with you after class sometime, but you're always in a huge hurry—when I see you there," I add. I have to remind myself to sound concerned, not annoyed.

"Things have been kind of crazy. I was sick for a little bit, and it was just a mess." She starts walking, and I join her without asking if it's okay because I might never get an opportunity like this again. She's wearing the look of somebody who wishes they had decided to skip the iced coffee this morning.

"Hey, I heard a rumor about you," she says with a grin, elbowing me. "It's crazy, but I see that ring you're wearing, so I guess it must be true. You got married?"

"Oh, yeah," I confirm with a shrug. That's not exactly what I want to talk about right now, or ever for that matter. After all, I have her to thank for it in part. "It was sort of a crazy, whirlwind kind of thing."

"Yeah, that's what I heard. I didn't even know you had a boyfriend." Meanwhile, I'd like to know who told her. Who would care or know me well enough to spread rumors? Maybe somebody overheard us in the office when we came in to talk about me staying enrolled.

Or maybe she heard it through her family. I doubt she'd admit it if that was the truth.

"I didn't," I admit with a shrug. "It's like they say: when you know, you know. I always thought that was bullshit, but now I understand." I wish it was true. I really do. The ache in my chest is excruciating, but I smile my way through it.

"That's really cool. You missed a lot of school, though, didn't you? You just kind of fell off the face of the earth for weeks."

"I worked something out. I can make up all the assignments I missed as long as I have the work finished by the start of next semester."

"Oh, that's great." I'm waiting for her to say something else, but she doesn't, and silence falls between us. I wonder what she's thinking. She has to be curious, doesn't she? Does she want to ask me about what happened at the warehouse and what came afterward? I wish she would. I'm already exhausted enough, and keeping up the pretense of being friendly and normal is only making things worse.

"So where did you meet your husband?" she asks, sipping her coffee and checking her phone even though we're in the middle of a conversation. But that's how she always is. She can't keep her mind on one thing at a time.

"Oh, um, it's kind of a long story. The kind of thing we'd have to sit down and talk about."

"Well, who is he?" she prompts with a smile. "What's he do? Is he from here? Does he go to school here, or is he older?"

"He's a little older," I murmur, trying to think beyond the haze of fatigue I'm fighting. It was hard enough when I was alone but having to maintain a conversation is so much harder.

"Good move there. Guys our age are a joke."

"Yeah, he's a lot more mature." He's a lot of other things, too, but I'll keep that to myself.

"You know," I offer, talking fast once I see we're approaching the sciences building, where she probably has a class coming up, "you should come by for dinner sometime. You're probably my only friend here at school, and I think you two would get along well."

"Oh, I don't know. I don't want to, like, impose on you guys when you're still in the honeymoon phase or whatever they call it." She drops a big wink, and I have to force myself to giggle, even if that's the last thing I feel like doing. If she only knew.

"But I kind of want to show off a little bit, too," I insist, thinking on the fly. "I'm, like, a married woman now. I want to show you the house and everything."

Her jaw drops. "You already have a house? Damn, girl. Who is this guy?"

"Well, it's his house. He already had it." I need to make this sound as normal as I can. "And you know it's not like I've ever really had a reason to show off. You know how it was for me."

If there was ever a time for her to mention sending me to the warehouse, it would be right now. And something does pass over her face, something that resembles guilt, but it vanishes quickly. I guess we're supposed to pretend that didn't happen, that she never sent me there, and that nothing ever went wrong. She hasn't even asked me how it went that night. Or if I went at all.

It's that thought that makes it easier for me to get insistent. The fact that she's never really been a true friend. A true friend would have checked in with me. A true friend would have wanted to be sure everything went well. When I vanished off the face of the earth like she mentioned, a true friend would have at least texted or called to see if I was okay, but she never did. And here I was, chalking that up to the idea that she might not be able to reach out because of her family or because she wouldn't want to get herself in trouble.

Now, alone with her on campus with nobody breathing over her shoulder, I realize she just doesn't care. Nothing is stopping her from asking me right now what happened that night, but she won't bring it up. I can't help but feel a little sad over that. I really thought she was my friend at one time.

"You have to come. And I won't be cooking, so at least I can tell you the food will be good."

She turns to me with a sigh—then, all of a sudden, something over my shoulder grabs her attention. My heart sinks even before I feel his touch on my shoulder before his hand closes over it.

Still, it's not Enzo I'm most concerned with. I knew he would find me anyway; it was only a matter of time. Now I'll get to sleep in a bed, at least.

It's Elena I can't take my eyes off. All of a sudden, it's like this transformation comes over her. She stands a little taller, pulls her shoulders back, and thrusts her boobs out as she tosses her hair over one shoulder and pouts her lips for no reason other than to look hot, I guess. "Oh, yeah," she murmurs. "I'll come to dinner. Just text me when and where." I don't have time to say anything before she turns on her heel and speed walks into the building. Is it my imagination, or is she swinging her hips more than she was before?

His hand tightens, and I know what it means.

But now that I'm too busy wondering what Elena was thinking when she eyed up my husband, I can't bring myself to care very much about what he's going to do to me.

VOW

22

ENZO

"You don't have to hold me so hard."

As if I give a shit what she thinks about the way I'm holding her. As if I'd have to hold on so tightly if I could trust her. I know better than to try to speak, so I merely tighten my grip on her shoulder, my arm around her. Anybody who sees us would think we're a normal couple walking side by side. I could be comforting her, supporting her through a difficult time.

In reality, any difficult time she's going through is the result of her selfishness.

"I got to talk to Elena, didn't I? That's who that was."

I had assumed since she's already made it clear that she had few people in her life. Is that supposed to make me feel better? Is that her way of apologizing? No, she's not apologizing. She's trying to cover her ass. She got caught, and she knows I'm furious. She has to. We didn't first meet yesterday. She knew precisely how I would feel about this, but she did it anyway.

And now, she wants me to be merciful. As if she deserves mercy.

Prince is waiting in the car and lifts his brows in a silent question when he sees us approaching. I shake my head—no, I most certainly do not need help with her. She's the one who needs help.

And damn, is she fortunate she's carrying my child. I've never been one to beat a woman, but I would definitely make her feel it. She wouldn't sit for a week by the time I was finished with her. Running away. Making a fool out of me.

I want to say all of it and more. I want her to know exactly what she's done. What a fool she turned me into—to think, I was looking forward to seeing her. The anger and betrayal blazing in my chest are almost enough to choke me, but I somehow manage to get her into the back seat without losing my grip. To her credit, she didn't do anything stupid, like try to alert someone to the trouble she's in.

Without saying a word, I reach over her once she's seated and snap the belt in place. "I can do that myself," she whispers, and I slam the door closed in response. I can't trust her with even something as simple as that now. She may not give a damn what happens to her, but I do. And she can't care, not after this little display.

What good could she possibly have imagined that would do? Running away? She has nowhere to go. I would have found her sooner if the campus wasn't so big. But I knew she was here because it's the only place she has. How pitiful.

Yet she tries to run away from me? From a comfortable home, a lifestyle she could never have known without me? It's unfathomable.

Prince drives the route, quiet for once. Smart enough to keep his mouth shut. I have no doubt I'll hear about this later, though if he knows what's good for him, he'll pretend this never happened.

Then again, how can he pretend? He has to oversee the cleanup efforts back at the house.

Alicia's quiet, too. Another small miracle. What's she doing now? Plotting her next escape attempt? When is she going to get it through her skull? There's no escaping me? She is in way over her head and totally outmatched, but it seems she hasn't gotten the memo.

Perhaps now she will. Now that we've arrived at the house. She makes a point of unbuckling herself, but I take her by the arm the moment she's out of the car with her bags in hand. Instead of going through the front door, I hang a right, walking around the outside of the house, through the gate of the tall privacy fence, then back to the garage.

She doesn't say a word, but she's trembling. Probably wondering why I would bring her back here.

"I thought you would like to see this. The results of your actions." I can barely get the words out, but I force myself through it because she needs to hear it. She deserves to.

She gasps once we're inside, and I can admit to myself we couldn't have come at a better time. Those guards still alive after this morning's debacle have stacked the bodies on top of a plastic sheet and are now cleaning up what looks like a lake of congealed blood.

I hold her in place when she tries to turn away. "Look at it," I mutter, holding her close to me, taking her by the jaw, and turning her face toward the grisly sight. "The least you can do is look at what you've created. These men didn't need to die. You took advantage of them because you were feeling childish and irresponsible, and thanks to your rash decision-making, they're all dead."

"I didn't... I mean, I never..."

"It's a little late for all of that now, isn't it? Because you did. Eventually, you're going to learn your actions have consequences." She's looking green and swaying on her feet, but that's good. She needs to remember this. If self-preservation isn't good enough and protecting her unborn child isn't either, perhaps she'll take this more seriously now that she's seen the very real aftermath.

"So you killed them? It wasn't their fault. They didn't help me."

"They didn't stop you, though, because they were either asleep on the job or fucking off somehow. I should thank you for revealing their unsuitability, really." She only moans softly, an almost pained sound. "Eventually, you'll understand this isn't a game."

She offers no protest when we leave the garage. Her deep gulps of air tell me she's fighting to keep herself together. "Buck up," I mutter. "You can handle it. I bet you don't even know any of their names." Her only response is a shuddery breath.

"Out," I bark upon entering the house. Prince is in the living room talking to a couple of the men, and he leads them outside. I hear him giving them instructions on how to dispose of the bodies while Alicia tries and fails to stifle a whimper.

"You're lucky I don't make you help them," I mutter, leading her down the hall.

"You know I would never want anything like that to happen."

"But it did, didn't it?" Once we're in my study, I close and lock the door.

She backs away from me, finally bumping against the desk. "Why are we in here?"

"Oh, I don't know. I thought we would revisit the place where I first watched you sneak out of here last night via the security footage. Would you like to watch it? It's right there on my laptop."

"No, thank you," she whispers, wrapping her arms around herself. "I just—"

"Did I ask you to speak? I don't want to hear a word that comes out of your lying little mouth." I'm on her in a flash before she can scurry away. She moans in dismay when I take her face in my hand, digging my fingers into her cheeks. "There are so many things this mouth is better suited for. Maybe we should get down to some of that right now. You could relieve some of the tension you're putting me through."

"On second thought..." I let go of her in favor of taking her T-shirt in both hands. Seams rip somewhere on the garment as I pull it over her head, and I laugh when she crosses her arms over her tits. "What is this? Feeling modest and shy all of a sudden? I've seen every part of you, wife. There's nothing you could possibly hide from me now." I take her by the wrists when she refuses to drop her arms and yank them apart.

"Stop, please," she whimpers. Doesn't she know by now that I only become more excited when she begs?

I turn her in place, grinding my already-stiffened cock against her ass. With one hand, I grope her tits, while with the other, I rub her stomach. "Still flat," I grunt. "But not for long."

I wish she was showing. I wish it was that evident she belongs to me, that she's carrying my child, my flesh and blood inside her. Mine, both of them.

"You don't have to do this anymore, you know." I can't tell if she's sullen or resisting or both.

"Don't tell me what I have to do." I squeeze her tit until she sucks in a pained breath. "I do what I want when I want."

"I'm just saying, I'm already pregnant. So there's no point to any of this."

No point? "Are you sure about that?" I slide a hand inside her shorts, beneath her underwear, and it's no surprise to find her slick with anticipation. "Your pussy tells a different story. Which one of you is lying?" She leans against me, and that's good; that's what I want. I want her to be docile and pliable, and this is how to make that happen. No matter what she tries to tell me—or herself—this is what she wants. To be taken, to be ravished, and even defiled.

She offers no resistance when I bend her over the desk, holding her down with a hand against her back, while with the other hand, I pull down her shorts and panties. She's glistening, her lips enticing me, and I can't help but drag a finger through her slickness before licking the nectar away.

I could sink to my knees now and eat her until she drips onto the floor and begs me to stop, but no. She doesn't deserve that. I don't want her writhing in ecstasy. I want her pinned beneath me, screaming her obedience, weeping in pain and humiliation for what she's done.

Yet she still carries my child.

So I settle for shoving my cock inside her all at once, pushing her forward across the top of the desk. The dread in her groan makes me laugh before I can help it and only makes me hold her down more firmly than before. I want to see my handprint on her back when I'm finished. With the other hand, I slap her ass, making her squeal.

But not loudly enough. "Come on," I grunt between strokes. "Let me hear it." I slap her again and again until my palm stings, and her ass is beet red. And still, I pound her pussy, now holding her hips in place.

She's going to learn. She's going to remember this. She belongs to me. Every thrust, every time her ass jiggles when I slam into her, is a statement. Mine. She's mine. No matter how she tries to get away and no matter why—that will never change.

I look down and watch my cock pump in and out, coated with her juices. "No matter how you try to run," I rasp, "you get wet for me. For this. Don't you?"

She doesn't answer, forcing me to wrap her hair around my hand and pull. "Say it."

"Yes!" she sobs. "Yes! I do!" The sound falls on my ears like music that sizzles its way through me, lifting my balls before tingling at the base of my spine.

"And your cunt gets tighter the worse I treat you, doesn't it?" As if on cue, the walls of her tunnel tighten around me while her cries rise in pitch. When I take her by the hips again, gripping her reddened flesh, she bites her lip to stifle a scream that translates to a fresh rush of hot juice. It coats me and runs over my balls, betraying her.

It's almost enough to make me think she drives me to this point on purpose.

But now is not the time to think. Not when she's clenching around me and screaming out her orgasm. Her muscles ripple like her greedy pussy is determined to milk me. I close my eyes and let go, allowing the rush of release to wash over me.

"Fuck... yes..." I stay locked in place for a moment, gripping her the way her pussy grips me until our mixed cum begins leaking out, thanks to her quivering muscles. I pull out and watch as the pussy I've claimed once again spasms, sending fluid leaking from her.

"This is mine. You aren't taking it away from me." After delivering one last slap against her reddened ass, I pull her to a standing position. "Now get out of here. I don't want to look at you. Thanks to your actions, I have a ton of shit to clean up."

She pulls her clothes together quickly and dresses without a word, her eyes downcast. "By the time I'm finished with you," I add, "there will be no question about who you belong to. No one will be able to look at you without knowing."

Let her pretend all she wants, but I catch the way her cheeks flush at my statement before she flees the room.

VOW

23

ALICIA

It looks like I finally figured out a way to get Elena's attention for good.

There's a text waiting for me when I get out of the shower, only a couple of hours after I chatted with her on campus.

Elena: Don't forget, you invited me for dinner. I'm available any night this week, so whenever you want, I'll be there. And let me know if I can bring something, too.

All it took was letting her get a look at my husband. It's probably for the best that Enzo has no intention of staying married to me once he gets what he wants because I'm not sure I could spend the rest of my life feeling this jealous. I mean, he's hot, but does that mean all the women around me have to be sluts about it? And I know that's why she's suddenly so interested. I knew it the second she tossed her hair and thrust her chest forward like she was on the front of a ship or something. She's got her eye on him now. How could I ever have thought she was an actual friend?

Any guilt I might have felt about luring her here dissolves when I look at it that way. She's so interested in him? Then let her learn who he really is, what he's really like. And how he wants to use her.

I'm not exactly proud of myself, but that's what's going through my head once I've dried off and gotten dressed. Instead of hanging out in my room—hiding, plain and simple—I go downstairs, my phone in hand. It isn't easy for me to look over at the spot where that guard was sleeping when I snuck out. He's dead now, and I'm the reason for it. I had no idea Enzo would do anything like that. I need to stop underestimating him.

"I'm sorry," I whisper to the spot on the couch where the man slept. Even though I'm not the one who pulled the trigger, I know I'll carry that guilt around with me for a long time. Probably for the rest of my life.

Enzo is in his study, and he lets out a frustrated little grunt when I tap my knuckles against the door. "What? I have a lot of things to work out here."

"I thought you would want to see this." I hold out the phone as I cross the room and place it in front of him on the desk. "What should I say? When do you want her here?"

He scans the message, his narrowed eyes widening a little as he does. "That didn't take long, did it?"

"No, it didn't." I have to fight back the rest of what I want to say. I don't need him thinking I'm jealous, even if I am. Just one more thing for him to hang over my head and treat like a big joke.

"Good job." He looks up at me, wearing a genuine smile that warms me up inside. "You reeled her in like a pro."

"I just jumped at the opportunity when I saw her, is all. It's a good thing I was on campus when I was."

His mouth tightens as he sees through me. "All right, don't overplay your hand. I'm not going to praise you for running away. But at least something good came out of it." He looks back down at the message, tapping rhythmically on the desk with the fingers of one hand. "Thank you for bringing this to me right away." Like I'm one of his employees.

"Sure." Shouldn't this be less awkward by now? He's my husband, and I'm carrying his baby, but I still don't know how to act around him sometimes. I don't want to get overly familiar because he'll only throw that back in my face. "What do you want me to do now?"

He pushes back from the desk and stands, sliding his hands into his pockets before he begins slowly pacing back and forth in front of the windows, where yet another guard was posted last night, one who is now dead. I clench my hands into tight fists and will myself to stop thinking about it. I can feel as sorry and as guilty as I want to later, but right now, I'm sort of fighting for my life. I need to do this well, to gain back a little bit of goodwill. Or else I'll end up spending the rest of my pregnancy as a prisoner, and I don't want that.

"She seemed interested, didn't she?" he murmurs. At first, I don't know if he's talking to himself or me. It's only when he throws a look my way, arching an eyebrow, that I know I was supposed to respond.

"In coming to dinner? Yeah, she did. At first, she tried to make excuses, but..." My tongue is suddenly too thick and awkward to let me get the rest of it out.

So he does it for me. "But then she saw me and changed her mind pretty fast, didn't she?"

That's what he meant when he used the word interested. My blood pressure is rising by the second. Isn't that bad for a baby? I've got to find a way to keep myself calmer when it comes to things like this. "Yes, she did."

"Some friend." He laughs before glancing my way again. I can't tell why he frowns. It can't be because he feels guilty for basically laughing at me.

"I've learned a lot of things the hard way, haven't I?"

He comes to a stop, staring out the window with his hands clasped behind his back. "Yet you still need to be reminded not to cross me. I would think you would have learned by now."

"Let's not get off topic. What do I say to her?"

"She said she's available any night this week?"

"Yeah." Sure, she's plenty eager, isn't she? I can barely keep my voice neutral. I don't want to give away how I really feel about this, how jealous I am. It doesn't sound like he's particularly interested in her, but I can't say how he'll react once she decides she wants to charm him. And considering the way she looked at him, she's going to do everything she can.

"Tell her to come by tomorrow night. It'll give me a little time to make sure everything is in place."

Tomorrow. I almost wish it was tonight, so we could get this over with. Whatever method he has in mind to use her to get back at Alvarez, the sooner it's over with, the better.

I make a move to reach for the phone, but his head snaps around, a sly smile tugging at the corners of his mouth. "Tell her to dress up."

"You want her to dress up? Like, formal?"

"I don't care what you have to say, exactly. Imply this is a special evening, and we'll all be dressing accordingly. How do girls say that kind of thing to each other?"

"Why are you asking me?" I blurt out. I wish I hadn't said it when he laughs, but it's the truth. I don't have the first idea of how girls talk to each other in situations like this. I haven't had that many girlfriends.

"You can figure it out."

"Can I ask why you want her dressed up? I'm only curious," I add when he turns around with a heavy sigh like it's such an inconvenience to have to explain something to me.

"Would it make a difference if I told you that's my business, and your only job here is to do as I say?"

"Like I said, I'm only curious. Wouldn't it be smart if I had the slightest clue what you're planning, so I can go along with it once she's here?"

The muscles in his jaw twitch when he locks eyes with me, but I will be damned if I back off now. His intimidation tactics don't have the same effect on me they used to. I think he senses that, too, since he lifts a shoulder in a half-hearted shrug. "I suppose. The bottom line is I want her to have every opportunity to get all tarted up. If she thinks she can attract me, she'll have even more of a reason to show up here tomorrow. If you give off the impression that we normally dress for dinner, she'll take from that the idea that I have money."

"You do have money."

"Yes, thank you for reminding me. I want to drive the point home. I want her thinking about nothing but getting her claws into me. The less she questions this or asks herself exactly where you happened to meet me, the better. I need her focused on how she's going to take me away from you."

How can he talk about it so casually? We could be discussing the results of last night's ball game or something; he's that removed. It doesn't even occur to him that it might hurt my feelings a little, the idea of somebody I thought was my friend being so intent on taking my husband away.

He's not wrong, though. I saw the way she looked at him. I might not have a lot of experience with men, but I know women very well. I've done a lot of observation in my life. The way she changed, her posture and her expression, all of it, told me immediately she had only one thing on her mind—even without considering how she changed her attitude about coming over here so quickly once she got a look at him. What, did she think I married some loser? Probably. The second she found out otherwise, however…?

"You figured all of that out without ever talking to her, did you?" I mutter, folding my arms.

"Girls like her aren't hard to read. And this isn't my first time at the rodeo. She'll be easy enough to manipulate, don't worry about that."

"I'm not worried."

"Good. Because this isn't over yet." He's wearing a wide, almost happy smile when he picks up my phone and hands it back. "Go ahead. You have an invitation to extend. Everything will be all set for Miss Elena when she shows up tomorrow night. And you'll get your revenge."

It isn't my revenge he's thinking of, not while he has that bloodthirsty look in his eye. I almost felt good about this until I saw that look because I know what it means. He wants to hurt her. And while she's not exactly my favorite person, I don't know that I want her to be hurt, either. Not the way I know he'll be able to manage it.

It's too late now. He's already set on this, so I have no choice but to do as he said and text Elena back.

Me: Dinner is at 7:00 tomorrow. Just to let you know, we usually dress up for it.

Thinking fast, I type out another message.

Me: It's a habit he picked up from his family. I guess they were always kind of formal. Don't worry, not black tie or anything, but maybe cocktail or nicer.

I include the address and send the text, hoping it does the trick. And it does.

Elena: *I can't wait.*
Me: *Neither can we.*

VOW

24

ENZO

Never in my life have I felt so much like a spider, waiting in my web for my prey to become ensnared.

Everything is perfect. Our food is keeping warm in the oven. The dining room is set beautifully, complete with flowers I ordered this morning as a finishing touch.

"What do you think?" Alicia steps back from the table, her head tipped to the side as she studies her handiwork. She needed something to do today to keep her occupied. My impulse was to lock her in her room as punishment for what she pulled yesterday, but I decided against it at the last moment after giving it some honest thought. I need her feeling good tonight—nervous, I have no doubt, but she can't be resentful or distant. I need her fully with me if we're going to pull this off.

If Elena grew up in the Alvarez family, even along the fringes, she'll be able to smell trouble right away. I won't pretend I'm not appealing, especially when I put my mind to it, but even I might not be charming enough to compensate for my wife's unease.

I look over the table and nod. "Nice work. We'll play up how careful you were with the setting tonight, make it seem like you do this all the time but wanted it to be special for your friend. The happy little housewife wanting to show off how lucky she got."

"And what will you be doing during all of this?"

There's an edge to her voice I can't help but respond to, right or wrong. "I'll be flirting with her, obviously. I might take her on the table between courses."

"Cute."

"A little finger banging after the salad course never hurt anybody." She rolls her eyes and folds her arms, and for a moment, I feel a twinge of guilt. I have no intention of doing any such thing, but she doesn't know that. I've kept it that way on purpose, haven't I? Because she's the liar responsible for my grandfather's assassination. Isn't she?

"You know I won't do that," I confess with a sigh. "But she needs to think I will. We want her defenses down."

"In other words, I'm going to have to sit here and take it while she tries to seduce you."

"Have you always harbored jealous tendencies, or is this new?"

Her eye roll screams derision. "Please. It's insulting, end of story."

I'm no longer joking when I round the table and place a hand against her stomach. "I don't want you upsetting yourself for no reason. She's nothing." I receive a quick nod and the ghost of a smile before she leaves the room, and another moment passes before her footsteps ring out in the kitchen. Elena is due in a few minutes, and the woman of the house has to at least make it look like she's used to serving up our dinners.

I gaze down at the flowers she so carefully arranged and reflect on the effort she took with her hair and makeup tonight. It strikes me as sad in a way. This is all a show, an act. She might wish it wasn't. What girl doesn't want to show off her new home to a friend?

But this isn't the average marriage, and Elena is no average friend.

I only hope Alicia can put on a good performance—then again, I, of all people, should know how good an actress she is when she puts her mind to it. The memory stiffens my spine in time for the pealing of the doorbell. I cannot afford to forget who she is and what she's put me through.

Alicia is wiping her hands on a dish towel as she hurries through the living room, breezing past me without so much as a glance. The girls do the typical squealing and hugging at the door while I busy myself opening a bottle of wine. A glance at my reflection in the mirror hanging over the sideboard tells me I'd better loosen up. Right now, I look like I'm ready to kill.

"And you can see through to the kitchen." Alicia sounds upbeat, cheerful, happy as she gives Elena a tour.

"Wow, this is gorgeous!" She can't hide how impressed she is. "You got lucky, babe. Really lucky. Does he have a brother?"

Alicia's laughter is light and teasing, and the sound grows louder the closer the girls get to the dining room. I wait with my wine, smiling. The spider seated in the center of the web.

"Wow," Elena breathes once she enters the room and sees the elaborate table, flowers, and candles. "All this for me?" Her smile is a bit disbelieving as she turns my way.

And then it hardens until it's almost brittle. She sees what she wants and is determined to get it. "We meet again," she announces in a decidedly softer voice.

"So we do, but now we'll be introduced." I hand her the wine, and she brushes her fingers over mine upon accepting the glass. "Elena, my name is Enzo. It's a pleasure to meet you."

"Likewise. I've been looking forward to this."

"As have I." I raise my glass to her. "You have no idea."

Alicia clears her throat, now wearing a brittle smile of her own. "I'll see about bringing out the antipasto." I nod but maintain eye contact with Elena. She's a beautiful girl—curvaceous, too, and dressed to accentuate the fact. Her neckline is low enough to almost be indecent, and if she bent over, I'd have a nice view of her ass and perhaps her pussy, as well. Her diamond earrings and bracelet, and the designer label on her purse, all send a message. *Your wife isn't in your league, but I am.*

She catches me checking her out and flashes a knowing smile. "I hope I look okay. Alicia told me you usually get dressed up for dinner."

"You look great. That's a nice dress."

"You like it?" She treats me to a slow turn. "I bought it for tonight."

"It was a good choice." And now I'm glad Alicia has those expensive clothes from the shopping trip I took her on. I'm glad she looks just as good as her so-called friend—no, better. This little slut looks trashy. Eager.

Alicia enters carrying a platter of meats, cheeses, marinated vegetables, and crackers. "Dig in, please. I think I went overboard." She sets the platter down in the center of the table before taking a seat at my right while Elena settles in on my left. "I never know how to estimate how much people are going to want to eat at once."

Elena either doesn't notice the way Alicia avoids the wine and soft cheese, or she doesn't care. "My appetite changes all the time, anyway. I can never predict what I'll be hungry for or how much." She pops an olive into her mouth, her attention focused on me.

Then she turns to Alicia. "Where did you find him? Where can I find one?"

Alicia blushes but says nothing, her glance at me speaking volumes. Right. We never planned how to respond to that question. "I first set eyes on her at a club in town," I explain, grinning her way but placing most of my attention on our guest. "It was... one of those things."

She lifts an eyebrow, clearly unimpressed. "Love at first sight, huh? You usually only hear about stuff like that in the movies."

"I would never have imagined it, but it happened."

"I hope the magic stays alive through real life." She swirls the wine in her glass, eyeing me all the while. "Sometimes these sudden romances get sour once enough time passes. My dad's been married four times, and my mom is between husbands right now."

"There's been... drama in my family, as well. Relationships take work."

"You'd better be careful." She winks at Alicia. "He's right. Relationships can take work. Which means your ass better not get fat. I can give you my personal trainer's number if you want."

Who does this bitch think she is? I cannot believe the intensity of the desire to slap the smirk off her face. And Alicia thought she was a friend? Did she ever have one before this? I'll have to ask her about it when we're alone.

"He never lets me skip leg day," Elena continues. "And check out the work he's done on my arms and shoulders." She takes my hand and places it on her bicep before flexing.

"I'm impressed." I allow my hand to linger, no matter how it repulses me to do so. She isn't who I want. I could find a hundred women just like her here in Miami.

I glance at Alicia, who's staring at my hand. "Shouldn't you go grab the salad?" Elena's eyes light up when I turn back to her. My dismissiveness is giving her confidence.

Alicia gets up. "Anything else I can get you?" She's sullen and soft-voiced. Is it all part of the act? I can't imagine so, now that she's witnessing a friend going out of her way to catch my interest.

I remember almost a moment too late not to watch her ass as she walks away. Instead, I slide my hand down Elena's arm. "What do you like to do in your free time?"

She tosses her dark hair over one shoulder and purses her already pouty lips. "I don't know. Whatever catches my interest. What about you?"

"My interests sometimes change from day-to-day, I admit. It's always been a problem."

"What are you interested in today?" She leans in until her tits are maybe a deep breath away from spilling out. "Maybe I can help you out with it."

"I think you can, now that you mention it. I have this deep craving that nothing has filled."

She bites her lip. "I bet you can fill a lot of cravings."

There's not a doubt in my mind that I could have her in any room in this house, this very night. I could vomit all over her. Nothing turns me off like a slut who reeks of desperation, but the disloyalty is leagues worse.

When Alicia returns, we turn our attention to the meal for a while. There's no end to the double entendre, but at least we get through the salad and lasagna without me wanting to shove a knife in the girl, so she'll shut up for once.

And all the while, Alicia eats mechanically. Dutifully. Eyes downcast, disappointment plucking at the corners of her mouth. I can't help but feel for her, and it's even more reason for me to hate this brazen skank. I have no regrets over what I'm about to do to her, not by the time we're finished.

"So..." Elena's knowing smile would be irritating enough without the playfulness in her voice. "What's next? Dessert? I don't know if I can afford any. This dress is tight enough." She runs both hands over her chest and waist.

"I had something a little different in mind, to tell you the truth." I look at Alicia, now sitting bolt upright, her eyes darting back and forth between us. I can all but hear her heart racing.

"Oh?" Elena smiles slyly. "I'm always up for an adventure. What were you thinking?"

I raise my voice, looking toward the door. "Prince? We need you in here."

Elena looks at Alicia, her brows raised. "Do you know anything about this?"

"No," I answer, waving Prince in when he appears. "No, I came up with this on my own."

She sizes Prince up in a single approving glance. "Wow. This is my night," she declares with a laugh. "Here I was, thinking Enzo was the only hot guy around here, but now I find out he's been hiding you."

Prince spares a faint, condescending smile.

He then pulls out his gun and strikes her over the head with it, knocking her unconscious.

VOW

25
ALICIA

Is that what it was like for me? When Prince so coldly and smoothly came up from behind and hit me over the head? Did I drop like a sack of potatoes after letting out a soft cry the way I just witnessed Elena doing?

There are voices nearby, but over the rush of blood in my ears, they sound distant, muffled, like I'm listening to a conversation through a wall. I can't take my eyes off her, slumped in her chair, eyes closed and mouth partly open. Is that what I looked like?

The muffled voices get louder until, finally, someone touches my shoulder. A soft scream tears its way out of me before the world comes back into focus again.

And when it does, Enzo is leaning over me, scowling. "Stay with me here. Are you all right? Do you need something?"

Yes. For one thing, I need to know how they find it so easy to do things like this. Prince didn't so much as hesitate before striking Elena on the back of her head. How did he do that? I could never do that. Or if I did, I'd have to close my eyes and turn my face away. I wouldn't be able to look.

But Prince only stands there behind the chair, staring at me. He looks like he doesn't know whether to feel sorry for me or to laugh. Of course, he would find this funny. To them, none of this is a big deal.

"Alicia." Enzo's stern voice finally cuts through the noise in my head. I shake myself out of it and force myself to meet his gaze rather than shrinking away.

"I'm fine," I tell him since he seems genuinely concerned. For the baby, of course—I'm still not under any illusions.

I can't help looking over at Elena. "Is she...?"

Prince understands me, and now he does laugh. At least it doesn't seem like there's any bitterness or nastiness to it, which is a change. "She's fine. Just sleeping." That doesn't exactly soothe my fears, though.

"Check her pulse if you want to," Enzo offers. "She's unconscious, the way you were." I look at him, and our eyes meet, and it's clear the mention of that night has him thinking back. He's wearing a thoughtful expression, searching my face like he's looking for a sign of something. Recognition? Understanding?

"So long as I didn't just witness you killing her."

"So what if you did?" There's the Prince I remember from before. I guess his close call didn't change much about him. If I were him and somebody had almost murdered me, I might think about changing a few things in my life. But not him. He's blithe, almost gleeful. Like it had been too long since the last time he knocked a girl out.

"Are you really all right, though?" Enzo pulls me to my feet. "Do you need some water, maybe?"

Yes, I'm sure water will help me forget the sound of Prince's gun making contact with the back of Elena's skull. She is pretty far from being my favorite person, but she's still a human being. "No, I'm fine. Though I could use a trip to the bathroom. I want to splash water on my face." And maybe throw up.

"Why don't you do that, then go to your room?"

My heart sinks, and a soft moan of dismay stirs in my throat. I should have known. Now he's going to get me out of the way and do terrible things to her while I'm not watching. He doesn't want me to see.

"I don't know," I whisper.

"Oh no. You have the wrong idea. You look like you could use some rest." He steers me from the room, and I don't miss the way Prince smirks as we pass him. Enzo gives him a filthy look that wipes the expression off his face before we walk through the living room, then up the stairs.

I can't believe I just witnessed that. I basically took part in a crime. It's not like I thought we were inviting Elena over out of the goodness of our hearts or anything. I knew something was going to happen once she got here.

But now she's unconscious, and she can't defend herself, and part of that is my fault.

Would you have done anything differently if you knew? That question taunts me, echoing in the back of my mind as I stand over the bathroom sink and splash my face with cold water. Would I have done anything differently had I known what they'd do to her?

Maybe I didn't think about it enough, or at all. I only saw the importance of getting her here. Just like before, in the beginning, when all I saw was a way to quickly and easily get out of the trouble I was in with school, with my tuition. I never thought about what might happen, all the reasons I might not want to take such a risk.

I can barely look at myself in the mirror after splashing my face one last time.

I expected him to go back downstairs, but instead, he hands me a towel and watches as I pat my face. "Are you going to be all right? You're not sick, are you?"

"Just feeling a little shaky. But I'll get over it."

"You're sure?"

I lower the towel. "Sure, yeah."

He runs a hand through his hair, tousling it a little as he backs away so I can step out into the hall. "I only want to be sure."

It's almost sweet how worried he is. And I don't think that after everything he's put me through, there's anything wrong with me feeling a little smug. He could have killed me more than once throughout this whole nightmare. Who could blame me for enjoying his concern a little bit?

But I'm not a monster, either. "You don't have to worry about me every minute of the day, you know. We have a lot of months ahead of us. You're going to wear yourself out with all this worrying."

"This isn't exactly easy for me. I don't have anything to do with carrying the baby. I'm standing on the outside, looking in."

Right, and he's not used to being the one standing on the outside, being out of control. Now I'm starting to get it. This isn't only the concern of a first-time father—which would be bad enough. He feels like his whole life, his whole purpose, is wrapped up in this. And it's driving him out of his skull not to have control over every last aspect of it.

It seems wrong for so many reasons, having a conversation like this while Elena is downstairs, unconscious. Like the last thing on my mind should be my relationship with Enzo. And I'm surprised he's taking the time to talk with me when he has so many things to do now.

The intensity in his eyes when he stares at me, though, tells me he's not distracted. He's fully here in the moment with me. "I promise, if anything seems even slightly off, like just a little bit, I'll tell you about it right away. No secrets and no stalling. You'll be the first to know."

"I appreciate that. And you know I'm going to hold you to it."

"I wouldn't expect anything else."

He looks toward the stairs, remembering what else is going on, I guess. "I'm going to need you to stay up here now. In your room."

Wanting to argue with him is reflex; that's all because, deep down inside, I don't want to be around for whatever happens next. But still, a part of me wants to fight back because I hate it when he orders me around like this.

He lowers his brow when I hesitate, and a familiar rush of heat blazes through me. Now is not the time for my hormones to go on a rampage. "You're going to need to get this through your head. You are carrying my child. Right now, you are the most important person in the entire world. And that's why, while I'm dealing with this, you're going to stay in this room and not come out until I say it's safe. I have a lot on my mind, and I want to be able to deal with it while knowing you're safe. Do you understand?"

Right. He cares this much because of the baby. Not because he cares about me. I'm actually glad he said it, so I don't get any crazy ideas. Once the baby is born, that's it. I won't matter anymore.

I can't even be annoyed, not really. Because as sad as I am, knowing his concern isn't really about me, it's still one of the sweetest things he's ever said to me. And my heart is just that vulnerable, that needy for him, that I can't help but reach out and grab his words and cling to them. I even force a smile I don't feel in hopes of easing his worries. "Okay. I'll stay here."

I don't know if it's because he doesn't believe me or he's being overly cautious, but he puts a guard at my door anyway before heading back downstairs.

I wish he would stay here with me. I feel so mixed up inside. Guilty and conflicted, and annoyed with myself on top of that. Annoyed that I feel bad about Elena, annoyed that I'm so lonely, and most of all, that I crave Enzo's love the way I do. It's pointless, but I can't seem to convince my heart of that.

What are they doing to her down there? I hope it's not more than she deserves. I'm not even sure what I think she deserves, honestly, no matter how disgusted I am at the way she acted during dinner. She couldn't have been more obvious. I was sitting right there, but that didn't stop her from flirting with him like crazy.

In the end, no matter what happens, there's one thing I believe: he's doing this for his family, meaning our child. That means everything. "Don't you worry," I whisper, rubbing my belly. "Everything will be fine. You just keep growing, and your daddy will make sure everything is safe for you." It feels good to say that. It feels right.

Not another minute or two passes before the door opens, and Enzo steps through. "I have her phone. I want to contact Alvarez through it, but I can't get it unlocked."

"I think she uses the face recognition thingy. I've seen her do that before; she holds it up to her face before she uses it."

"That didn't work. Is it because her eyes are closed, do you think?"

I snap my fingers when the memory becomes clearer. "No, she uses that along with her thumbprint. I think you have to do both at the same time." It's almost cute that he needs my help with this. It's a nice feeling, sort of like I'm part of the team.

"Thank you." Instead of hurrying back downstairs, he pauses and looks at me. "We're going to make things right. For both of us."

I hope so. I hope once this is over, he finds a little peace. I want that for him because I love him, no matter if it's right or wrong. When he's gone and I'm alone again, I place a hand against my belly. "He's going to make things right for all of us."

VOW

26

ENZO

"If this doesn't get his attention, nothing will."

I take a slow walk around the couch, studying our captive. She's looked better, I would guess, but for this evening's purposes, she looks absolutely perfect. As an extra touch, I reach down and run my thumb over her lips, smearing her lipstick onto her cheek.

Prince steps back, her ankles now bound. Her wrists have already been secured behind her back. The way she's positioned, half her ass is showing, and her nipples are barely covered. "She looks like she's been through a rough night," I observe with a humorless chuckle.

"Though it's not exactly the kind of rough night she had in mind." Prince looks as disgusted by the memory as I am. "I'm surprised she didn't offer to take us both on at once."

My lip curls in a sneer at the memory. "Maybe she'll learn a lesson from this. Don't throw yourself at a man unless you at least know his last name. I thought girls like her were supposed to be smarter than that."

"Well, she trusted her friend."

"Yes. The way her friend trusted her." Her friend, who is now upstairs, as ordered. I don't know what's going to happen next precisely, but I know she would do better to stay where I put her unless told otherwise. "I think this shook her. Seeing what you did."

"She's tough. She can handle it." From Prince, that's the closest thing to a compliment one can hope for.

"Let's see what Uncle Josef thinks about Elena's night out." I brush the hair back from her face to make sure he gets a good look at her before snapping one picture, then another, and several more. She looks sloppy, like after a long night of being used, which is precisely the look I'm going for. Let him wonder what we've done to her. Let him come to the worst possible conclusion.

Once I'm satisfied, I open her contacts—sure enough, there's an entry for Tio Josef. There's no going back from this, not that I want there to be. "Everything else is in place?" I ask Prince, and to his credit, he doesn't roll his eyes or smart off about me not trusting him to take care of things as ordered. Too much is riding on this to leave anything to chance.

"We're all set," he grunts, and that will have to be enough for me. I type out my message, keeping it short and sweet.

Me: *It's time for us to have a little talk, Tio Josef.*

With that, I attach a few of the worst photos, then hit send. There's no going back now.

I should have started a countdown clock. Prince and I exchange a surprised look when no more than ten seconds pass before her phone buzzes with a call from none other than her uncle. I didn't imagine he would check the text right away.

"That was fast," Prince murmurs before I answer the call, bracing myself for what comes next.

"Who the fuck is this?" Alvarez growls. "Where is she? Who are you?"

"Calm down, Tio Josef," I murmur, unable to keep from smiling. All this time, he's considered himself on top of things, having a good laugh at my expense when I believed he was Alicia's father. I would ask him how it feels, but that seems a bit heavy-handed. It's enough satisfaction to listen to him melt down, ranting in Spanish once he recognizes my voice.

"You motherfucker," he growls. "I'm going to cut off your balls and feed them to you, you piece of shit."

"You underestimate me," I tell him with a sigh. "Again, I've never been one to fuck my mother. Have you ever considered going to therapy to work out this fixation you seem to have?" Prince snorts at this, and I wish he could hear better, but then Alvarez isn't trying to be quiet.

"Where is she?"

"She's safe with me. And lucky, too."

"Lucky? How the fuck do you work that out, genius? She doesn't look so lucky to me."

"Simple. She is completely at my mercy right now yet is relatively unharmed. I could do any number of things to her—then again, for all you know, I already have. Me and all of my men."

"You'd better fucking hope not."

"Or else what?" I drop the humor, now mirroring his attitude. "You're going to bring an assassin here and shoot someone close to me? It's a bit too late for that one."

"What do you want?"

"Exactly what I asked for in the text I sent. I want to have a talk."

"So talk."

"Right. As if it would be that easy." I glance at Prince, who only nods firmly, his gaze steady. "I want to see you in person. Face-to-face. Tonight."

"And you'll bring her with you?"

"Of course I will. Unlike you, I'm a man of my word. You want her back; you meet with me. And I promise…" I look down at her, still sleeping away, thanks to Prince's efforts. "She'll be more or less in the same condition she was in when she arrived. Really, someone should have taught her not to leave herself wide open to an attack like this."

"You fucking watch your mouth. You don't talk about her that way."

"Or else what?" I ask again, this time with a laugh. "What, all of a sudden, you want me to be a gentleman? After the shit you've done? Please, don't pretend to be a loving family man now."

Behind him, there's shouting in Spanish, a language I'm not fluent in. But I don't need to be. The obvious anger, frustration, and confusion are easy enough to interpret. I can't help but savor the knowledge of the disarray the family has been thrown into.

"I want a face-to-face meeting in a neutral location," I explain. Prince pulls out his phone, prepared to arrange our guard. "I'll even let you name the location, but it has to be in neutral territory with which I'm familiar."

"Fine," he barks. "You know the old brewery?"

"I think I do." I hold the phone out so Prince can hear better. "Exactly where is that located?" When Alvarez rattles off the exact location, Prince nods, typing furiously into his phone while I bring my phone back to my ear.

"We'll be glad to meet you there."

"You'd damn well better be."

"Yet I'm afraid I have to make one more request."

"The fuck you do." Is he honestly surprised? As if I would leave it there.

"Fine. If your niece matters that little to you, that's your family situation, not mine. My men are already frustrated with me for not allowing them to play with her. I'll give them what they want if it doesn't matter to you either way."

"What do you want?" he shouts.

"A single person. Frankie Morris. You know who I mean and why I want him."

"Frankie Morris? I don't know anybody by that name."

"Spare me the stalling bullshit. This isn't some child you're speaking to, and you're wasting valuable time. I know he's with you. I've seen him on your property. I know he defected to your side the minute my grandfather was dead. And I know that fucker killed him. I want him, and I consider this a fair exchange. You hand him over, and you can have Elena."

"You bring me Elena, and I bring you Frankie."

"That's correct."

"Fine. On one condition."

"You're not the one setting conditions here. You are the one whose niece is in a rather unflattering position at the moment. I could bring her back to you smeared with much worse than makeup, Alvarez."

He only growls at this. "I want you to bring that wife of yours with you."

My body goes stiff, and my heart clenches, which is precisely what he wants. "And why would I do that?"

"To make sure you and that temper don't get out of hand."

As long as he continues to breathe, this bastard will find a way to surprise me.

"Fine," I reply because there's no way around it. This is the last thing I want to do, but it's a means to an end.

"We'll see you there in half an hour. And don't get any ideas. Elena is counting on you. I don't think I need to describe the amount of damage that can be done to a woman's body in a mere thirty minutes."

"You just remember how easy it would be for me to hurt that little wife of yours." He ends the call, and I do the same, trembling with rage.

"Everything all right?" Prince asks, guarded.

"Just about." I stare down at my phone, then look up at Elena. "He wants us to bring Alicia."

"He would." He snorts. "Like a rat, always looking for a way to save his ass. I almost admire him for it."

"I'm going to need you to make it your mission to protect her."

"You know I will."

"No," I snap. "Swear it. You will protect her tonight."

His brows draw together when he frowns. "I will. I swear it."

That's all I have to hang on to as I climb the stairs, then knock on Alicia's door while Prince handles the logistics of this meeting. As I swing the door open, it occurs to me that I don't normally knock before entering. One of the small things that have shifted between us.

She jumps up from where she is seated on the bed, still fully dressed in her dinner attire. I wonder if she's sat frozen like this since I left her in here. "Well? What happened?"

"Alvarez took the bait," I murmur, noting her bright eyes and flushed cheeks. She's in the moment with me, going through it by my side. This is the sort of wife a man in my position wants. She cares deeply and wants what's best for the family.

She heaves a sigh of relief. "That's great. I was worried he'd try to call your bluff somehow."

"But…"

"But?"

"He wants you to come along to the meetup. That was one of his conditions."

What did I expect? For her to break down crying? To beg me not to put her through this?

If I did, I should have known better. That's not her way. She rolls her shoulders back, her lips set in a smirk. "Of course, he did. Why not use me as a human shield while he's at it?"

I don't think I've ever admired her more than I do now. "I don't want you getting upset. This could be dangerous." I place a hand over her belly, though my words more than likely convey the message without the addition of my touch.

"I understand, but you need to do this. I'm not going to hold you back."

I could be snide now. I could make a comment about my child giving her extra strength and fierceness, but that would be disingenuous. She was already fierce, strong, and willing to stand up to me time and again. What once frustrated me most of all about her now fills me with pride.

Rather than take her here and now, I give her a firm nod. "Let's go."

27

ALICIA

"You know if anything happens to her, I'll fucking kill you." Enzo stands face-to-face with Prince after they load Elena into the back seat of the car. She's awake but still a little groggy. I remember that feeling. This is bringing everything back to me in vivid and almost sickening detail.

Right down to being dragged into a meeting with Josef Alvarez. The first time, that meeting never happened, and Prince was nearly killed. This time, somebody Alvarez actually cares about is involved, so I doubt things will go exactly that way.

But I don't doubt he'll try to throw a curveball somehow.

It's no secret Enzo feels the same way, which is why it's killing him to have me along for this.

Prince doesn't back down, merely nodding at Enzo's threat. "I know. She'll be fine. You have my word on that." I'm not sure it's enough for me, but it seems to be enough for Enzo. I'm going to have to trust him on this.

Now to get over the final hurdle, the one last thing I was dreading: having to get in the car and face my so-called friend. I have to remind myself there's nothing for me to feel guilty about. In the end, she's going to be fine—nobody wants to hurt her. She's only leverage. I don't feel quite as bad when I remind myself of that.

And when she hits me with an absolutely filthy stare, all I have to do is remember how obvious she was about trying to seduce my husband right in front of me. That helps a lot, too.

She's staring daggers at me by the time I buckle myself in. "How could you do this to me?" she hisses as the men get in the front seat.

"I didn't do anything to you," I whisper back. "So don't blame this on me."

"You didn't do anything?" she asks with a harsh laugh. "Are you serious? You're the reason I'm in this mess."

"No," I counter. "You're the reason you're in this mess. Don't put this on me." I fold my arms and stare straight ahead as Prince takes us out of the development.

"How is any of this my fault?" she whispers. "I didn't do anything."

"Keep telling yourself that." I am not going to engage. I refuse to engage. Enzo and Prince are silent, but of course, they're listening. I don't know why I care, but I would rather not have this fight in front of them.

Clearly, she doesn't care. "What did I do to you? All I've ever tried to do is be your friend."

That's it. That's the last straw. "Oh, really? For one thing, that's bullshit. A friend doesn't walk into another friend's house and flirt with their husband."

"Please. You're that insecure?" Suddenly, the car swerves, and she falls against the door because she can't balance herself with her hands and ankles tied. There was no reason for Prince to swerve. I think he did it on purpose.

"You admit that's what you were doing. And I was just supposed to sit there and take it?"

"So you set me up like this? Because I can't help but respond to somebody I think is hot?"

"That's not what this is about." And if she wasn't such a thirsty slut, she wouldn't have come to my house with the intention of fucking my husband. "Are you really that self-absorbed that you think anybody would go to this kind of trouble for something like that?"

"Then why? How could you lie to my face and pretend we were friends?"

"Are you serious? I mean that. Do you honestly have to ask me why?

Are you that clueless?" When all she does is gape at me, I can't help but growl my disgust. "You got me into this mess. You sent me to that damn warehouse and left me for dead. Or have you forgotten all about that? Because you never once asked me. You never once texted, you didn't call, and you never followed up in any way. And when I finally saw you at school, what did you do? You deliberately avoided me. You ran away from me before I could catch up with you after class. That's not how somebody acts when they're someone's friend. So stop pretending."

"I figured you were fine. What, you couldn't even handle a simple job like that?" The car swerves again, more sharply this time, and Elena cries out in pain when her shoulder hits the door. I should be ashamed of the satisfaction that ripples through me, shouldn't I? Yet I'm not. I like the sound. I'm not going to pretend otherwise.

"Do you honestly believe what's coming out of your mouth? Or are you only telling yourself that to feel better? Because that was not a simple job. And when I didn't show back up at school, you should have known something went wrong. A friend would've cared enough to reach out. But no, because we aren't actually friends. You don't care about anybody but yourself. So drop the act."

"Is that really what this is about?" She jerks her chin toward the front seat. "Are you even married?"

"Yeah, I am, and that's your fault, too. This is all your fault. You thoughtlessly sent me into that warehouse and acted like it was no big deal, then you don't even have the nerve to check and make sure I'm okay? No, you would much rather try to steal my husband from me. And you're sitting there acting like a victim? It's pathetic."

"You would know all about pathetic. Maybe if you had your life even slightly under control, you wouldn't have been in a shitty situation in the first place. Ever think about that?"

"No, you're right. I should have been born into a mafia family, so I could grow up thinking the whole fucking world revolves around me while never having to work an actual day in my life. Yeah, you definitely made the smarter decision."

Even now, in the position she's in, she tosses her head. "What, am I supposed to apologize for how I was born?"

"No, clueless. But you could try realizing you didn't earn a single thing you have. At least I could say I took care of myself and did the best I could. Nobody gave me anything I had. And, of course, somebody like you would look down on that."

"You're such a crybaby. You always were. Oh, poor me, poor Alicia, what am I going to do?"

It's like I've never known the real Elena before now. I may as well be sitting here next to a stranger. And all it does is rid me of any lingering sense of guilt I might have carried around.

"Crybaby? Do you want to hear about some of the things I've been through since that night? I've been beaten. Knocked out and thrown into a trunk. Tied up. Humiliated. Locked in a room for days at a time. I also had to save somebody after they were shot. And yeah, I had to marry a man I barely knew. But sure, I'm a crybaby. You couldn't last through an hour of what I went through because you've never really had to face a challenge in your entire life. Congratulations, you're facing one now. How's it feel?"

"Fuck off."

"After you," I mutter back, turning my face away from hers and staring out the window, ready to boil over with rage. Pathetic. She thinks I'm pathetic. I'd love to knock a couple of teeth out of her mouth. She wouldn't look so pretty then, would she? Maybe she would think twice about trying to steal somebody's husband.

"Are you girls finished?" Enzo turns his head slightly to look into the back seat.

"What about it?" I snap. Prince snorts but says nothing, while Enzo turns back around without a word. I have no doubt he'll want to talk about that later, but I'm too damn angry right now. Because this is just as much his fault as it is hers. They're both to blame. Now is not the time for him to throw his attitude my way.

Pathetic. I'm pathetic? All I ever did was try to make the best of what life handed me. And I'm pathetic. Some spoiled, pampered little princess thinks she can judge my life? Never had to work a single day, had all her decisions made for her, and then she acts like a backstabbing little slut—

and I'm pathetic? I could tear every strand of hair out of her scalp right now, the snide bitch.

But I've already given the men enough entertainment. And I'm not going to stoop to that level, either. I have to try to show a little dignity. I almost want to laugh at myself. Dignity? Now? That's sort of like closing the barn doors after the horses have run out. These two have seen me at my most undignified. That doesn't mean I have to make a fool out of myself for their amusement.

It's better for me to ignore the things Elena is muttering to herself as we ride through the darkness. I know better than to ask where we're going, and I just hope we get there soon. I need to get this over with.

We arrive first, pulling into an empty parking lot that doesn't look like it's been used in years. Tons of weeds are coming up through the cracks in the pavement, and colorful graffiti decorates the walls of a building with boarded-up windows. How do these people know about places like this? Is there a list somewhere? I can see no other cars anywhere in the vicinity, though it's pretty dark. When our headlights wash over the area, there's nothing but thick, dense wooded area behind the building. In other words, Elena has nowhere to run if she gets the idea in her head. I wouldn't step foot in there in the daylight, much less on a moonless night like this.

Now she's quiet. Afraid. I want more than anything to taunt her, to ask how it feels and remind her I've been through this, thanks to her. I know what it means to arrive somewhere and have no idea if I'm going to make it out alive.

"Come on." Prince yanks the back door open and is rougher with her then he ever was with me. Enzo, meanwhile, helps me out from the back seat even though I don't need the help. If it makes him feel better to hover over me a little, I'm not going to argue. Especially not when it feels sort of nice.

"You up to this?" he asks.

"Does it matter if I am or not? Alvarez was never going to show up without you agreeing to bring me along."

"Just a little longer. We'll get this wrapped up."

I try to offer a brave smile, but it isn't easy, especially when Elena won't shut up with her complaints.

"I hope you know my father will kill you for this," she mutters as Prince holds her in place beside the car. I see what he's doing: if somebody happens to be watching from the darkness, he's got her with him. In other words, they need to be careful if they decide to open fire.

"Your father won't kill anyone," Enzo retorts. "And if he wants you back alive, he knows that. He might not be the head of the family, but he knows how this works. And your uncle? If he even gives a shit, he'll still know better."

There's a sound somewhere in the darkness, beyond where I can see. The hair on the back of my neck stands up.

We're not alone here. I feel it. I sense it. Just because I didn't see any cars doesn't mean we're the first to arrive. Enzo wouldn't take a risk like that, I realize. He would also never tell me the specifics—he'd either decide I don't need to know, or he would rather keep it quiet, so there's no chance of me giving anything away. Regardless of the reason, I'm sure he wouldn't risk my life or the baby's showing up here without somebody to watch our backs.

"At least I know the answer to one question," Elena mutters with a laugh. She cranes her neck to look over her shoulder at me. "I couldn't figure out how you landed somebody like him."

Enzo is either too surprised that she would say that, or he doesn't figure I'll do anything about it. Either way, I am able to walk up to her without either he or Prince trying to stop me. Forget being the bigger person. Forget holding myself back.

All I know is my fist makes contact with her face, and she falls back against the car. "Shit!" I squeal, grabbing my fist. I'm pretty sure I hurt myself worse than I hurt her. But damn, it felt good.

"Hey! What the hell do you think you're doing?" Enzo pulls me away from her and puts himself between us. "What are you thinking? Why would you do that?"

"I'm sorry if I'm supposed to stand here and take that, but I can't."

"You want somebody punched, you tell me—or Prince, and we'll do it for you. Got it?"

That's the problem? That I did the punching myself? It's almost enough to make me laugh, but the pain in my fist won't allow for that. "Got it," I grit out, shaking my hand. I won't bother arguing since I doubt he'd understand, but there's something about doing a job like that yourself. What's between Elena and me is personal. It wouldn't be nearly as satisfying to watch one of the men punch her for me, even if it meant sparing my fist.

Still, knowing I have backup is nice.

28

ENZO

The hair on the back of my neck rises at the sight of approaching headlights. Prince left our car's headlights on, and they are the only thing currently illuminating this spot where we stand waiting. Though we're standing outside, it feels like all the air has been sucked away. This is it. Everything hinges on this.

"If you know what's good for you, you'll keep your mouth shut," I warn Elena. "Unless you would rather be gagged." She gives me a dirty look but doesn't protest. Maybe a few brain cells are rattling around in that head.

Alicia stands behind the open driver's side door, which I hope shields her if things get out of hand. I'm going to do my best to see to it that isn't the case, but I can't speak for Alvarez and his crew. "If anything happens," I murmur, "I want you to get behind the wheel, and I want you to leave. Do not hesitate. Don't worry about me. You are to leave immediately. Do you understand?"

In the light from the car's interior, I see her frown and can almost hear the arguments she wants to make. Yet instead of voicing her complaints, she merely nods. Once again, I have to admire the way she's bearing up under this. I had not intended to put her through this sort of strain, especially in her condition and especially so early in our union. The wife of a cartel boss has to be prepared for anything, but normally we can shield our women from the worst of it. She's been granted no such protection thus far, yet it seems she has a backbone of steel. I can't help but wonder if fate knew what it was doing when it stepped in and placed her in my path.

Now's not the time for fantasies. I step away from her, and Prince takes his place by her side. I have no doubt he will guard her with his life —and if he doesn't, he'll lose his life anyway because I will gladly kill him.

"Come on," I murmur, taking Elena by the arm. "Behave yourself, and this will all be over soon."

"Go to hell," she mutters.

"Have you already forgotten that I promised to gag you? It doesn't have to be as simple as that. Don't make me hurt you." She glares at me, eyes blazing, but holds her tongue. With my hand around her arm, she won't be able to get away. And even if she tries, I would be a fool to open fire on her—that would only give Alvarez an excuse to do the same.

Several cars approach, rolling past us in a wide arc before swinging around and coming to a stop in front of where I stand with Elena. I raise a hand to shield my eyes from the glare of the headlights, and two of the cars flip them off, making it easier to see. A handful of men emerge, guards by the looks at them, surveying the area before giving the signal for their boss to emerge.

Then he does, followed by a man who looks a lot like him. A man who makes a move as if to lunge for Elena before Josef thrusts out an arm, barring the way. Elena whimpers, and I know that must be her father, Josef's brother.

"Nice to see you again," Josef calls out. "And where is that lovely wife of yours? My daughter for a day." The man drips sarcasm when I would much rather he drip blood.

I thrust a thumb behind me. "She's there. Just as you requested."

"You would be wise to remember her presence."

"You would be wise to remember you're in no position to tell me what to think or do, you son of a bitch. You put my grandfather in the ground."

"I'm telling you I didn't."

"Then give me the man who did!" I scream. His head snaps back, eyes widening. "Because even if you didn't, you fucking benefited from it, you bastard. And that cowardly murderer defected to your side, so tell me again how you had nothing to do with it."

"Cowardly murderer? I take it you're referring to Frankie Morris."

"No, I only wanted you to bring him here because I miss seeing his face."

"I didn't summon him. He came to me of his own free will, knowing he would need protection from you."

"And like the piece of shit you are, you took him in rather than hand him back to me. The way you should have, the way anyone with a grain of character would have done. Accepting him into the fold is tantamount to an act of war. Has no one ever told you that? By sheltering him, you've made a move against my family."

He touches a hand to his chest. "Sheltering him? Is that what I've been doing?"

"I've had eyes on you. I know that's what you've done."

"So typical of you, believing what your eyes tell you."

"And what is that supposed to mean?"

"See for yourself." He waves a hand, and one of the car doors opens. I watch as a guard reaches in and pulls something out—no, someone. Someone who I can't quite make out in the darkness.

I don't need to make out his face to see he's in terrible shape. His legs sag, and he practically has to be carried out until he's in front of a pair of headlights, illuminating his face.

His battered, bruised face. Alvarez goes to him, taking him by the hair and pulling his head back so I can get a good look. "Is this the man you were referring to? Frankie Morris?"

Once again, he surprised me. The man's face is swollen, but I watched him long enough through that drone camera feed to see through the damage. "What have you done to him?"

"See, not all of us take things at face value the way you do." The frank amusement in the man's voice makes my blood boil. "Certainly, I accepted him into my compound, but not as an employee. Information is all that matters in our world, little boy, and I knew he would have it. After all, why else would he have come to me?"

"For protection."

"Bullshit," he snaps, letting Frankie's head drop again. He staggers a little but stays on his feet. "He was sent to me. It was obvious. If he wanted to get away, if he wanted protection, he could have easily arranged that for himself."

"And how would you know that?"

"Our friend, Frankie, has a loose tongue. And a very, very beautiful, brand-new car. It still smells new, for fuck's sake. Now, exactly where did he get that money? And why couldn't he have used it to get far, far away from you?" Alvarez casts a disgusted look his way, and I can't pretend not to share the sentiment. That's what he used my grandfather's money for? The fucking fool.

"No," he continues, removing a handkerchief from his pocket and wiping his hands after touching the sweat-soaked and bloodied Frankie. "It was obvious something more was happening. So don't pretend to be surprised that I found out."

"Very well." The fact is, I am surprised, and puzzled on top of that. "Why not kill him, then?"

"That was always the plan, but first was the matter of extracting any information he could give me about you or your family or why he would choose to assassinate the man he was supposed to protect." He casts a look toward Frankie, swaying on his feet. "Unfortunately, it led me nowhere, though I did enjoy watching and listening as my men worked him over. After all, a traitor is a traitor."

He shrugs, grinning. "I hope you don't mind. I'm sure you would like to take a piece of him yourself. But there's still plenty left for you or your men to have a go at."

"I want my daughter," his brother calls out. He hasn't stopped staring at Elena since this began.

"Patience, brother," Josef murmurs, still staring at me. "You'll get what you want. Young Enzo here isn't foolish enough to make a mistake like harming our Elena."

"She is unharmed," I confirm. "A slight bump on the head, but as you can see, it hasn't affected her."

"So?" Josef folds his arms, his feet planted at shoulder width. "Are we making an exchange, or are we not? I have nothing else for you. And if you are looking for revenge, you've come to the wrong person. I can only say it so many times. I had nothing to do with the old man's murder."

The guards draw their guns when I tighten my grip on Elena's arm and jerk her slightly closer to me. All eight of them have their eye on me. Alicia's soft gasp rings out behind me, followed by Prince's equally soft grunt as if he is forbidding her from moving or reacting.

Now I know what I'm up against, which of course, was the plan all along. To draw them out, count them, and be sure of what we're up against.

"I'm nothing if not a man of my word." With that, I release her, and she runs to her father. "Take her, and get her out of here," I call out as the man wraps his arms around her and leads her to one of the cars. Immediately, he puts her inside and pulls away without hesitation. Smart man.

"See?" Alvarez gloats. "I knew you could be reasonable. It's not that difficult. Now, why don't we put all of this behind us once I hand this loser back to you to do with as you wish? And we can both go on our merry way."

"That does sound like a good idea," I muse. This bastard. He's so full of shit I'm surprised he can move. "My family has been through a lot. Too much, if I'm being frank."

"There's no reason not to be. And I know losing your mentor, the man who raised you, must have been difficult. But I am not your enemy in this. What would I have to gain by killing him? It makes no sense and only causes turmoil. Now..." He offers a shrug and a smirk. "I wouldn't call myself a foolish man, but I'm no one's idea of an evil genius. And I don't get off on killing. I had nothing to gain. I hope you see that now."

He gestures toward Frankie. "I give him back to you alive as a gesture of goodwill. I didn't want to take the pleasure of dealing with him away from you."

"That was very thoughtful of you. But I have to admit, it isn't Frankie I'm most concerned with now. Don't get me wrong," I add, glaring at the beaten, bloodied man as his head swings back and forth between us. "We're going to have a long talk, and he's going to tell me everything he knows. But I'm still worried about one thing. Maybe you can help me with it, being as experienced as you are."

"Please, by all means. What can I do to help you?"

"You can return everything given to you upon my marriage."

He blurts out a disbelieving laugh. "You can't be serious."

"You made that agreement under false pretenses. You pretended to be Alicia's father because it served your ends. And because you wanted to get your hands on what she took from the warehouse that night."

His eagerness betrays him. Let him pretend all he wants, but he isn't nearly as calm and cool as he pretends. "Where is it?" he barks, and now the mask falls off completely. No more pretending to be the gregarious, experienced adversary. "It belongs to me. It always has."

"Don't worry. I'll take good care of it."

"You couldn't possibly know what to do with that product, how it's manufactured, any of it."

"But I can find out, can't I? And I'm already in the process of doing so. I sent a sample to a laboratory, and they're working on the chemical composition as we speak. Before long, I'll know exactly how to replicate the product."

"But it's mine!" Spittle flies from his lips, illuminated by the headlights behind him.

"Relax," I tell him, savoring his rage for as long as I can. "It's not like you'll be around to do anything with it, anyway."

And that's when I withdraw my gun and lodge a bullet between his eyes. He didn't even see it coming.

Alicia's soft scream as his body hits the ground only punctuates my satisfaction.

As predicted, the remaining guards raise their weapons, but I hold up a hand. "I wouldn't do that if I were you," I call out over their grunts of surprise and anger, and as if by magic, a series of lasers appear, bright red in the darkness, their points trained on the chests and heads of the men now aiming their guns at me.

"We're surrounded," I announce with a smile as my snipers reveal themselves, closing in on us from all sides. "So if one of you fires at the ground, you're all dead. It's as simple as that."

Either he does it out of anger or because he couldn't protect his boss and wants to prove himself.

No matter the reason, one of the men raises his weapon and fires.

The sound makes me flinch, crouching instinctively with my own gun raised. I fire before thinking, and he goes down, clutching the wound in his stomach. I'm fine, I realize—before realizing it wasn't me the guy was aiming for.

My head swings around, my eyes searching frantically for Alicia in the semi-dark. She was standing behind the open car door, and I look that way now, expecting to find her.

What I find makes my heart stop: her body, prone on the ground, Prince lying on top of her.

Just like that day. The wedding. Lying on the ground after the gunshot rang out. Covering her. Thinking she was hit. Thinking my world was shattered—unaware of how correct I was, even if she was safe and unharmed.

How much longer can her luck hold out?

I'm haunted by the sense of the past and present overlapping as I lunge for the car. She can't be hurt. She cannot be hurt. I won't allow it. How do I live if she's gone? "Alicia!"

VOW

29

ALICIA

I barely know what happened. One second, I was trying to make sense of Alvarez dropping to the ground. Then the next thing I knew, I was on the ground with Prince over me, shielding me. I can hardly breathe with his heavy frame on top of me. I bat at him with both hands. "Can't breathe!" I gasp.

Enzo pulls him off me, maneuvering me into a sitting position. He takes my face into his hands, and the light from the car's interior shows me the panic in his eyes.

"Are you injured? Were you hit?"

"I'm fine." But I don't think he hears me. Not over his heavy breathing—it sounds like he just ran a marathon, and now I'm afraid he was hurt. But there's no blood to be seen on his shirt or his pants. He's okay. Thank God.

"Sorry about that." Prince is grim as he sits up and brushes himself off. "Reflexes."

"No, thank you. You don't have to apologize." Even though I don't think the bullet came anywhere near us. If it had, it would've at least hit the car. He was only protecting me.

"Get her out of here," Enzo orders Prince, but I shake my head.

"I want to be here," I insist. "I'm fine." When I look over to where

Alvarez's men are now gathered in a cluster, I see Enzo's guys disarming them. "See? They're no threat now, and plus, I don't want to leave you."

He exchanges a look with Prince, who nods. "Finish this." Enzo's jaw tightens, but he doesn't offer any further argument, helping me to my feet before turning back toward the man he killed.

I watched it happen. I see the man with my own eyes. Somehow, I still can't believe it. Enzo killed Josef Alvarez. Shot him dead. The act was so simple, like brushing his teeth or putting his shoes on.

And now I understand why Enzo didn't want to give me any specifics about the plan. I could've guessed he'd try to have Alvarez killed, but I didn't know he'd be the one to do it himself. Not right in front of me.

The Alvarez men look in all directions, heads snapping back and forth, muttering in confusion and anger. They have to know there's no hope. They're dead men, like the guard now bleeding out on the ground after firing a shot. He could've killed my baby. I'm almost consumed by the impulse to walk over and spit on him.

"I'm not an unreasonable man," Enzo announces, holding his hands up. "I understand you're all here to do a job, and I respect that. I also respect intelligence, which all of you need to exercise now, or you'll end up like the stupid bastard drowning in his own blood. I want you to get the hell out of here. You don't have to die tonight, so long as none of you do anything stupid. I would rather you live, in fact. I want the men now in charge of your family to know I showed mercy here. I returned the girl to her father and am prepared to let you go."

Then he points at Frankie. "I only want him. We need to have a conversation. The rest of you, get out of here and be grateful I'm giving you the chance."

The men exchange looks like they're wondering whether they can believe this. I'm not sure I do, honestly, but after a few moments, they all do what they're told. The guards from our side wait, though. They don't open fire. And eventually, when the Alvarez men start to move away, they let them go.

Because they left Frankie behind.

He falls to his knees once nobody's holding him up anymore and raises his folded hands like he's praying. "Thank you, thank you. I thought they were gonna kill me. He only hired me because he knew I was the one who pulled the trigger, but it was—"

He doesn't finish before Enzo backhands him hard enough that he falls over. "You pulled the trigger? You would admit that to me so easily, like it means nothing? You son of a bitch!" He hauls Frankie to his feet and throws him over the hood of his car, then pulls out his gun and shoves it into the man's already bloody mouth.

I've seen Enzo at his worst. At his most violent and cruel. This? It's on a whole other level. I'm torn between wanting to turn away and being unable to tear my eyes from it.

Frankie screams around the gun. "What's that?" Enzo shouts over him. "You don't like the taste of metal? That's a real fucking shame. My grandfather didn't like having lead shot into him, either."

He pulls the gun out far enough for Frankie to speak. "He told me to do it!"

"Alvarez? No big surprise there."

"No! The boss! Mr. De Luca! He told me to do it!"

I didn't expect that. I know Enzo didn't, either. "Bullshit. You're a lying piece of shit, and I should blow your fucking brains out right now."

"It's true! It's true, I swear. He planned the whole thing. I was supposed to shoot him, then get hired by Alvarez once I told him it was me. I swear!" he adds once Enzo presses the gun's muzzle to his forehead.

"He put you up to this, didn't he? Alvarez."

"No!"

"I'm supposed to believe that? You want me to believe my grandfather asked you to kill him?" He uses the butt of the gun to hit Frankie's face and head, and I almost feel sorry for the guy. He was already wounded before he got here.

But he killed the old man, and Enzo's not going to stop until he punishes every person responsible. This is his family he's fighting for. I can imagine him going to these lengths for our kids one day, and I can't pretend that doesn't excite me a little. At least I'll always know my children are safe with him.

"Please, Enzo, please!" Frankie's blubbering isn't easy to understand now that both lips are split, and I think he's missing teeth. "Stop, man. I only did it because he told me to. I swear."

"My grandfather told you to kill him."

"Yes! I swear!"

Enzo shakes him until his head bounces off the car's hood. "Do you understand how insane that sounds? Why would he tell you to do that? He had everything in place, finally. He had everything he wanted."

"Please, stop hurting me." Frankie's crying, I realize. "I'll tell you about it. I will. But I can't take any more of this. Please."

Enzo pulls him in close, baring his teeth. "You'd better start telling the truth, you worthless shit. Because if you think you know what pain is, I'll be more than happy to show you how wrong you are. I'll make it last a long time. Got it?"

"Yes... yes, I get it." When Enzo lets go of him, Frankie slumps against the car. "Thank you."

"Don't thank me. Start talking."

Frankie fights to catch his breath for a few seconds before spitting blood on the ground. The sight of it makes my stomach churn, but I can't lose it now. That would only distract Enzo, and he needs to hear whatever it is Frankie has to say. If Enzo can be strong, so can I.

"We worked it out before the wedding," Frankie explains in a voice tight with pain and fear. "He told me where to stand so I'd have a good angle. He made me swear to go to Alvarez after that and get a job with him."

"Why did he want you to do that?" Prince asks. I think Enzo is beyond the point of speaking right now.

"So I could get in close with Alvarez and kill him, too. That was the whole point. For Alvarez to die so you could take over. I swear!" he almost shrieks when Enzo aims his gun again—this time at his balls.

"Why did he need to die for that to happen? Tell me that. Why couldn't he have lived? That's where your story falls apart, fucker."

"He was sick!"

I clamp a hand over my mouth, but not before my gasp rings out. Nobody seems to notice. Prince's brows knit together, and he immediately looks at Enzo, whose face flushes a deeper red than before. "Convenient."

"It's the truth! He didn't want you to know. I'm the only one he told."

"Also convenient."

"He knew he was gonna die anyway. I swear, he didn't want you to know, and he didn't want to look weak or anything, so he didn't tell anybody. Just me. He paid me to do it all."

Is he telling the truth? I feel worse for Enzo than I ever have since he has to be just as torn as I am. No, more. It's not like I can't believe an old man was sick, especially not this one. He didn't look great, no matter how he tried to pretend he had it all together. He was imposing and well-dressed and everything, but he was also pretty thin and drawn.

It's easy for me to look back and see that. Enzo's a different story. This is the man who raised him we're talking about. A man he clearly respected and revered. It can't be easy to hear he was sick enough to pay someone to kill him.

One part of the story makes me believe it's true. He decided to use his inevitable death as a way to boost his family's position while eliminating an enemy. That's the shrewd sort of guy he was. He wouldn't get emotional or reflect on making things right before he left. He wouldn't think back on his violent life and where he could've done things differently. No, he used his remaining time to plan his own murder in hopes of killing somebody else. I could live a hundred years and never understand it.

Enzo doesn't understand it either, judging from his anger and confusion. I want to go to him. My heart's aching for him, my arms aching to hold him, to tell him everything will be okay even if, right now, he probably doesn't feel like it will.

I might be his wife, but it's not my place. Not right now. Besides, I don't want to go near him when he looks the way he does. Like he's about to explode. And good luck to anybody who happens to be in the vicinity when he does.

He shakes himself slightly like he's coming back to his senses. "Looks like you didn't do a very good job with the second half of your assignment. I had to kill Alvarez myself."

"I know." Frankie hangs his head. Sweat drips from his hair, and blood from his chin. "I don't know how they knew. Somehow, they figured out it was a setup. But I didn't tell them anything. I swear to God, I didn't tell those guys anything."

"I believe you since I'm sure they would have killed you if they'd gotten the information they wanted." Enzo backs away. "Stand up. Be a man. This won't take much longer."

"Please, man. I only did it because he told me to. He would have just had somebody else do it if I didn't."

"You could be right about that," Enzo allows. "But we'll never know, will we. Now stand the fuck up." He's not talking to me, but a chill runs up my spine just the same. I know what's coming next.

From the resigned sigh Frankie lets out, so does he. He fights his way to his feet, breathing heavy and swaying slightly once he gets his balance. For a breathless moment, the men stare at each other.

Frankie lifts his chin, and Enzo nods. "You've done your job. Unfortunately, this was only ever going to end one way for you." He raises his arm and aims at Frankie's head. There's no more begging, no more blubbering. Frankie stares down the gun, silent.

The shot rings out loud and sharp, and Frankie drops to the ground.

I let out my breath slowly, shakily taking one last look at Frankie before turning to Enzo. He doesn't move, his hand hanging by his side, the gun gleaming in the headlights. I want to go to him so much, it hurts. But I know he would hate it and hate me for it. Whatever he's going through, he doesn't want me to be a part of it. Not unless he invites me in, and I doubt he would ever do that. It would mean admitting he needs help.

"Get rid of the body," he grunts. "Alvarez, I want you to keep on ice. I might have other plans for him." I'm not sure I want to know what that means, and I doubt he would tell me if I asked. While his men get to work, he tucks his gun away. I can breathe easier once he does. Not that I think he would ever turn it on himself, but people are capable of all kinds of things when their world shatters.

And I think his just did.

VOW

30

ENZO

I'm not certain how I thought I would feel once the whole thing was over. On the way home, with my enemies dead.

I'm not a child. I left naïveté behind a long time ago. I didn't expect to feel elated. There was no fantasy about this being the end of anything. I never imagined a touching scene with my wife, gathering her into my arms as emotional music swelled. That kind of shit only happens in the movies, and this is all too real.

I did, however, expect answers. A sense of closure. Understanding of what happened that day, my grandfather's last day, a day meant to be a celebration that ended in tragedy. I hoped when all was said and done, I'd be able to grasp what went on in my grandfather's head.

I forgot there's no understanding of what went on in his head. That attempting to understand him was always a fool's errand.

At the moment, something bigger is on my mind, anyway. I can set my questions aside in favor of focusing on Alicia. "You're sure you're all right? You didn't get hurt at all?"

Instead of smarting off the way she might have done any other time, she offers a soft, understanding sort of smile. "I'm fine. You don't have to worry about me."

That's what she'll never understand. There will never come a time when I don't worry about her. Even if she were to walk out of my life, never to be seen again, not a day would pass when I wouldn't ask myself what she's doing, how she is, or where she is. Certain things, you don't need to experience to know for sure. That's one of them.

Even though Prince is driving, able to hear every word, I place a hand over my wife's stomach. "You're sure? Sometimes, things can happen, and a person doesn't know until it's too late."

"I fell on the ground. I didn't actually get hurt."

"Just the same. We're taking you to a doctor first thing in the morning," I tell her, needing to make sure she and our child are okay. She rolls her eyes and clicks her tongue, but I'm not budging on this. "I mean it. I'm taking you to a doctor, and they'll do one of those ultrasound things."

"If it makes you feel better." She covers my hand with hers, and her smile widens, making something ache deep inside my chest. It isn't a painful ache. It's rather nice—warm, almost sweet. I don't know what to do with it. And when I withdraw my hand, rattled by the intensity of my reaction, her smile slides away, and I know I've ruined something. There's no undoing it. I pull farther away, returning to my side of the back seat. I shouldn't have sat back here. I should have stayed up front instead of being so determined to make sure she was safe, whole, and well.

There's one thing I keep forgetting. I'm not meant for this life. Doting husband, concerned father, that shit. I've gone so far over the edge I can hardly remember why it was important to stay away from her. Moments like this remind me that I don't have what it takes. I'm not built the way I should be. I'm broken.

And we aren't in this for a relationship. Once she gives me what I want, that's it. Those were my terms, weren't they? I can't even stick to my own terms around her. She's worked her way that deep into the heart I was sure I didn't have.

Once we arrive at the house, I leave her at the foot of the stairs and gesture up toward the hallway. "You've had a long day. Go take a bath and get ready for bed; you need your rest."

"I'm pregnant," she reminds me while wearing that same soft, understanding smile. "Not dying."

"For once, could you do something without arguing? I have a lot that still needs to be taken care of. Word is going to spread of what happened tonight, and—"

"Enough." She raises her hand, her brows pinching together while disappointment radiates from her eyes. "Next time, all you have to do is say you want to get me out of the way so you can get some work done. It'll save us both a lot of time."

"Wait a minute."

She pauses after placing a foot on the stairs. "Which is it? Do you want me to go, or do you want me to wait a minute?"

Why is she like this? I have to grit my teeth against what threatens to spill out, thanks to her attitude. "Just go. And don't forget, I'm making you an appointment in the morning, first thing."

"Yes, sir." It's the fatigue in her voice that gets me as she walks slowly up the stairs. I know I'm right—she has to be exhausted.

You asshole. Thank her. Tell her how it felt when you didn't know whether she was hurt or safe. Tell her everything that went through your mind. Tell her how pointless everything would be if she was gone. I wish I could. I do. What's stopping me? Knowing how unfair it would be to make her care for me more than she already does. I'm no good for her. I'll only ever fuck things up, and she needs more than that. Better than me.

And I need to clear my head of these distractions. A lot of people will be asking a lot of questions after what went down tonight. I expect Rosa Martinez to be one of the first people to reach out. I promised her a lot, and she won't want to wait to collect.

I head straight for the bar and pour myself a healthy glass of whiskey before turning to Prince, holding up the bottle in a silent offer. He nods, and I set about pouring him a drink.

"You were keeping tabs on the Martinez cartel, right? They came through for us, didn't they?"

He doesn't answer right away, not until I give him a pointed look. "Well? Yes, or no?"

"Yes," he grunts. "They had the warehouse raided and hijacked a shipment last week. I gave you a report on that."

Did he? I'm starting to think I'm the one who could use a good night's sleep. The days blend together, so much so that I can't remember how long it's been since Rosa visited me here at the house. "Right, of course you did. I know she'll be on my ass to settle up now that she did her part."

"I'm sure she will, but you can handle her." He's giving me a funny look as I hand him his glass. When I raise my brows, he reads my expression for what it is. "That's what's on your mind right now?"

"Obviously. Word's going to get out, and there's going to be a lot of questions and offers and maybe a few demands for a piece of the Alvarez businesses. We have to be prepared for that." I gulp down half of my drink all at once on my way to the study.

He follows without question, waiting until I've settled in behind my desk before clearing his throat. "I'm only asking because tonight..."

"What about it?"

"Nobody would blame you if you needed a little time to wrap your head around what happened."

"What happened?" I lean back in my chair, grinning. "I won. We won. That asshole is gone. We're going to absorb his businesses after cutting off a chunk for Martinez."

"What about the rest of it?" Rather than take a seat in a chair, he perches on the corner of my desk, swirling the whiskey in his glass without having consumed any yet.

"What about it? What are you trying to get me to say?"

"It's not that you have to say anything. But I don't think anyone would blame you if you needed a minute to process what Frankie said."

"Fuck Frankie," I snarl, my reaction making his gaze widen. I'm giving myself away, but I don't care, at least not this second.

"Okay," he murmurs. "I wouldn't trust him as far as I can throw him, either. But what if what he said was true?"

"What about it? It doesn't change anything."

"Are you sure you mean that? Because personally, it changes things for me."

I ignore the tightness in my chest in favor of glaring at him. "How so? My grandfather's still dead, regardless of whether he arranged for it to happen or not."

"This isn't her you're talking to." He glances up at the ceiling. "Maybe she would believe that—though I doubt she would. But I know better. And it changes a lot for me, thinking he might have been dying, which was why he set the whole thing up. Tell me that doesn't sound like something he would do."

Everything inside me feels like it's on fire. "I can't talk about this right now."

"Eventually, you're going to have to."

"And exactly who are you all of a sudden? My therapist?"

He sips his drink, lowering the glass with a sigh. "I disagree with how he handled this. He should have been honest. He could at least have left a note, something to explain what he was thinking."

Why won't he let it go? "Too much is going on right now for me to afford the time to think about this. I'm going to need you to accept that. Do you think you can?"

He nods slowly. "Sure. Just be careful it doesn't eat a hole in you when you aren't paying attention."

"I'll keep that in mind." I empty my glass, which I then slam onto the desk. "Anything else?"

He turns the glass around in his hands. "Do you really want to know?"

"Something tells me I don't."

He snorts. "Too late. You already asked." He tosses back the rest of his whiskey, placing his glass beside mine before facing me head-on. "Why don't you give up the act and tell that girl you care about her? What's it all about anymore?"

I'm ready to punch something or, better yet, someone, and Prince is looking real tempting. "Get the hell out of my study."

"Make me."

I can't help but laugh. "Fuck off. Seriously, enough of this. We'll talk about it another time."

"I think we need to talk about it now because something became crystal clear to me tonight. You don't have to agree with me, but don't insult my intelligence by denying it. You have the right to remain silent," he adds with a smirk.

I lean back in the chair, dread swelling in me though I do my best not to show it. "Speak. But make it good."

He squirms a little like this makes him uncomfortable. "Things have changed. For you, for her. I'm the first to agree that it's bullshit how you were tricked into marrying her. Yes, I said, tricked," he's quick to add when I lower my brow. "Can we please speak plainly? I think we know each other well enough to do that. I'm not her. I know you too well. And I know that when you threw yourself at her and pushed me out of the way, she was the most important thing in the entire world. Nothing else mattered. Not Alvarez, not Frankie, not even your grandfather. Only her."

"She's carrying my child."

"I said what I said. I have never seen you like that. I didn't even know you had it in you. And I'm sure she saw it too. She's not a stupid girl, not even close. It might be a good idea to decide how you want this fucked-up relationship to go once and for all. Because I was watching her in the mirror on the way here, and when you changed your attitude, her face... crumpled."

When I remain silent, he rolls his eyes and lets out a heavy sigh. "I don't know who I'm becoming. I'm no matchmaker. But it seemed like you were being unfair to yourself, and I felt like I had to say something about it. Even if you don't see it, I do. It's all right to want her. Nobody would blame you for that. You're nobody's fool. But you'd be a damn fool to push her away if you actually care about her."

With that, he stands. "I'm going to get some sleep. If you need me, try to at least wait until morning to bother me." I hate the fact that I can't come up with something to throw in his face. I want to—badly—but I'm too tired to lie. Too tired to make sense of how far I've fallen.

I learned this evening that my grandfather was quite possibly dying and decided to use his impending death to further our family's position. I murdered our strongest rival and have every intention of absorbing his family business. I'm supposed to reflect on how deeply I've come to care for my wife?

And how much I regret hurting her?

It's a relief when my phone rings. This, I can handle. This, I can do. I clear my throat before answering. "Ms. Martinez. I thought we'd speak this evening."

31

ALICIA

"Did you sleep at all last night?" I can't help the concern that blooms in me when I look at Enzo the next morning. I had a hard time falling asleep, so I wasn't expecting him to be all fresh-faced and chipper this morning, but it's clear he never got a wink of shut-eye.

"I had a lot on my mind. Still do." He pours himself a cup of coffee and gulps down half of it before topping it off. "It wouldn't be the first time I went without sleep. Not to worry."

I'm not worried—about that, anyway. I don't know if I could put it into words even if I tried. I'm still afraid of him throwing my concern back in my face, so I won't bother.

Inside, though? I know he has to be hurting this morning. He doesn't want to think about Frankie's confession or what it means.

I want so much to ask him about it. To offer support. I'd listen to anything he has to say for as long as he wanted to talk. I only want to be here for him, the way a real wife would be. Instead, I pull water from the fridge.

"Do you want something to eat?" he asks.

I can't help but remember how protective he was last night. Why can't he be this way all the time? I could learn to like him being so concerned if I knew he wouldn't swing back and forth between caring and pushing me away. Otherwise, here I am, wondering if I can afford to let my guard down. If he'll make me regret it again.

At least I don't need to think too hard about whether I want breakfast. "No, thanks." The thought turns my stomach. I'm not such a fan of the smell of coffee right now, for that matter, and I usually love it. *Who doesn't?*

"I contacted a highly respected obstetrician with an office downtown." When I look at the clock, he reads my mind. "Office hours don't matter much when you know which strings to pull. He'll see us this morning before the office opens. Which means we need to get going soon."

It's hardly seven thirty, but I've learned to expect the unexpected. I'm already dressed for the day, and since I took a bath last night, there's no need for showering.

"I'm good when you are," I announce.

"No arguments for once?"

I hear the humor in his voice and appreciate it, but I can't manage more than a weak smile. "I'm too worn out to argue. Catch me once the morning sickness passes." And the guilt that's been eating away at me over Elena's disappearance I can't shake it. She's safe now, I'm sure, but I'm sorry for how far things went. Even when she was a nasty bitch last night—my hand is still sore from when I punched her. But damn, it felt good at the time.

Still, I know the fear she must've gone through. I felt it, too. Knowing my life was in the hands of a stranger. Being used as a pawn. I wouldn't wish that on anyone, even if she tried to seduce my husband. Maybe she learned a lesson.

The car ride might've been a bad idea, but there's no way around it. The motion from the car isn't doing me any favors. "We'll stop and get you some ginger ale if you want," Enzo offers when I can't suppress a miserable groan.

"Yeah. That might help." Even if I didn't want the soda, I wouldn't refuse. Not when he's being so sweet.

I sip it slowly on the rest of the way to the doctor's office and feel a little better once we're out of the car in the adjoining garage. It's practically empty, thanks to the early hour.

I know better than to think I'll have a moment's privacy with the doctor, so I don't bother mentioning it once we're in the office. A pretty pissed-off-looking nurse takes my vitals and asks questions in a short, businesslike tone. She doesn't look at Enzo once as he stands against the wall, arms folded. When I glance his way, I decide it's better if she doesn't look at him since he wears the expression of someone who'd throw her out the window if she makes a mistake.

Thankfully, the doctor doesn't leave us waiting long once the nurse is out of the room. "Mrs. De Luca," he says with a smile when he enters the room. "I'm Dr. Greene. It's a pleasure to meet you." I have to shake myself a little and remind myself he's talking to me. Has anybody ever called me that before?

"My husband, Enzo." I'm sure he would have introduced himself, anyway, but I sort of feel bad for this guy. Something tells me he wasn't given much of a choice whether or not he wanted to open his office this early in the morning. He's smiling, even jovial, but he's also sweating a little. It makes me wonder exactly what kind of strings Enzo pulled.

"Let's get you looked at, shall we? I understand you are a little concerned about your baby." Rather than tell him that isn't the case, I nod mutely while he wheels over the machine. He asks me to lie back and lift my shirt a little. He gives me a reassuring smile while tucking a towel into my waistband before squirting gel all over my stomach.

"Come on over, Dad." I have to turn my face toward the wall when I can't help but grin at the doctor's casual attitude. Enzo is clearly in over his head here, shifting his weight from one foot to the other and rubbing his hands together.

It's touching. I wish we had the kind of relationship where I could reach out and pull him closer to me. Where I could squeeze his hand and look into his eyes and tell him everything is fine and there's nothing to worry about. I wish. I wish it so hard.

The doctor touches the wand to my stomach, and immediately my attention goes to the monitor. Enzo stands beside me, and I'm pretty sure he's not breathing. Now I do reach for him, brushing my fingers over the back of his hand, and he's quick to grab for me.

"From what you told the nurse, you should be around twelve weeks along. Is that right?"

"I think so." After a few moments, a ghostly image appears.

"There you are," the doctor says with a smile. "There's your baby. Stay still for me, baby, so I can take some pictures and do some measurements."

"See?" I whisper to Enzo with my heart in my throat. "Everything's fine." That's my baby. Our baby. I tear my eyes from the monitor to look up at him and find him staring with his mouth hanging partly open. What is he thinking? What is he feeling?

"Can you tell yet? The sex, I mean?"

Oh, I wish that hadn't been the first thing he asked. My heart sinks, and my eyes sting, but I blink back the tears threatening to well up. I'm not going to do that here.

Dr. Greene chuckles briefly before seeming to remember who he's dealing with. His spine straightens before he clears his throat, suddenly serious. "I'm afraid not. It's a little early for that yet. Give it several more weeks, and we'll have a better idea." He moves the wand around and clicks the keyboard a few times. "It does look like we're right around twelve weeks, according to the development. Everything seems to be in order here." He asks me a few more questions about how I'm feeling, whether I'm spotting, and if there's any cramping. When I tell him everything seems fine, he appears satisfied.

Enzo, on the other hand, is not. "She's healthy? They both are? No problems?"

"None, Mr. De Luca, though I would be glad to schedule blood work to be on the safe side."

"Why can't you take blood now?" Even I cringe at the way he sounds. The poor doctor almost jumps out of his white coat.

"I-I would prefer your wife fast in advance. We could do it as soon as tomorrow morning."

"That would be fine." I look up at Enzo, who nods, satisfied.

The whole thing doesn't take more than ten minutes, with him finishing up by advising me to get rest and giving me information on diet, vitamins, and ways to help with the morning sickness. Otherwise, he leaves me with a printout from the ultrasound—granted, it doesn't look like much, but I can't help feeling like it's the most precious thing anyone's ever given me. Baby's first picture. Maybe I should start a scrapbook.

After all, if Enzo decides to take the baby and send me off somewhere, I'll want something to remember them by.

"You aren't the first father to worry like this," the doctor assures him. I want to tell him not to get the wrong idea, that he's not freaking out like this out of love.

God, I wish this could all be different. I wish I could look at him with a loving smile and know his concern was out of caring and tenderness. Luckily, the men are too busy talking to each other to notice me struggling to keep my emotions in check. I have a grip on myself by the time we leave, and I thank the nurse one last time before we go. Poor woman. I'm sure she didn't feel like coming in early.

"See?" I venture as we leave. "Everything's fine. We don't have anything to worry about, and now we know for sure how far along I am. Twelve weeks."

"There's a long way to go. Seems like forever." For somebody who just got good news, he sounds awfully grumpy.

I knew this was how it was going to be, didn't I? I have no right to act surprised now. It's not like he ever lied about the way this was going to go. He only wants to know how long it will be before he gets his heir.

I might as well not even be here.

The photo is in my lap as I sit in the passenger seat, staring down at it. *I want more for you*, I tell my baby, as tears blur my vision to the point where I can't see anymore. They roll down my cheeks and drip onto my shirt while Enzo drives, oblivious.

It isn't until I can't help but sniffle that he notices. "What's wrong? Are you in pain? Are you sick?"

"No!" I didn't mean to shout it, but I'm almost glad I did. I'm tired of having to hold everything back and pretend anything about this is normal. "I'm perfectly healthy."

"Then what is it?"

"Hormones, I guess. Don't worry about it." I turn to look out the window, knowing I should stop but knowing I can't. This is supposed to be a happy time. All I want is for us to be happy together, like a normal couple. Why do I have to want him like I do? I hate myself for it. He's never going to care.

"Hey." He pulls over and puts the car in park before touching my leg. "Are you sure nothing else is going on? What do you need? Are you hungry? Or just tired?"

"Both of those things."

"We can take care of that." My head bobs up and down because I don't trust myself to try to speak. He's so clueless. And I'm too afraid to set him straight.

"I just want—" No, I can't say it. I can't bring myself to put it into words.

"It's going to be okay." His awkward, unpracticed attempts at offering comfort make me feel worse than ever. We may as well be on two different planets; we're so out of sync.

"I just want to be happy," I finally whisper, wiping away my tears with the back of my hand.

"You will be." If only it were that easy. "Come here." He pulls me in for a tight, warm hug—and when he doesn't let go right away, another spark of hope flares to life. I close my eyes, bury my face in his shoulder, and cry for everything I'm missing. Everything we're missing. He can't even give in to happiness over being a father because he's too busy thinking about what it does for his position, his business. I don't know who I feel worse for as fresh tears begin to flow.

"I'm going to make sure you have everything you need," he promises as he strokes my hair. "You and the baby. You're going to be just fine."

"Are you glad everything's okay?" I pull back, searching his face.

When he smiles, my heart sings. "Of course I am. It's a huge relief, too. Now we know everything's going the way it's supposed to, and it's only a matter of waiting. I'm not the most patient person," he admits, and it's the closest I think he's ever come to having a sense of humor about himself.

Yet I wait for more, my heart waits for more, but there is no more. He only offers a chuckle before turning back to the windshield and putting the car in drive.

So much for that. We always feel like we're so close to connecting, but then we miss each other again. At least he seems happy, which makes me happy. I'm not so close to crying anymore by the time we make it home. "I'm pretty hungry now," I admit. "I could fix us some breakfast if you want." Because I can't admit what I really want: to spend time with him. That's it. We just went through the first ultrasound together, and it seems anticlimactic to go our separate ways now.

"I could use something to eat," he admits. "But you shouldn't have to go to the trouble. The doctor said you need to rest."

"It's fine. I think I can handle fixing a little breakfast." And just for the hell of it, once we're in the kitchen, I take an unused magnet from the side of the fridge and use it to fix the ultrasound image to the surface. So we'll both be able to see it whenever we're in here. Enzo's grin tells me it was the right thing to do.

"Maybe you should try to get some sleep before you eat anything," I suggest when I notice the shadows under his eyes. "It seems like you need that more than food."

"No, I have too much to do. I'll make it an early night." He takes off his jacket and drapes it over one of the kitchen chairs while I pull out a pan and the butter dish. Maybe French toast—I suddenly have a craving for it.

Until his phone rings, and my heart sinks, and what might have been a nice breakfast slips through my fingers. I turn in time to find him reaching into his pocket for his phone. "Do you have to?" I whisper.

"What do you mean, do I have to?"

"I just thought... we could spend a few minutes..."

He scowls before pulling out his phone anyway, checking to see who's calling. I wish I could see. "I have to take this."

"What's the point of being the boss if you're still jumping the second the phone rings?"

"Who are you to tell me when I can answer the phone?"

"I'm just saying—"

"This is about my family."

"Your family?" Though I just put it up there, I pull the photo from the fridge and hold it up in front of him. "What about this family?" Then I fling the picture at him before fleeing up the stairs. I'm not so hungry anymore.

Before I close the bedroom door, I hear his smooth, cordial voice. "Sorry, I just missed your call. What can I do for you this morning?" Nobody would ever guess he had an argument—or that he cares about anything at all.

And I remember the problem with my argument: we aren't a family. We never were.

32

ENZO

"I appreciate you agreeing to see me this soon."

"Not at all. We made an agreement, didn't we?" And I already know Rosa prefers to conduct business face-to-face. Her request for a meeting this afternoon didn't come as a surprise. "Please, come inside. Can I get you something to drink?"

"No, thank you." She looks me up and down in a cool, appraising sort of way while her men follow her into the house. "I have to say, I would never guess by looking at you that you're the man who killed Josef Alvarez last night."

"It wasn't a particularly strenuous task." I lead the way to the study, where Prince waits. "Now that all is said and done, I have to thank you for playing your part."

"As promised." We enter the room, and Prince stands, buttoning his jacket. "Now, Mr. De Luca, it's your turn to fulfill your promise."

"I appreciate people who get straight to the point." Prince extends his hand as he crosses the room. "Ms. Martinez, it's a pleasure to meet you. I'm—"

"Hello." She offers her hand but hardly makes eye contact. Distracted and perhaps not impressed with Prince. I cough to cover up a laugh as she turns to me. "So? Shall we get started discussing the terms?"

"Yes, of course." I glance at Prince, whose narrowed eyes and tightened jaw tell me he sees a challenge and wants to pursue it. He thinks he could handle her, and he's the one giving me advice about women? It's baffling.

"I've compiled information on the Alvarez shipping routes." I offer a folder to Rosa, then to Prince. "You're welcome to verify the information if you prefer."

"I prefer." Her lips twitch in the beginnings of a smile. "You've been quite thorough. I appreciate that."

"I don't believe in breaking promises." I sit on the edge of the desk, between the chairs in which she and Prince sit. "You'll find that, should we decide to continue working together, I'm not the guy who doubles back and conveniently forgets what he offered in exchange for a favor."

She nods slowly, lips pursed. "What about contracts?"

"Pardon?"

"How do you feel about them?" Her head tips to the side. "I was unaware your family drew up a contract with Alvarez but heard about it through various channels. He was due to take a slice of your transporting revenue, and now he's dead. What happens if you decide you don't like the terms of our contract?"

Prince shifts in his chair, wearing a scowl when he turns her way. I clear my throat before he can say anything stupid. "That was an entirely different situation." Dammit. I should've prepared for what would happen if the time came when the marriage contract was discovered. It was never going to stay a secret forever.

"A private situation," Prince adds.

"Alvarez signed that contract in bad faith. He knew very well he was lying on his side of the terms and made no attempt at even pretending to have misunderstood." I lift my shoulders. "It was null and void before the ink dried."

She nods slowly, her gaze locked on mine. "I see. I'm willing to let it go at that."

Prince snorts, but I ignore him. "Thank you." I make a mental note to come up with an official explanation should the subject come up again, but considering the suddenness of the question, I think I did all right. Every word was the truth, and it was enough to remind me how badly the man needed to die. He might not have killed my grandfather, but he committed other crimes against my family. We don't let that sort of thing go.

There's a knock on the study door, and in a heartbeat, Rosa's guards block the way with their bodies. "Wait, please," I call out, standing. "That's my—"

"Who are you?" Alicia demands from the hallway after finding two strange men in front of her.

"Who is this?" one of the men grunts, looking over his shoulder at me.

Instantly, my blood begins to boil. "I respect your devotion to your boss, but this is still my house. And that is my wife." The word feels foreign on my tongue.

The men step aside when Rosa waves a hand, but instead of entering the study, Alicia remains frozen in place. She's staring at Rosa, who offers a brief smile at me. "I apologize, I forgot about the arranged marriage. Congratulations again. You De Luca men know how to keep things under wraps." I can't tell if she's annoyed by that. She strikes me as someone who appreciates the value of information and doesn't like missing out.

"We kept it private," Alicia adds. Of all times for her to come downstairs and look for me. I thought she was taking a nap after disappearing upstairs for an hour. I go to the doorway when she doesn't move after another few moments.

"Can this wait?" I murmur, aware of the people behind me.

"I should've known." At least she keeps her voice low. "No wonder you had to answer the phone. She was calling."

"What?" Jesus, this is going sideways fast. "No, it's not what you think, but I don't have time to explain. We'll discuss it later."

Her dark gaze darts to Rosa and back to me. "Right. You have a lot going on right now. I wouldn't want to interrupt your time with her."

She's lost her fucking mind. Is this what I have to look forward to over the next several months? "Do us both a favor and find somewhere else to be." She's damn lucky I'm feeling patient. Still, her face crumples before she turns away, and I have to ignore the impulse to run after her.

By the time I return my attention to Rosa, she's standing. "I don't want to take up any more of your time. You were gracious enough to accept this meeting at the last minute, after all, and I'm happy with the information you've provided. I'll verify it and get back to you within a few days."

"You don't have to go," I assure her as calmly as I can. Damn Alicia for this.

"There's nothing else for us to discuss until I confirm this information." She places a hand on my arm, smiling. "Congratulations on your marriage." I don't know whether that's a sincere sentiment or if she's being sarcastic after witnessing our whispered spat. All I can do is maintain a neutral expression, confirming Rosa's promise to reach out within a few days before escorting her and her men through the front door.

Then I whirl around and immediately start for the stairs, and Prince is smart enough to stand aside. "I'm going to kill her," I growl, knowing the words are empty but needing to vocalize them just the same. I've taken as much of her bullshit as I'm willing to take.

The door is already open, and Alicia stands in the center of the room, arms folded. Before I can draw a breath, she roars at me. "What was she doing here? How can you bring her here while I'm in the fucking house?"

I'm too surprised to do anything but gape at her. "What are you talking about?"

"That woman! She's the one who was here before, isn't she? I smelled her fucking perfume before I saw her." She snorts, tossing her head. "Somebody should tell the bitch you're not supposed to take a bath in it."

"You have no idea what you're talking about."

"Did you let her kiss you this time?" Her eyes are blazing, and bright red spots color both cheeks. "Did you? Sorry I interrupted before you could do any more than that."

I'm starting to get it—and while I'm still displeased, I'm not as furious. "Are you serious? This is about you being jealous?"

"Damn you! You do not get to laugh at me!"

"It's ridiculous, though. Being jealous of her?" I look her up and down, curious. Is this the pregnancy hormones talking, or does she genuinely feel this way? When I think back, I remember she wasn't pregnant the first time Rosa paid a visit but was just as pissy over it.

"I told you, I'm not..." Her chin quivers. "I'm not..."

Can she mean it? Does she care enough to feel jealous? I can't imagine it, yet here she is, on the verge of tears. As much as I want to torment her after embarrassing me the way she did, there's a much bigger part of me feeling otherwise. Like I might want to comfort her. Clear a few things up.

I don't want to hurt her.

What the fuck is happening to me? This is the woman who lied more times than I can count. She made a fool out of me.

She's the world to me.

"Did you look around the study? Did you see we weren't alone?" I ask, quieter now. She shouldn't get this upset in her condition, but I know better than to remind her of that to calm her down. She would do anything but calm down.

She blows out a disparaging sigh. "Yeah, she had those assholes with her."

"And Prince. Prince was there." Her head snaps back. "It's true. You were too busy getting the wrong idea to notice. That was a business meeting. Rosa Martinez is head of another cartel, for fuck's sake."

Her eyes bulge. "A woman?" she whispers.

"Stranger things have happened."

"I can't think of many."

I can. Such as how much I want to hold her and laugh over this. If we were any other couple, I might be able to do that. Just a misunderstanding, honey, no big deal. I even take a step toward her—then stop myself short when she flinches. I deserve that. I've given her no reason to think I'd do anything but hurt her now.

I couldn't have fucked this up any worse if I tried.

"Why didn't you tell me that before?" she murmurs, sinking until she's sitting on the bed.

"I didn't think I had to. It's my business."

"But I'm your wife. Why am I not allowed to know?" Her brows draw together. "And don't tell me it isn't done because there's a chick leading a cartel out there. So not everybody is afraid of talking to women in your world."

"Because..." I can't remember why. I know there has to be a reason, but something in her shining, tear-filled eyes makes me forget everything I believed.

"Is it because you still don't trust me? After I've done everything I can to show you I'm sorry? I set things up with Elena and dealt with her hanging all over you even though I wanted to scratch her goddamn eyes out—"

"Did you?"

"You know I did," she snaps. "And if you don't... I don't know what to say. I thought I made it clear, but maybe I didn't."

"Made what clear?" I step in front of her, but she stares at my knees rather than look at me. "Tell me, Alicia. What did you think you made clear?"

The sound of her broken whimper goes straight to my chest, stirring an ache. "That I'm in this with you. For real. You can trust me. I'm your wife—and even if you don't love me, maybe we can still at least build something together. I could be a good wife to you. I could be who you need me to be. I only need you to give me the chance."

I don't know what makes me think there's more to it. The way she hesitated? How miserable she sounds? That could be genuine sadness. Why is it so difficult to believe her? Is it because I don't want to? Why would she want that kind of life with me after everything I've put her through? All the things I've done to her?

She lifts her head slowly. "I want more than what we have right now. I want a family. We already have all the pieces in place. Can we stop acting like enemies who live under the same roof?"

This time, she doesn't flinch away. I take her by the arms and put her on her feet before sliding my hands over her shoulders, coming to a stop when I'm cupping her face.

I don't know what to say. I've never been here before. So close to something real wanting to fall from my lips.

Instead of risking that, I pull her in and inhale her scent—better than Rosa's perfume, better than anything—before pressing my lips to hers.

33

ALICIA

I don't know what this means. Is he accepting me? I want to believe it. Why else would he kiss me?

He isn't just kissing me, either. To call this kissing would be like calling Mona Lisa a painting—true, sure, but it hardly scratches the surface. No, he's caressing my mouth with his, pouring himself into me, waking me up with every stroke his tongue makes against mine. He's kissing me like I've never been kissed before, like I didn't know was possible. My knees are weak, and my heart feels fluttery, and I hope he never stops.

I wind my arms around his neck and hold on tight to keep myself on my feet. His dick is already hard, and it presses against my hip and sends jolts of pleasure through me. He doesn't need to be threatening or hurting me. It's not only my reaction that gets him off. I'm enough.

Right now, it's enough for him to run his hands over my back, my ass, my thighs. He slides them up again and works them under my T-shirt. Every touch makes me hungrier for more, leaving me moaning into his mouth so he'll know how much I love this, need it, and how good it feels. He lifts the shirt, and I raise my arms so he can pull it off.

Once it's gone, he wraps an arm around my waist to pull me closer while his other hand cups my breasts, moving back and forth. My head falls back, and he licks the length of my throat before tracing his path back down to my collarbone—then farther south, over my chest. I arch my back, offering myself to him. I need more. I need him all over me.

He sits me on the bed and strips off his jacket before lowering himself to his knees. I pull off his tie and unbutton his shirt, kissing him and pulling him in with my legs. My hands touch bare skin, and my hunger deepens while I open his shirt, sliding it over his shoulders and down his arms. He groans when my nails move over his back and across his shoulders, so I do it again, both for him and for me, since his reactions double what I'm already feeling.

And what I'm feeling is heat. Growing, burning, raging heat that's got my pussy throbbing—but not as strong as my heart, thudding against my ribs. Not only because it feels incredible when he cups my breasts and lifts them to suck like he's starving, and I'm the only thing keeping him alive.

Because it's like it was before the wedding. When I started feeling something could be growing between us. Like he wanted me as more than a pawn. That feeling is back, and I didn't know until now how much I missed it. How much I need it. How much better it makes every kiss, touch, every flick of his tongue over my nipples. He wants to give me pleasure as he takes pleasure in me, not just take what he wants and get me off at the same time. That's everything.

And it makes me lift his head until our mouths align again. I can't kiss him hard enough. I can't hold him tight enough.

He lowers me onto the bed and follows me until we're side-by-side, facing each other. He tugs down my leggings and thong—a little clumsy, in a hurry, and I help him.

But for once, I roll him onto his back and straddle him instead of lying back and letting him take the lead. His eyes widen, but his hands continue to tour my naked body. "This is different," he whispers with a grin.

Everything's different. I'm different. I reach down between us and undo his belt, his waistband, and his zipper. Concentrating on the task at hand is difficult once he works his fingers between my lips. My pussy clenches when two thick digits enter me, sliding in deep.

"Oh... God." I close my eyes for an instant and let my attention dwindle to that single spot, to the thrusting of his fingers, before he focuses on my G-spot, pressing and massaging. I rock my hips, lost in him and the sensations he's setting off. The building heat. The delicious tension.

"I could watch you like this all day." He fondles my breasts with his other hand, rolling his thumb around my nipples before flicking and twisting them and driving me insane. His dark, knowing laughter blends with my moans. "Fucking gorgeous. So hot. Let me see you come, baby."

I was already close, but his words push me the rest of the way over the edge all at once. Suddenly, my insides are quaking, and the most mind-blowing waves of pleasure roll through me, but he won't stop fucking me with his fingers, rubbing my clit with his thumb, coaxing another orgasm from me. Greedy for the sight and sound of me, and I don't know if I'm coming again or if the first one never ended, but my back arches, and a cry of sheer relief fills the room when bliss explodes again deep in my core.

I fall forward with palms on his shoulders, gasping for breath, dazed. "So wet," he groans as he pulls himself from his shorts. "You soaked into my pants. Should've had you sit on my face so I wouldn't miss any." The thought alone makes me moan, and he chuckles against my neck.

"Are you ready to ride my cock?" He drags his head through my wetness, and I shiver as much with anticipation as from the pressure against my sensitive, quivering entrance. The promise of more, more, that's all my body wants. It's all I want. More of this. More of him. The magic of it. The way I feel fully alive and connected.

He plunges inside me and lifts his hips to fill me, sinking in deep. I bear down on him, grinding my hips, and we both moan when I reach his base. "That's right." He takes me by my hips. "Ride it. Fuck yourself on me. Let me feel you come."

I don't think I could do anything else if I wanted to. I'm helpless against him, helpless against this. With my palms on his chest, I raise myself, using him as leverage. "So nice," I whimper, grinding hard, searching for release again.

"That's right. Take me deep. Take what you need. Soak my cock." He's watching me, staring up at me as I work myself into a frenzy. I close my eyes—his grip on my hips tightens instantly, and forcefulness leaks into his voice. "No. Don't hide from me."

I can't help but obey. I never can. I watch him watching me ride, and now I'm not embarrassed. I'm not shy. I roll my hips and laugh at the way he groans. The power shift is hot, too. Everything about this, him, us together.

And he wants this. He wants me. He could've shut me down and told me he didn't want anything to do with me. He could've reminded me of the deal we made and how us being together was not part of that deal.

Instead, he kissed me. I'm moving with him inside me, working my way to another orgasm while he urges me on. He swells inside me, and his hips start to jerk like he can't help himself, and I'm going to come again. I feel it; it's happening—

"Yes!" It's a strained whisper when what I want to do is scream. I fall forward and sink my teeth into his shoulder and sob out pleasure almost too intense to handle.

His fingers dig in tighter than ever, and he groans in my ear; an instant later, a rush of warmth signals him coming. "Alicia... my God..." His arms wind around my back, and that's the best part, the way he holds me to him like I matter. He doesn't want this to end any more than I do. I wish I had been honest with him sooner.

Then again, no. Maybe it had to be this way. We had to go through what we've faced together to make this so sweet. No, it's not a declaration of love, but it's a start. It's better than living as strangers and pretending neither of us cares or wants anything better.

I'm still coming down when he gently slides out of me, then coaxes me into climbing off him. Instead of getting up and dressing, he finally gets rid of his pants and boxers, then slides between the sheets and gestures for me to join him. This is new, too. I'm almost afraid I'm going to wake up from this dream.

But by the time I'm in bed with him, his arms around me, and my head on his chest, the spell hasn't broken. I guess this must be real.

He laughs softly with his lips against the top of my head. "I should let you do the work more often. Especially when I haven't slept in days."

"Days? As in more than one day? You never said anything."

He snorts softly. "Are you surprised? I don't share much. I couldn't sleep the night before our dinner with Elena, either. Too much on my mind."

"Now you can relax a little and let go, I hope."

"Not something I'm used to doing, but I could try." His hand moves over my back in long, slow strokes. "You're the one who needs to relax now. For at least six months."

"I'll do my best."

"No getting jealous over other cartel leaders."

He can't see when I roll my eyes. "I'll do my best, so long as you don't get jealous—"

"Not gonna happen, so don't waste your breath." No, I know better.

He falls silent for so long, his hand going still, that I figure he must've fallen asleep. I wouldn't wake him up for anything and could use a nap myself, so I'm fine with drifting off like this. Even if I wasn't tired, I wouldn't move.

I'm starting to fall asleep when he speaks again. "I don't know how to do this."

"How to do what?" I whisper, opening my eyes.

"This. Us. I don't know how to do it. I want you to know that. I'm not trying to withhold shit or make you feel bad. I honestly don't know how to do this right, and that's not your fault." He grunts like he's frustrated. "I shouldn't have said anything. I'm making it worse."

"You aren't. Tell me what's on your mind." I push myself up on my elbow. "If you want to. I'm here."

"It's something I feel like you deserve to know. I... told you my mother was killed."

"Yeah, the night in the kitchen."

He nods. "Right. She was murdered." He pauses to take a deep breath. "By my father."

Instinctively, I know he won't like it if I react too strongly. I would normally gasp and get upset and tell him how sorry I am. I catch myself before that happens and murmur, "That's terrible."

It gets worse. "He tried to kill me, as well. He left us on the side of the road like we were trash."

"Oh, Enzo." I can't help the tears welling up in my eyes. There's no stopping them.

He stiffens at the sight. "I'm not looking for pity."

"I don't pity you." I pity the little boy. I'd ask exactly what his father did, but he'd tell me if he wanted me to know. I'm not going to pick at the wound. Maybe he'll tell me one day.

"You deserve to know, is all. I don't have the first idea of how to be a husband or a father. But... I want to be. I want our kid to know how it feels to have a family. Not a bunch of bodyguards who work for him, either. Parents."

"I understand. I want that, too."

"With me?" he asks as if he doesn't understand or is afraid to believe it. "You're sure about that? Even after what I just told you? Christian, my brother, he's a lot like me. Whatever is fucked up about us has to be partly genetic, right? Are you sure you want me after knowing that?"

"I'm sure." I run my hand down his face before letting it come to rest on his chest. His heartbeat is strong and steady. "You're you. You aren't what happened to you. Not unless you want to be. And as for genetics... we'll work with what we have."

He takes my hand and lifts it, pressing his lips to my palm. "Thank you."

"For what?"

The arm around me tightens, pulling me closer to him until my head is on his shoulder. I wait for an answer, but none comes—and when I cautiously lift my head to find out why, I find him sleeping.

VOW

34

ENZO

"Wow."

I look up from the stacks of boxes crammed into the living room to find Alicia frozen in surprise halfway down the stairs, wearing nothing but a nightshirt and a stunned expression. I didn't expect her to come down this early in the morning and had planned on carrying everything to my study to have it out of the way before she was awake.

Now her eyes bulge at the stacked boxes. "You said you were sending for all of his files, but I didn't think it would be this much."

I can imagine how she wouldn't. There are thirty-seven boxes, all of them delivered less than an hour ago by highly trusted men who've been on the family payroll for years. It took a great deal of trust for me to allow them to load the files into boxes, then to fly with them across an ocean and unload them here.

"You know the older generation," I remind her with a sigh. "He liked to do everything on paper."

"Now I know why he needed that big house, to store all that paper."

"There's a good chance I didn't need most of this, but he wasn't the greatest at keeping things organized."

"What a combination. Fully analog, and he had no organizational system."

"What did he care? He wasn't the one who would have to comb through everything once he was gone." Even though I'm more than slightly irritated with him, I can't help but experience a twinge of fondness. He did things his way and refused to bend to pressure. He must have been doing something right since he grew our business to what it is today almost single-handedly.

"I give him credit. I do. I know I sound critical." She runs her hand over one of the boxes before turning to me with a quirked eyebrow. "Well, it seems like we have a lot of work to do."

"You don't have to help me with this."

"What, I'm going to let you go through a million boxes all by yourself? Please. Just tell me what to look for, and we'll get the work done twice as fast."

She pauses in the act of lifting the lid from one of the boxes, turning to me, her teeth sinking into her lip. "That is unless you don't want me to. I understand if you don't."

"No, that's not it." And it isn't, which in itself is surprising enough. "I didn't expect you to want to help."

"You don't have to do everything all by yourself." With that, she removes the lid from a box and pulls out an armful of files. "So what are we looking for?"

"That's the thing. I'm not exactly sure."

"Ah, so we're looking for a needle in a haystack, but we don't know what the needle looks like? Even better." But she's grinning as she sinks to the floor, sitting cross-legged with the files stacked beside her.

I can trust her, can't I? It seems like I should. She is my wife. She's witnessed me doing terrible things.

I've done terrible things to her.

Yet here she is, eager to help. I'm not sure I'll ever understand her.

"You see, shortly before his death, he made a series of large payments. I know two of those payments went to Frankie." His name curdles in my mouth, even now that he's dead. Just because he paid the price doesn't mean my attitude toward him has softened any. I'm still not completely sure I believe his story. Why would the man want to die? Was he sick? If he was, why wouldn't he tell me? That's the question at the heart of all of this, the one that sticks in my craw and keeps me up at night, thinking. Didn't he trust me? Shouldn't I have been let in on the secret, considering I was meant to take his place? It might have been nice to be clued in so I could prepare myself. This could all have been done so much more intelligently.

Instead, I have hours' worth of searching to do with no clear goal in sight.

"The payment went to someone with the initials D.S.," I conclude. "So that's where I'm starting. Anything to anyone with that name. An invoice, a receipt, anything you can find."

"You've got it." Using the scrunchie on her wrist, she gathers her hair into a bun on top of her head, then cracks her knuckles before flipping open the first folder. My chest swells at the sight.

The next couple of hours is spent mostly silent, with only the sounds of flipping pages and the occasional frustrated sigh punctuating the quiet. The guards on duty are outside the house—that was my specific request since I don't necessarily want them hanging around while I go through Grandfather's private things. For a moment, I can almost pretend we're a normal couple working to solve a problem together. It isn't as easy to believe that when we're surrounded by bodyguards.

"Wow, some of this is older than either of us. It looks like it was typed out on an actual typewriter." She shakes her head in wonder, thumbing through a stack of stapled pages. "Old contracts."

"He didn't believe in throwing anything away—which I suppose is part of the reason we're surrounded by a forest worth of paper."

"It's interesting, though." She runs her fingers over the page she landed on and smiles. "It's like touching history. I know this isn't exactly the Declaration of Independence, but it is an old contract signed more than thirty years ago. I wonder what life was like back then."

"Probably not very much different than it is now—only back then, he had no choice but to keep everything in hardcopy." I, on the other hand, am going through files from a few years ago. "This? Could have been scanned and shredded."

She pulls an empty box down beside her and refills it, then pushes it aside before tackling another. "Be careful," I warn, glancing up from my work. "I don't want you lifting any of these boxes while they're still full."

"I promise I'll be careful." Is that fondness in her voice, in her smile? Do I want it to be?

She settles in with another stack of folders, and the pleased little noise she makes grabs my attention. "This is a lot more recent. Thank goodness."

"Yes, there aren't even any dates on the folders."

"No offense, but I can almost imagine him laughing to himself over what a mess he knew he was leaving for you. I know he probably wouldn't do that," she's quick to add when I frown. "But it would be kind of funny if he did."

"That wasn't his way. It's more likely he thought he was going to live forever."

"I can imagine that, too," she decides, and we exchange a smile before diving back in.

It isn't another few minutes before she gasps. "Wait a second. You said D.S.?"

My head snaps up, and I nod. "Yes. Why?"

"What if it stood for Doctor something?" she asks, holding up a bill. "Like Dr. Santoro?"

"Let me see that." I all but rip the page from her hand and scan the print. It's a bill for a treatment, though the nature of the treatment isn't specified.

"It would make sense," she muses as I read. "If he was sick like you-know-who said."

"Frankie. You don't have to tiptoe around his name."

"I wanted to be sure, is all."

"I appreciate that." I can't tear my eyes away from what's before me. Is this it? Is this what he was hiding?

"Let's start looking at more recent files," she suggests. "Pare this down some. If he was this meticulous with his records, he would've saved every bill and correspondence."

"Good thinking." We get to work identifying files from the past few years, which greatly reduces the number of folders to look through.

"I thought there was like universal healthcare in Europe," she muses as we pull files.

"To a point. Some services aren't covered."

"What if this guy was a specialist of some sort?" Yes, that would explain why Grandfather would be billed for services. I don't like the implications, but in the end, the result is the same. The man is dead.

Within twenty minutes, we have a stack of folders between us. Now it's almost like a game, finding the doctor's letterhead and pulling the pages free once we do. My heart sinks a little each time we find the name, however. I can't help it.

Was my grandfather dying all that time?

By midmorning, I'm left holding a stack of bills. "He visited the doctor twice a month by the end," I murmur, staring at the dates once we've organized everything chronologically.

"That's not something someone does when they're well." She touches my shoulder, allowing her hand to linger. "I'm sorry."

"For what? You didn't do anything." I regret it as soon as it's out of my mouth. What a shitty thing to say. Yet she doesn't back down, only tightening her hold on me a bit.

"I know it isn't easy, but I'm sure he had a good reason for not telling you."

"That doesn't matter. I don't care what his reasons were." My fist clenches and crumples the page I'm holding. "He should've told me. Why did he keep it a secret?"

"Was it a secret, though? Really?"

Her gentle question cuts me to the core because she's right. I heard the man's coughs. I even noticed once or twice how much thinner he seemed toward the end. Why did I say nothing? Because I knew he would lash out if I did. "If I so much as hinted at him looking poorly or sounding bad, he would've had my balls in a vise."

"I have no doubt about that," she murmurs. "Men like him don't want to be seen as weak, even by their own family. Especially not, I think."

"Why do you think that?"

I look up from the papers to find her frowning, thoughtful. "He'd want you to believe he had everything under control. When you live your whole life giving off this strong, powerful aura, who does it make you when you aren't strong or powerful anymore? Who are you? That's a big, scary question for anybody to wrap their head around. He might not have wanted to admit it even to himself that he was sick."

"I should've said something."

"Hey." She sits beside me in the middle of so much paper, so many mementos from a life now over. "Don't do that to yourself. You know he would've told you to fuck off or something like that."

"Yes, something like that," I admit. "But I could've tried."

"You can't blame yourself. He had his reasons for keeping it from you—and in the end, isn't that his right? It was his life. He had the choice of whether he wanted anyone to know."

"I would've appreciated a heads-up, at least. He knew what his death would mean to me." I drop the rest of what I'm holding in favor of lowering my head into my hands and closing my eyes. It's all so complicated. He lied to me. Alicia lied. Where's the truth? Is there such a thing? How do I know who to trust?

She ponders this for a silent moment while rubbing my back in slow circles. I don't have it in me to make her stop. I don't want her to, either. "He believed you could face whatever came next."

"That's generous of you, but you have no way of knowing that."

"Don't I?" She nudges me until I look at her. The softness and warmth in her smile take my breath away. "Let's say Frankie was telling the truth, and the assassination was set up by your grandfather. Do you think he would've gone through with it if he didn't think you could handle the family once he was gone? I can't believe that. He trusted you. He knew you would step up and take control. And you have. Look at how you've risen to the occasion."

Is she for real? How can she mean that after everything she's been through? After everything I've put her through? Is this another lie, a way of getting closer to me so her life will be easier?

Something inside me recoils from the question. There's nothing but sincerity radiating from her smile and gentle touch. I find myself leaning into that touch, into her, before I know what I'm doing. I didn't mean to allow her to wrap her arms around me, but that's what she does. I settle in against her, and she holds me, not saying a word. She doesn't need to. This is more than enough. I can almost believe she has what it takes to heal my blackened heart when she enfolds me in her arms and allows me to process everything.

"I'm with you," she whispers after what feels like a long time but isn't nearly long enough. "I'm here. And we'll get to the bottom of this together."

Yes. I want that, too.

35

ALICIA

"I wish I understood. It doesn't seem like something he would do." Enzo joins me at the stove while I scramble eggs. One of the few things I'm actually good at cooking. Since he pulled back the number of guards around the house, it's easier to feel comfortable hanging around in nothing but a nightshirt. We could be an actual, normal couple getting ready to eat brunch.

Except for the way he can't let go of his grandfather's final wishes—and whether or not things actually unfolded the way it's looking more and more like they did. He can't accept it. "It doesn't make any sense."

"Maybe because you've known him for so long."

"What do you mean?" There's a difference in the way he asks that. No demand, no edge of a threat in his voice. We've come a long way. I wonder if he notices.

"It's easier for me to understand. And I do. I got it right away." He grunts, and I glance his way. "I'm sorry. But it's true. Everything clicked into place for me as soon as I heard it."

"That makes one of us because I can't make it click into place."

"I know. And I'm sorry." I take the eggs off the heat and slide bread into the toaster. I don't think it's ever been used before—it's practically sparkling. Like so much of this kitchen is only for show.

He sips his coffee, staring at nothing. His brows are knitted together in frustration, and he keeps shaking his head slightly. "I just don't get it. Doesn't seem like something he would do—at least, not to me."

"Like I said, it's because you knew him. And you loved him, and that's good. You're lucky you had somebody like that in your life."

He laughs softly, like the word love never came into it, while accepting the plate I hand him. "I should be cooking for you. You need your rest."

"I'm pregnant, not sick." And even though the thought of eating breakfast earlier was enough to turn my stomach, today's bout with morning sickness has passed. Now I have a raging appetite. "And no offense, but we both know you can't cook."

"What, you mean there's more to it than ordering something on an app?" I'm surprised at his little joke. It sounds good, and it feels good. I don't like to think of him wallowing in this. If he can make little jokes, he's not completely gone, not totally lost in his troubled thoughts.

And he's sharing them with me. He's opening up to me. It's probably wrong for me to revel in that, considering how upset he is, but there's no stopping that little part of me that cheers every time he shares a little more of his inner thoughts.

We sit down at the table, facing each other. "This is very good," he grunts between forkfuls of egg. He then slathers butter and Jelly on a slice of toast. It's good to see him eating with gusto. I'm sure knowing Alvarez isn't a problem anymore goes a long way toward his change in mood.

"I can fumble my way around the kitchen if I have to. I guess I never had much of a chance to learn how to cook."

"We'll have to give you the chance."

"You want to keep me barefoot and pregnant, is that it? Chained to the stove?"

His smile widens. "Using a chain just long enough that you can make it to the bedroom." I almost choke on my eggs, and he laughs softly. "I used to hear that one sometimes, growing up."

"Let me guess. One of your grandfather's pearls of wisdom."

"Yes, actually. I did hear that from him."

"He was a charmer."

He nods, smirking. "He had his good points, too. I know that might not be easy for you to accept, but he was a good man in his own way." He's still grieving, so I'm not going to argue. I find it hard to believe that man had a shred of goodness in him, no matter how many diamonds he gave me for my wedding.

"Like I said, I didn't know him like you do, so it's easier for me to imagine he would make a move like that. If he knew he was dying—" he flinches, and I hate to see it "—and I'm sure if he was as devoted to your family as I think he was, he'd want to find a way to make his death benefit you somehow."

He stares down at his now empty plate, his fists sitting on either side. "And he never thought about what that would mean or how it would make me feel. Witnessing his assassination."

True, and I can't get past that part, either. Talk about cold-blooded. But still… "He knew you could handle it. He knew you would do the right thing when the time came, and you have. I'm sure he would be proud of the way you've handled all of this." I take his plate and mug and put them in the sink along with mine.

He's still sitting at the table when I turn around, and I go to him, placing my hand on the back of his neck. "I wish he hadn't done it this way," I whisper. "And I'm sorry he did. But he knew you could handle it. He trusted you. He believed you could lead this family."

He turns in his chair all at once and winds his arms around my waist, resting the side of his face against my stomach. It takes my breath away, how suddenly it happens, how my heart swells, how joy fills me. I take the chance of running my fingers through his hair, and when he doesn't pull away, I close my eyes and focus on soaking in the moment, not pushing anything, just being here. Right now, there's nothing but the two of us holding each other, and nothing in the world has ever felt so good. Like this is how it's meant to be, the way it's supposed to be for us. Holding each other, taking refuge in each other when we need to.

It isn't long before something else flares to life, and all it takes is the slightest shift of his hands over my back. The way his fingers press in with need before he lifts his head, staring up at me. He pushes his chair back but remains seated, pulling me around in front of him between his spread thighs.

He nudges me back slightly, and I follow his lead, sitting on the edge of the table. For a while, it's enough for him to just touch me, neither of us saying a word. I lean back on my elbows and watch him as he works my nightshirt over my thighs. The familiar heat is there, sure—it takes nothing for him to wake my body up. There's more to it, though, a tenderness I've never felt from him. Not now, not while he's touching me and kissing his way up the insides of my legs. There isn't that sense of demand or ownership. As much as I like it when he takes me forcefully, I like this, too. I could learn to love it.

I hold my arms out to him because there's nothing I want more now than to hold him. To touch him. I can't put a finger on why or where any of this is coming from exactly. Maybe it's all the feelings I've had for him all along coming to the surface, rushing forward now that all the walls between us have crumbled. All the pent-up, held-back emotion is free, and we have so much time to make up for. It's scary, giving into this, letting myself feel this way. I don't know whether this is going to end up hurting me worse than ever, opening myself and letting him into my heart. I only know nothing could stop me.

I could scream with happiness when he stands and lowers himself over me. Instead, I sit up and wrap my legs around him while my arms do the same. He buries his hands in my hair and covers my mouth with his, kissing me deeply before breaking the kiss and tipping my head back so his lips can trail over my throat.

"Oh, Enzo..." I breathe, and he shudders when the evidence of his arousal makes contact with my aching pussy. I can't get enough of touching him, my hungry hands running over his shoulders and back, over his ass, anything I can reach. It's the sweetest indulgence, made sweeter when he teases my breast with one hand. He groans, and so do I, both of us grinding our hips, gently humping each other.

He lifts his head just far enough to meet my gaze and what I see there makes my heart skip a beat. "Alicia..." he whispers, already breathless, his voice already strained. I tighten my legs, drawing him closer, and he sighs before capturing my mouth again, plunging his tongue inside, enfolding me in his arms. I moan into his mouth, and he responds in kind, the pressure from his dick increasing. It's so sweet and so hot at the same time. My pussy is aching to the point of pain, and wetness flows from me in anticipation of what's about to happen.

He pulls my panties to the side and frees himself with the other hand. I gasp, straining against him when he drags his head through my wetness. I've never needed anything so much as I need him right now.

And he rolls his hips and fills me all at once. I could scream, I could cry. I could roar out my triumph because this is what I needed. The two of us locked together like this, moving as one. I needed him staring deep into my eyes as he connects us again and again, his lips brushing over mine, our breath mingling between us as the heat builds and grows. As he touches me deep inside, so deep. Every time he grinds against my clit, he pushes me higher until there's nothing that matters but the tension building in my core and what I see in his eyes. Something I always wanted to see, something I wished so hard was there. I see it now, and my heart is so full, swelling, making it difficult to breathe.

I'm going to come. I feel it, just beyond my fingertips. I cling to him, and he holds me close, rocking me slowly, every stroke bringing me closer to the edge. And when I fall to pieces, it's in his arms, shaking and moaning his name.

I'm still trembling from the aftershocks when he pulls out. My heart sinks a little until he holds out his hand. "Come with me." I place my hand in his and put my feet on the floor, ready to follow him anywhere. Only my legs are still a little shaky, so he takes pity, lifting me in his arms and carrying me through the kitchen, the living room, then up the stairs. He doesn't say a word. I don't need him to.

Instead of taking me to my room, he walks passed the open door and to his suite, where he sits me down on the bench at the foot of the bed and drops to his knees. Now he undresses me, his hands roaming my body as he lifts the nightshirt over my head, then lowers my panties. He kisses his way up my body, and I lean back until my head is on the bed. He buries his face between my breasts, and I hold him there, whimpering, moaning out my pleasure. Pleasure he gives me, lapping at me, teasing my nipples with his tongue and even his teeth, then moving farther up to my throat and finally my mouth.

He plunges his tongue inside again, in time with his dick entering me. He takes it slow, almost torturing me with every inch he gives me, then takes away. I tease him back with my tongue, breaking our kiss to flick the tip over his lips until he groans helplessly. His eyes open and lock on mine, and a shudder runs through me, curling my toes. I close my legs behind him, pulling him deeper, demanding more. More of him, more of this, more of us.

The familiar pressure is starting to build again, the unbearable tension, and I want him to come with me. I move my hips, grinding them with every stroke, every time our bodies connect. He picks up his pace, and I know he's getting close, too. I run my hands through his hair, gasping every time he drives himself into me harder, faster. "Come with me..." I gasp, so close.

"Look at me. Just at me." With his face inches from mine, he stares into my eyes, and I do the same, lost in him, lost in this. I'm torn between craving release and hoping this never ends.

But it's going to end, and soon, the tension is building until I can't take it. I want to come—I chase it. I need it. I need to come in his arms again.

And when my whimpers turn to cries, he follows me until the wave builds to its peak—then crashes, leaving me sobbing his name as delicious waves roll through me. He buries himself deep, grunting out his release and filling me with his cum. It leaks out between us, but he doesn't pull away, holding us together, breathing hard against my neck, pressing his lips to my skin again and again.

"Alicia... oh God..." he groans. I only smile, nuzzling him, holding him close. So close.

If we have nothing else, we have this. And I intend to hold on for as long as I can.

VOW

36

ENZO

"You didn't have to do this."

"Sure, I did." Alicia lifts an eyebrow at me as the jet's landing gear touches down. "What, did you think I was going to miss a chance to fly to Italy again?"

"You know what I mean. You're missing school."

"I've already missed plenty of school—and we made an arrangement with them, right? I'm not worried about it."

It seems no matter how many arguments I make, she has a counter-argument prepared. If I didn't know better, I would think she'd already thought this through before we ever took off.

Who am I kidding? I know she has. It's who she is.

"You can wait at the house. I can have you driven—"

"You're not getting rid of me, so you might as well not bother trying." I recognize the firm set of her jaw and the steely look in her eyes. I'm not getting around her. I'm not sure I want to, either.

At the end of the day, there might be something to be said for having someone by my side at a time like this. Is this what it means to not be alone? Is this why it's so important for some people to have someone in their life? I always told myself I was beyond that, that I was a curse. It isn't like I ever had a solid example of how to be a good husband. I imagined anyone I met would be better off without me.

But no matter how I try to push her away, she keeps coming back. She insists on being part of my life, standing beside me as I go through this.

"So long as you can stand back and allow me to do what needs to be done."

"I won't get in your way."

I'll have to take her word for it.

We're silent along the way to the doctor's office. There's nothing to be said, really. She knows what I'm thinking—if anything, it's unnerving, the sense of being seen so thoroughly. Understood. Yet she has the tact and intelligence not to make a thing of it. She keeps to herself, as I do, but that's all right. I prefer it that way.

I already did my homework on where the office is located, the doctor's history—everything I could find online. It seems he's highly respected and handles a rather exclusive clientele. In other words, patients with the sort of money my grandfather had. He operates out of a small villa on a lake not twenty minutes from the estate. Convenient for all those trips grandfather took.

When we enter, an attractive middle-aged woman immediately jumps up from her chair. "*Scusi—*"

"Do you speak English?" She nods. "Good. I would rather my wife understand without my having to play interpreter. I'm here to see the doctor."

"What is your name?"

"Enzo De Luca." Her eyes widen as I expected. "Yes, my grandfather was a patient. That's what I've come here to discuss with the doctor."

"It is… confidential." Yet I can tell from her sort of vague, half-hearted reaction that she knows it's no use. She's only saying what she knows must be said. If this woman is at all familiar with my family, she has to know it's no use trying to dissuade me from getting the answers I want.

I'm ready to draw my gun in case that convinces her, but a door behind her swings open before I can make a move. A gray-haired gentleman in a suit and white coat regards us. "Mr. De Luca. Your grandfather told me to expect you."

He's an old man, around the same age my grandfather was. A doctor of his age would be full of secrets. I wonder how many of them he plans on taking to his grave, a grave he'll reach much sooner than planned if he so much as considers withholding information from me now.

He steps aside so Alicia and I can enter his office, and I get a quick look at his worried assistant before he closes the door. "So my grandfather told you to expect me?"

"He spoke very highly of you." He has a gentle, paternal energy about him. I'm sure he thinks that will get him somewhere.

"He didn't think highly enough of me to be honest with me, though, did he?"

The old man winces in obvious discomfort. The light on his desk reflects in his glasses as he removes them, cleaning them on his necktie. "He did not share his inner thoughts with me, Mr. De Luca. I cannot say for sure what they consisted of."

My patience is already wearing thin. "What about his physical condition? Are you in a position to discuss that?"

"Mr. De Luca, you must understand. Confidentiality is key."

"What about this?" Alicia gasps softly when I pull my gun and aim it at the old man's head. "How does this stack up to confidentiality?"

He holds up his trembling hands. "Please, there is no need for—"

"Don't tell me what there is and isn't a need for," I snap. "Now, you listen to me. I want you to tell me exactly why he was seeing you. What was wrong with him. All of it. Or else you and that woman out there won't live to see tomorrow. Do you understand?"

"He was very ill."

It turns out confidentiality doesn't matter so much when a man is staring down a gun. "In what way?"

He sighs wearily. "Your grandfather suffered from late-stage lung cancer. Inoperable and too far gone by the time he came to see me. Perhaps if he'd been here sooner... there is no way of telling."

The coughing. Dammit, I knew there had to be something to it. Alicia barely chokes back a groan.

"But people live with lung cancer all the time, don't they? It doesn't mean—"

He shakes his head slowly, his already wrinkled face more deeply lined, thanks to the way it sags. "I'm afraid not. At maximum, he had a month left—but I'm afraid he would have been heavily medicated all the while."

He sits back in his chair, sighing again. "As it was, he required a rather high dosage of narcotics to simply remain upright, to keep from living in bed."

My hand is shaking, and the gun along with it. Why is my hand shaking? "He was in that much pain?"

"I'm afraid so. You see, the cancer had already spread to his bones. Before long, he would have been unable to function at all due to the amount of medication it would have taken to keep him out of pain. He would have been unaware of his surroundings. Hallucinating."

"Jesus," Alicia whispers. I can't bring myself to make a sound. He was dying. He had a month to live, and that month would have been spent in excruciating pain. I might not be a doctor, but I know what happens when cancer spreads to a person's bones. I've heard of the pain. No doubt he wouldn't have wanted to go out that way. He only wanted to be in control of the way things ended. The way he always needed to be in control of every aspect of his life. His family.

"I am going to pull your grandfather's file," the doctor explains. He hasn't taken his eyes off the gun yet, and I can't say I blame him. "Inside is a letter he instructed me to give you if and when you came to me." He glances down at one of his drawers, then back up at the gun. "I'm going to open the drawer and pull the file out. I have no weapons here."

"Do it," I bark.

He opens the drawer slowly and breaks eye contact only long enough to look down to where the file waits. He places it on the desk—it's fairly thick—then slides it across. "The letter is inside the folder. It's sealed in its original envelope." Yes, an envelope bearing my grandfather's handwriting, so neat and precise.

"Everything you need to know is in that folder," the doctor tells me. "X-rays, scans, all of it. He paid me to keep this quiet. If you wish to have the money back—"

"Shut up. This isn't about the money. Do you think my family can't afford it?"

"No, of course, that isn't what I was thinking."

I stand, and Alicia follows suit. "If I am in any way dissatisfied with this, I will make a return visit. Do you understand?"

"Yes, Mr. De Luca." His voice shakes slightly now, but that could be relief at knowing we're about to leave.

I don't acknowledge the assistant on the way out the door. All that matters is getting to the car, so I can read the letter in private. Alicia will be there, but I can't very well tell her to wait outside.

Still, it's as if she reads my mind. "Would you rather be alone?"

"No. There's no need for that." It's as if her offer spurs me to action. I open the envelope and withdraw a single folded sheet of paper.

Enzo,

If you're reading this, the plan was successful. I know you and your temper, and I'm sure you want to know why. I've done everything I could over the years to teach you to be the man you need to be to do what needs to be done. This is another one of those lessons. A man deserves to decide how his life ends on his terms, and that's no one's business but his own. If he can find a way to benefit his family when it is clear the end is inevitable, so much the better. That is what I've had to do. I'll be damned if I turn into some drooling, semi-conscious thing. I will go the way I want to go, and I will protect my family.

That means arranging for my assassination during your wedding, which will give you the ammunition you need to take down your adversaries. I leave this letter with the doctor prior to boarding the jet for Miami. I am well aware of what awaits and go into it of my own free will.

Now, it's your turn to do the protecting. I can think of no one better suited to take care of our family. -Grandfather

And that's it. No other thoughts, no further instructions. No advice, nothing. Not that I would expect him to give in to cheap sentimentality, not even now.

If anything, I'm proud of him. He went out on his own terms and didn't change anything about himself in the process. Yet somehow, I don't feel any better than I did before entering the doctor's office. It doesn't change anything. He isn't here, and he made something of a fool of me in the process.

Though in the end, the result is the same. I wanted to rid myself of Alvarez, and I did. I've also cleared the way for my family and our associates to absorb Alvarez's business, including the manufacturing of the product he was so proud of.

The thought of him has me pulling out my phone and calling Prince, waiting for word in Miami. "Send the body to the family. Include a message."

"What would you like it to say?"

"What was theirs is now ours. Either they comply or they die. Otherwise, they're safe. I have no more business with them."

"Consider it done." Then he adds, "And you?"

I reach out, finding Alicia's hand resting on the seat. She closes her fingers around mine, and the knot in my stomach loosens a fraction. "I'll be fine."

"Fair enough. See you when you get back."

Yes, because my life is more there now than it is here. That townhouse, which was supposed to be a temporary resting place, is almost home, and that's because of the woman seated beside me.

The woman I would have been able to do none of this without. The woman carrying my child. My future.

Our future.

EPILOGUE
ALICIA

Here I am again, surrounded by papers, books, and an endless list of work.

This time, I feel better about it. This time, I'm working like this in hopes of getting ahead of things for when the baby comes in a few months. I absentmindedly rub my growing bump as I scroll through a syllabus on my laptop with the other hand, making notes, trying to break the work down day-to-day, week-to-week so I know the milestones I have to hit.

I wouldn't have it any other way. Now that I'm back in school full-time, I have everything I need or want. An attentive husband, a healthy baby, and a future to look forward to.

At times, I still wonder if I should pinch myself. Can this be my life? There's no scraping by, no staying up late to go over my already stretched budget to see if I can stretch it just a little further before it breaks. Instead, if I stay up late, it's because my husband can't keep his hands off me. I don't have to think twice before making even the most everyday purchases. I don't have to deny myself anymore.

I still can't believe this is reality. Like my nightmare turned into the most incredible dream imaginable. I'd better never wake up.

"I thought I would find you here." I look up to see Enzo standing in the doorway, smiling at me. That's another thing I can't quite wrap my head around. My husband, smiling lovingly at me. Instead of locking me in here like he did in the beginning, we decided to turn this room into sort of an office. I have my desk, my computer, the whole nine yards. We still managed to keep the bed in case of any guests. The corkboard in front of me is covered in notes, reminders, and a calendar covered in ink.

And a sonogram image of our little girl.

I was so scared Enzo would be upset when he found out we weren't having a boy, but nothing could have been further from the truth. "We'll just have to try again," he told me at the time. Sure, I already knew he'd want to keep trying until we had a son, but there was no threat in what he said. No cruelty, no *silent or else* attached to it. He sounded like any other happy husband.

And in the weeks since, he's only warmed up more and more to the idea. Already, he wants to decorate the baby's room in nothing but pink, and he's wondered aloud more than once how old she'll be before he buys her first pony.

I can only laugh at those questions and his ideas, but it's always done with love. I love seeing him like this. I love watching him reveal a little more of himself to me all the time. He doesn't have to be anybody he isn't. He only needs to be himself. That's enough for me.

Not that he's changed his ways. Now that he's wiped out Alvarez and nobody else has stepped up to challenge the De Lucas, there's more work than ever and more people to keep in place. I might not have agreed with his grandfather on anything, but he was right about one thing: Enzo has what it takes to lead the family.

Right now, he's not thinking about the family—not that part of it, anyway. It's our little family he's more concerned with. "I'm busy!" I tell him with a laugh when he joins me, rubbing my belly from behind while nuzzling my neck. "Come on. I have to get this finished."

"You have months until the baby is born. Why are you in such a hurry?" He inhales deeply and growls. "Why do you smell so good?"

"I want to make sure I have all of this taken care of so I can enjoy her." And I'm not delusional. I know having a newborn is going to change my life in ways I can't imagine.

The way Enzo has changed my life. Enzo grunts and growls like an animal and starts tugging at my dress, pulling it up over my thighs and running his hands over my skin. No matter how many times he touches me, it's never enough. I still tingle every time.

"I want to enjoy you," he growls in my ear before finally pulling me out of the chair and pressing himself against me. There's no mistaking what's poking me in the ass.

"Yes, you feel ready," I observe with a snicker, even though I can't pretend I don't love it. He pulls me over to the bed, and I laugh and only pretend to fight him off.

"I can't help it." He works the dress up over my hips, then my belly, and I raise my arms so he can take it off completely. There's no point in even trying to pretend I don't want him—my hormones are off the charts, for one thing. For another, I can't pretend it doesn't feel good to be wanted like this.

He turns me around and drops to his knees, rubbing a hand over my belly while looking up at me. "I walk around with a hard-on half the time. Just the thought of you carrying my child like this. All I want to do is sink into you."

I run my hands through his hair, smiling down at him. "What was your excuse before I started showing?"

"Knowing you would eventually?"

By the time he nudges me onto the bed, I'm laughing helplessly. "I love you." I giggle.

Surprise steals my breath and cuts off my laughter. Now there's nothing but silence—that and the frantic beating of my heart. I didn't mean to say it. Neither of us has said anything close since the wedding. It just came out. I couldn't help it. Shit.

He goes still, staring down at me. Should I say something? Should I apologize? "I... uh..." I whisper, but I can't think of anything to say.

As it turns out, I don't need to come up with anything. "I love you, too."

I let out a shaky breath, staring at him, waiting for him to laugh or sneer or something. But he doesn't. All he does is smile, and it's warm, genuine, and sweet.

"Really?"

"Really. I love you." The words are a little strained, like he's not used to saying them. But he means it; I feel it in the way my heart swells, in the peace that washes over me. The last puzzle piece has fallen into place, and the picture is complete. We are a family, really and truly, and we always will be. And now I know in my heart we won't try for another baby just because I didn't give him the son he wants. We'll try again because we want to grow our family. Because we want our love to live on in our babies, and it will grow as they grow.

Happy tears fill my eyes when I sit up and reach for him. "Then you'd better get over here and take me right now."

"I thought you were in a big hurry to get your work done," he reminds me with a chuckle as I undo his belt.

"I have all kinds of work I need to get done," I tell him with a grin as I drop his pants. "Right now, you're at the top of my list."

And he always will be.

∽

Thank you for reading Savage Vow, if you haven't met Enzo's brother Christian yet, you can read his story in Perfect Villain.

Or start a new dark mafia series for FREE here.

About J.L. Beck

J.L. Beck is a **USA Today** and international bestselling author and one half of the author duo Beck & Hallman.

When she isn't writing you can find her sitting with a cup of coffee, in a comfy chair, with a book in hand. She's a mom (both kids and pups), wife, and introvert.

Learn more about her books on her website

WWW.BLEEDINGHEARTROMANCE.COM

About S. Rena

S. Rena (Sade Rena) is a *USA TODAY* bestselling author of dark contemporary and dark paranormal romance.

As with her contemporary titles, Sade enjoys spinning tales that are angsty, emotional, and sexy. But because she loves a villain just as much as she loves a hero, she also writes dark, diverse characters who are flawed and morally grey.

Visit www.saderena.com

Printed in Great Britain
by Amazon